The Prisoner and the Chaplain

Other titles by Michelle Berry

Blind Crescent

Blur

How to Get There from Here

Interference

I Still Don't Even Know You

Margaret Lives in the Basement

This Book Will Not Save Your Life

What We All Want

The Prisoner and
the Chaplain

MICHELLE BERRY

Buckrider Books is an imprint of Wolsak and Wynn Publishers.

Cover image: Ingrid Paulson
Cover design: Ingrid Paulson
Interior design: Mary Bowness
Author photograph: Fred Thornhill
Typeset in Minion
Printed by Ball Media, Brantford, Canada

Buckrider Books
280 James Street North
Hamilton, ON
Canada L8R 2L3

Library and Archives Canada Cataloguing in Publication

Berry, Michelle, 1968-, author
    The prisoner and the chaplain / Michelle Berry.

ISBN 978-1-928088-43-1 (softcover)
    I. Title.
PS8553.E7723P75 2017   C813'.54   C2017-904874-0

The publisher gratefully acknowledges the support of the Canada Council for the Arts, the Ontario Arts Council and the Government of Canada.

For Stu, Abby, Zoe, Mom and Dad

"My guiding principle is this:
Guilt is never to be doubted."

– Franz Kafka

The Road

There is a road that leads through two cornfields to a prison on the outskirts of a town. There are concrete walls thirty feet high. There are motion sensors and dogs. There are trenches dug into the earth. There are rolls of barbed wire, doubled, tripled. Steel doors that clang shut. Correctional officers in dark blue uniforms with numbers on their chests. Prisoners in orange jumpsuits and slip-on shoes. There are cells, ten by ten feet, with furniture anchored to the walls and floor. There are common areas – the day room, the medical centre, the chapel, the yard.

And there is death row. In death row, there are heavy, closed doors. There are no views to the outside. There is a slot through each door for food delivery and a small window that can be opened from the hallway for monitoring. There are no common areas. No socialization. On death row, the prisoner wears a white jumpsuit with the letters *DR* on the back. The prisoner is allowed two supervised showers a week and one hour a day alone in a cage in the empty yard.

And then there is the death chamber, painted green. There

is a digital clock on the wall, counting down the minutes and seconds until execution. There is a cot with a mattress on it. No pillow. There is a sink. Chairs can be brought in for the prisoner's chaplain or support worker. There is a door with a window in it. Five correctional officers sit and stand outside the door. This is the death squad.

And then there is the execution room. It is right next door to the death chamber. It is steel-walled and heavily sound-proofed. It is also painted green. There is sometimes a gurney, sometimes a chair, depending on what type of execution the prisoner has requested, depending on what is available to the executioner. There is a curtained, bulletproof glass window that, when the curtains are pulled back, reveals a gallery of seats. No more than twenty places to sit and watch the execution. There is a closet off the execution room with two doors for the executioner. He or she comes and goes anonymously; pulls levers, presses buttons, controls the execution.

If you walk away from the execution room, past the death chamber, down the hallway through death row, through the less constrictive regular cells, past the warden's office, out the front doors of the prison, through the armed gates, past the wall, down the road between the cornfields and turn left, you will come across the rest of the world. You will come across families sitting down to evening meals, a baseball game on the screen, the dog keeping one eye open for squirrels. If you keep walking, you will end up somewhere else, far from the prison, far from death row. You will be on the road.

The Woods

We are in the woods. A cabin somewhere. Sometimes it is made of wood. Sometimes it is made of glass. Or brick. Or steel. We are standing and sitting on a deck, or a porch, or sometimes on the ground, looking out into a forest, or looking out at a river, or a lake, or an ocean, as it rapidly churns and moves and sways. We are holding things – mugs of coffee, cans of beans, umbrellas. One time someone is holding a flamingo by a leash. It is mid-afternoon, the light in the sky is bright but low beyond the branches of the trees. A small boy drinks milk out of a sippy cup. There are children running around and splashing and jumping in the fast-flowing water, and there are dogs I've never seen before wandering around, roughhousing, snapping. A basset hound baying, a pug snuffling. A cat in a cage once. And a donkey grazing. Nothing makes sense, but everything makes sense. We are comfortable and the sun is hot and warm. The air feels thick, like the milk the boy is drinking. Our hands are sweaty. Someone drops a glass and it shatters and then reappears whole. We are in bathing suits. Some of us have towels wrapped around our waists as if we have just been swimming, which is odd considering the turbulent rapids below. Where would we swim? A woman's hair is wet and hangs in long tendrils down her neck.

Although it's a beautiful day, I can't shake the feeling that something is going to happen. There is an electric current running through the scene, amplified, turned up, made brighter and more colourful than real life. The donkey brays. The dogs bark. The forest is darker, greener, blacker. The water is violent, foamy, white. The tide goes out and in. The swimsuits are sleek and shiny. I am holding something in my hand. I look down but can't see what it is. A mug of coffee? A can of beans? An umbrella? I'm watching the small boy as he sips his milk. I'm watching the woman's hair as it drips on her shoulders. I'm watching the children as they tempt fate at the water's edge.

Suddenly mouths are open, but I can't hear what anyone is saying. I shake my head as if there is water in my ears, but there's no sound. Not even the low rumble of the water. No talking, not even muted humming. The dogs move silently close to the ground. The fur on their backs bristles.

And this is when it always happens. The familiar cry of a seagull comes into the scene, and everyone – even the small boy with his milk, even the children at the water – suddenly stops and looks towards the sound. The cry gets louder and louder, but no one can see it through the trees.

The cry becomes stronger, frantic. It is not the usual sound a seagull makes. I know, quickly, that this is the thing we've all been waiting for, the thing that made the day thick and hazy and silent. This is what made the trees still, the water wild, the people gather. This is that thing that was going to happen.

We watch the seagull fly. It doesn't look natural. It's much larger than a regular seagull, and it's veering towards us. Wings flapping quickly. Head straight. Closer and closer until it's almost at eye level. Everyone is frozen. The adults in their chairs, the children on the shore clutching the sticks they poke into the water. The gull is the only object in motion. There is no wind. The trees are still. The water is suddenly glass, and even the foam in the current has calmed. As it comes closer, we all see what we are meant to see.

Through the seagull – from back to belly, through feather and hide and blood and bone – is an arrow. We can see the fletching at the gull's back and the arrowhead at its breast. There is no blood. No other injury. Merely an arrow. Almost a joke, like those arrow-through-the-head hats. Or like the horses on a carousel with the poles that go straight through.

How can the gull possibly fly?

But the gull flies past us and continues through the trees, crying steadily. It continues on towards its death, flying until it collapses and dies with an arrow straight through its body.

We turn then, all of us, and look to the person next to us. We all look carefully and quietly at our neighbours, making sure what we saw was real.

No one says a thing. The wind picks up again, and I can hear the sound of the rushing water.

And that's when I always wake up.

PART ONE

12:01 a.m.

The Chaplain thinks the inmates seem strangely awake and alert, not a tired bone in their bodies. He walks beside the Prisoner. Corrections Officer 1 and Corrections Officer 2, their numbers blazing on their shirts, walk behind them. CO1 has removed the Prisoner's handcuffs, a small act of mercy, but he keeps his hand on his gun. The Prisoner walks at a leisurely pace, as if he's got all the time in the world. The Chaplain keeps pace with him, but the COs shuffle awkwardly, not used to moving so slowly.

No one on death row is allowed a name. Not the Warden, the Chaplain, the Prisoner or the corrections officers.

Take away your name, the Chaplain thinks, and you are nothing. You are no one.

The Prisoner is wearing regular clothes – work pants, a plain black T-shirt, canvas shoes. He is allowed work clothes for the occasion. No more white jumpsuit. Before the Chaplain arrived, the Prisoner was fingerprinted and allowed a shower. His hair is damp. He did not shave, and the Chaplain notes the stubble on his face.

The other inmates, hundreds of them, rows upon rows of caged men, shout as the group walks past. War cries. Wailing. Howling anger. They bang their bars with whatever they have handy, and the noise rains down upon them – the Chaplain and the Prisoner and the COs – like a sudden hurricane. It swirls around them. The Prisoner looks up at the chaos, and he lifts his hand slightly as if to wave goodbye. CO1 shouts, "Hands at your sides, Prisoner!"

He has been segregated from the general prison population for his entire stay here, for the ten years since he was sentenced to death, the ten years of appeal after appeal, and yet these other men, these strangers – these banging, shouting men – feel a solidarity with him tonight. The Chaplain marvels. Even caged, they perform a ritual to show support for their fellow man.

The COs brought him out at midnight hoping to avoid this. Hoping most of the other inmates would be asleep. But word travels fast – an execution is coming – and they wait to see the last of the Prisoner, bursting at the seams. Furious at the system. Adrenalin junkies high with excitement. The Chaplain can feel them. He can smell them, and it's not the smell of sweat or body odour. It's the smell of fear and rage. A sour, sickly smell.

The noise reminds the Chaplain of the soccer stadium, the games he watched in university, the gleeful anger of the masses, howling and chanting and sharing in the sport. He remembers Tracy then, as well. Of course he does. Before everything he did to her, when they were happy. Whenever he thinks of the past, he can't get away from thinking about Tracy. He remembers the way she was before he did what he did. Before he hurt her. And then he remembers her after. What happened between them is getting farther away now, getting more and more distant. But it's still there. At those soccer games, he remembers not paying attention to her. He was mesmerized by the sound around him, focused on everything else. As usual. She always tried to get his attention, talking, smiling, pointing things out, but inevitably left the game and went home by herself, back to their shared apartment to read a book. Whenever he thinks back to his time with Tracy, the Chaplain recalls not paying attention.

And he's doing this now. His focus on the Prisoner is shifting quickly. Has he not learned anything from before, from losing Tracy? Today, he wants to pay attention. He has promised himself he will. To the Prisoner. To the moment. To the last few hours of this man's life. The other inmates shout and rattle their bars as the Prisoner walks towards the death chamber. His last walk. The Chaplain reminds himself to pay attention. Even after his promise to stay present in the moment, he has failed already. Thinking of soccer, of Tracy.

Pay attention.

He figured it out yesterday after he met the Prisoner for the first time. How many minutes, how many seconds. There are 720 minutes in twelve hours and 43,200 seconds. He looks at his watch. It is 12:06. Six minutes gone already, 360 seconds.

The Prisoner is to be executed at noon.

On his way to the prison, before the Warden gave his lecture on not trying to "save" the Prisoner, the Chaplain stopped and bought a coffee at the all-night variety store. The clerk was startled to see him there so late at night. There were three other men in the store. One customer was buying a lottery ticket and cigarettes. Another was buying milk and diapers, and the third was looking at the antique adult magazines, pulling out the centrefolds from back when people dealt mainly with paper for their porn. The Chaplain bought his coffee and thought about how many seconds people waste shopping for diapers and milk and cigarettes and lottery tickets and porn. How many seconds does it take to stir his coffee and then throw out the stir stick and get back in his car and turn on the engine? How many seconds does it take to drive to the prison, the windshield wipers slapping, a summer storm hailing down upon him, the Chaplain cold and distracted from his dream of the seagull and the arrow. The black feeling that lasted until he stepped into the Warden's office. How many minutes wasted on a dark feeling? On a dream?

"Don't let him talk you into saving him," the Warden had said. "I mean, shit, you're supposed to 'save' him." The Warden used air quotes as he said it. "Like religiously and all. You're the chaplain, but I mean, don't think you can save him in the real way. You know what I mean? It's not possible. You know that, right? The execution is going ahead."

The Warden is aware of his past, the Chaplain knows this. He had to be made aware of it in order to hire him. The Chaplain still cringes at the memory of meeting the Warden for the first time. He had said, "Funny that you'd end up in prison anyway, even when the judge let you off." The Warden has never mentioned any details, never really come out with what he might know, but the Chaplain feels it lingering there in everything he says. The Warden toys with him, plays with his feelings, makes him ashamed and provokes the anger still within him. The Chaplain has worked hard the last several years to rid himself of all these feelings, to tone down the surging swell, to make himself worthier of what he has become, of his calling, yet the Warden has a way of making the hair on his arms bristle. It's almost as if the Warden wants him to fail, to satisfy his ridiculous certainty that everyone in prison is here for a good reason. That no one could make a mistake, or no one's circumstances could put them here. Or that someone could take the blame for someone else. The Warden is convinced that once guilty, you are always guilty. Because the Chaplain destroyed Tracy, because he let his anger get the better of him, the Warden thinks he deserves to be locked up.

"I will save him," the Chaplain had said, fingers up. "But I won't 'save' him."

Soon they have walked through too many heavy, metal doors to hear the shouting of the inmates, and now the only sound is the footsteps of the COs and the Chaplain and the Prisoner. Heavy footsteps. Two in boots, one in slip-on dress shoes and the Prisoner in slip-on canvas running shoes. No laces. The Prisoner swings his arms casually, freely. The Chaplain can feel CO1 and CO2 tense behind them, ready for trouble. But the Prisoner acts as if he's heading out to a club, going for a late-night drink with friends. He even has a shy, sly smile on his boyish face. But the Prisoner's eyes are deeply circled black holes. This is a man who doesn't sleep, no matter how much he smiles. The Chaplain wonders about Death Row Phenomenon. Men go crazy from years in solitary. Perhaps the Prisoner has already broken through this reality and is there now, on the other side. The Chaplain's primary job, he thinks, is to keep the Prisoner here, in the real world, in the present. His job must be to make sure the Prisoner doesn't stray into that other realm. A man might not go gentle into that good night, but he might at least go sanely.

"Fucking noise," CO2 says softly. "Shouting and banging. Every single fucking time."

"At least they aren't flinging their shit," CO1 laughs.

The Chaplain clears his throat and both men shut up quickly. Who are you, the Chaplain wants to say, to complain about anything? The corrections officers often forget he is there. The Chaplain thinks that it's because he is young. They are used to older chaplains, grey-haired and milky-eyed. In fact, the Prisoner seemed shocked to see the Chaplain when they first met. No one respects youth.

Again, silence and only the sound of their shoes. The Prisoner's grin is larger now, toothier, the Chaplain notices, as if he appreciates the COs' banter. The Chaplain can feel the tension around that grin. A spooky feeling, like when a dog bares its teeth. The tattoo around his neck gives the impression of a collar.

"Left here," CO2 says.

The Chaplain is suddenly distracted by the CO's title – CO2. Carbon dioxide. He thinks of the silliness of it and wonders how often he is teased. "You're sucking the air out of the room . . ."

The Prisoner doesn't turn wide; instead, he makes a sudden left and cuts the Chaplain off. They bump shoulders hard. The Prisoner swings his head quickly towards the Chaplain. He is as tall as the Chaplain, so their eyes meet squarely. The Prisoner looks as if he's going to kill him, but then his eyes focus on the terrified eyes of the Chaplain, and the Prisoner immediately swings his head back down and stares at the ground. The Chaplain knows that the corrections officers are armed with truncheons and pepper spray and guns and will keep any danger at bay, but for that one brief moment, he felt his insides contract, his heart speed rapidly, his throat seize. The look in the Prisoner's eyes was enough. This man, the Chaplain reminds himself, is here for a reason.

The room is small. Barely ten feet by ten feet. An underground parking space in a condominium building. Concrete walls. The ceiling seems low, but the Chaplain realizes that is only because there are no windows. You would think they would let him have a window, a last look out, to see the changing light, the weather. He thinks this oversight is unfair.

The floors and walls are thick. The walls are painted green, chipped with age. There is a small, rusty sink in the corner and a toilet with no seat beside it. A roll of paper rests on the floor beside the toilet. There is no soap for the sink. The Chaplain shakes his head. There is a digital clock on the wall, to count down the minutes. There are two chairs and a cot. Blue and green blankets, clean white sheets, the smell of bleach emanating from them. No pillow. The chairs are stiff, side by side. Black. They look out of place, like they should be in a dining room, or a modern living room. They should be in that condominium with the underground concrete parking space. Although the Chaplain and the Prisoner will spend twelve hours in these chairs, they look like an afterthought. The door has a small window in it, and at all times, he was told, the COs will be right outside, looking in. There will be five COs in each shift – a special, elite squad. Two shifts. The final shift will walk the Prisoner to the death chamber. The Chaplain looks at the window now and yes, they are all there. CO1 and CO2 have left. Their duty is over for now. Gone home to wives, babies, children, dogs, soft beds and open windows. They get their names back the minute they walk out of the prison. They will become human again. COs 3, 4, 5, 6 and 7 look back at him. Numbers on their shirts. No one smiles.

Although they didn't pass it, the Chaplain knows that they are directly beside the execution room. The final chair the Prisoner will sit in – be strapped into – is right next door. It's an eerie feeling, being separated by only a wall.

Not every prisoner requests a chaplain. He feels lucky. And also cursed. Sometimes a man's last twelve hours are spent on the telephone with family. Or alone. Or with the corrections officers. Watching. Always watching.

"Too bad about him," the Warden had said earlier, before the Chaplain met COs 1 and 2 and escorted the Prisoner to his cell. "Who'd have thought he was sick? I mean, the guy was the picture of health. And then he's down for the count."

"Cancer," the Chaplain said. "You never expect it, I suppose." His mentor, the Prisoner's original chaplain, had collapsed at work only a week ago, and the Warden had called the Chaplain into his office and asked him to take over. He was only halfway through his two-year mentorship, but there was no one else available on such short notice. The Chaplain had been ordained and certified and trained; all he needed was one more year with his mentor. But his time has been cut short. It couldn't be helped.

"Yep. I hear he doesn't look so good now. I always wonder, you know, if he hadn't found out he had cancer, would he look so bad so quickly? I mean, he looked fine, he felt fine, until he found out."

The Chaplain sipped his coffee and shrugged. Good question, he thought. The Chaplain's own mother looked good right up until she was told she had breast cancer. And then she started to look haggard and tired. He always assumed that the stress of knowing you were dying took a toll on your body before the disease actually caught hold.

"I've got COs 1 and 2 taking him down with you. They've been on death watch since he found out. They like this kind of stuff. Makes their lives exciting." The Warden laughed. The Chaplain cringed.

But the Warden took pity on the Chaplain. "So, you've only met him once?" the Warden said. "Yesterday?"

"Yes. Briefly. It's such a shame that his previous chaplain got sick now. Just when he's needed the most. And after all the years of preparation. All the time they spent together."

"Believe me, this guy won't really care who's with him. He's not a touchy-feely kind of guy." The Warden laughed. "In fact, he'll probably try to beat the shit out of you when he gets you in that cell." The Chaplain's face fell. "Sorry, I shouldn't have said that. It's just that he's a tough cookie. You saw that yesterday, I guess? He really doesn't say much, unless he's fighting."

The Prisoner was quiet when the Chaplain met with him. But the Chaplain could feel it bubbling under the surface. The tension in the Prisoner's jaw. One hour together, and the Prisoner said absolutely nothing. "Well, I suppose that's what got him into this situation."

"Your mentor has done this kind of work before, too. You haven't. It's pretty intense. It can really mess with you."

"Yes, well, I've been trained."

The Warden laughed and the laugh was like a soft cry, a gasp – like the seagull, the Chaplain thought, and shivered.

"Fucking training," the Warden said. "Sorry, Chaplain, but that ain't going to help you now." The Warden leaned forward in his chair and locked eyes. "Training for this is like being told how to handle a gun without ever having seen one, if you know what I mean. It makes sense logically, but shit, it's not the real thing."

"Yes, well." The Chaplain didn't really know what to say. The training was a bit of a joke. An appointment with the psychologist. And he has had enough of psychologists to last him a lifetime. A couple of hours. Here is what you do. This is what you say. Listen. Always listen. Keep him talking. Keep him calm. All made-up scenarios that never take the real situation into consideration. A few book recommendations and a pamphlet or two, but no one can prepare for something like this. It has to be an instinctual thing, a fly-by-the-seat-of-your-pants kind of thing. You have to have faith. There is nothing you can do to make it easier or turn things one way or the other. Just being there, the Chaplain thought, should be enough. Or not. In the long run, it probably doesn't matter at all.

The whole thing, the Chaplain realized, as the Warden chuckled like his demented gull, was an exercise in futility.

The Prisoner settles onto the cot, his shoes where the pillow, if there was one, would be. He puts his hands behind his head and stares up at the ceiling. A lazy day in the park under a towering willow. A farmer resting in his field. A small boy engineering shapes out of clouds. The Chaplain sits down quietly on one of the two chairs. He adjusts his body so that he is comfortable for now, but he knows the chair will soon get the best of his lower back, and he wonders if he should have brought his Formed Back Relaxer and if that would even have been allowed. This all happened so quickly he didn't have time to ask about small things such as comfort, food, bathroom breaks.

The Prisoner speaks. "Is my chaplain okay?"

"Pardon? Sorry?"

"The guy you replaced. The other chaplain. Is he okay?"

"Yes. Well, no. Not really. He's alive, if that's what you're asking." The Chaplain takes his foot slowly out of his mouth. He can't believe he just said that. "He's okay. Had surgery on his large intestine and they took out the tumour. They need to do chemo now. He's not that old, you know, so he's pretty healthy for the operation and such. He'll be fine. I hope." He curses internally – stop rambling, he thinks. Slow down. Breathe. "It's only been a couple of weeks. I don't really know all the details." Be honest.

The other day, when they met for the first time, the Prisoner said nothing. The Chaplain told him why he was there, what he would do for him, how the Prisoner could tell him anything, could talk or stay silent, whatever he wanted. The Chaplain told him it might feel good to get things off his chest. He asked the Prisoner to think about whether or not he wanted the Chaplain to deal with things – where his body should be buried or if he wanted cremation and, if so, where would the ashes go? What about his funeral? What about any property he owns or family he needs contacted? Think about this kind of thing and we've got twelve hours in which to deal with it all, he had said, and the Prisoner had only nodded.

So now, hearing his voice shocks the Chaplain. It's a clear, clean voice. No accent. Just a low thrum of a voice, almost like listening to a news announcer or a radio host. A confident, deep voice. Sure of himself.

"So he'll be okay, then? My chaplain?"

"No, not really." The Chaplain looks around the room again, as if he's missed something. "No. He'll die of his cancer. That is for certain. It's a bad kind. But he might have a few years left."

"Sounds familiar" the Prisoner says.

"Yes, I suppose it is. The waiting."

"Funny that he'd get sick right when I get called up." The Prisoner rolls onto his side and looks at the Chaplain. "Like he didn't want to spend this time with me. After all we'd been through."

"No, no. That's not true. It's not . . . that's not what happened. He got sick. It wasn't fate that it happened when your execution order came through. It just happened that way. He would have wanted to be here. I know that."

"Did you talk to him?" The Prisoner rolls onto his back again. "I mean, did he say that?"

"No. I didn't talk to him. But I know."

"Yeah. You guys are always so sure of yourselves, aren't you? Guess it's your faith or something. Guess it's just your way of looking at things."

The Chaplain doesn't know what to say to that. He is certain of many things, that is a given, but he's also very uncertain when it comes to a lot of questions about life. He questions many things, has always been curious. Just because he never questions his faith, because he never questions his God, it doesn't mean that he doesn't question other things. But then, the Prisoner is right about the Chaplain's mentor. He was always so sure of himself, so sure of everything. And he made sure you knew it. Made sure you heard him.

The Chaplain realizes that he's thinking about his mentor in the past tense, and then he thinks that this Prisoner before him, in a little less than twelve hours, will himself be in the past tense. He will be a *was*, as opposed to an *is*.

The Prisoner flops back and forth on the cot, attempting to get comfortable. The COs peer in the window, which, the Chaplain notices suddenly, has mesh between the glass. Not breakable, even if there was something in this cell you could break it with.

Two weeks ago, the Chaplain was working with prisoners in D block. Talking to them about forgiveness and guilt and empathy and faith. Telling Prisoner Dwight about the afterlife and about how to think about God and religion. Telling Prisoner Rusty about how he needs to forgive himself before others can forgive him. About how God will forgive. He was there to comfort the suffering. Two weeks ago, his life seemed fairly simple. A chaplain job at the prison. A few friends. His sister, Miranda, whom he loves dearly, and her two crazy kids and truck-driving husband, Richard. He had finally gotten past those things in his life that he needed to get past, those things that were torturing him. Simple. Until this. His mentor fell sick. Cancer. Death row. Twelve hours. An execution.

It's his turn now. A turn he never really wanted to take. How do you stay calm in the face of this? When you don't believe in what is happening? When you believe in forgiveness and acceptance and faith. *An eye for an eye* is not the way his faith runs. These are the questions he cannot cope with, the questions he isn't sure how to answer. But the Prisoner is right about the Chaplain's mentor. With his cancer, his many years in service over the Chaplain, his walk down this path before, the man always felt he had all the answers. He felt that his job was not to tell the system it was wrong, but to give hope and peace in those final hours. To smooth the head of the sinner and tell him everything would be all right. The Chaplain is not here to right the wrongs of society, but to comfort the sinner in his time of need.

Now he asks the Prisoner, "Why do you think he became sick right now?"

"I told you, man, because this is when I was called up. Maybe he just wanted to avoid having to talk to me for twelve hours." The Prisoner laughs. CO4 looks in the door at the sound. The number on his uniform shirt seems to glow through the window. Numbers on the front. Numbers on the back. The man is branded, nameless, until the minute his shift is over.

"No, really," the Chaplain says.

"I don't know. I don't really care. Maybe . . ." the Prisoner rolls to face the wall, ". . . maybe he's going to die before me in order to save me a place beside him at the dinner table."

He won't die that quickly, the Chaplain thinks, but says nothing.

The Chaplain looks at the digital clock on the wall. The Prisoner says, "You got somewhere to go?" even though he is facing away from him. How did he know he was looking at the clock?

"No. Of course not. I'm here for you. We can talk about anything you want. We can be silent. We can pray together. Whatever you want."

"What's the time?" the Prisoner asks, without looking up at the clock.

"Twelve-thirty-five," the Chaplain says. "Seems later than that, doesn't it?"

"Yeah, I guess." The Prisoner yawns and rolls back to face him, and then he sits up on the bed. "I was wondering if time would go fast in here or slow. It's something I've been wondering."

"Me too," the Chaplain says. "I couldn't tell you. Right now, it seems to be going slowly. That's good, I guess."

"Is it?"

A corrections officer knocks on the door and enters. He has a six on his shirt. "You got to fill out the form about your last meal and when you want it and all," he says, thrusting a piece of paper and a pencil at the Prisoner. He stands there, waiting, while the Prisoner looks at the form and then looks at the Chaplain.

"I've got to decide now? With you watching me?"

"I can't leave you with the pencil. The last guy tried to stab through his eyes to his brain with a pencil."

The Chaplain opens his mouth to say something, but can't think of anything to say. The irony of trying to stop someone from killing himself so that you can kill him yourself.

"Man," the Prisoner says. "That's fucked."

He writes something on the form and then hands it back to

the CO. CO6 leaves the room. Locks the door behind him.

The Chaplain wants to ask what the Prisoner ordered and what time the food will be coming, but he decides not to say anything. He wonders, though, if he'll have anything to eat himself. They didn't give him a form.

As if reading the Chaplain's thoughts, the Prisoner says, "I should have ordered you something," and lies back down upon the cot.

There is silence then. It fills up the room and the Prisoner's eyes shut. The Chaplain shuffles on his chair but tries not to make too much noise. He tries not to squeak the chair or move the chair over the floor. He isn't sure if the Prisoner has fallen asleep. Time clicks on.

"I suppose," the Prisoner says after about five minutes, his eyes still closed shut. "I suppose I should start with the beginning."

The Chaplain looks at him. "Sorry?"

"My story," he says. "That's what you're here for, right?"

"Well, I'm not sure. I'm here for whatever you want me to be here for. Whatever you want. Religious guidance? Comfort?"

"But you want my story, right?" The Prisoner opens his eyes and turns his head towards the Chaplain, curious. "I mean, why else would you be here?"

"You asked me to be here."

"I asked my chaplain to be here and I got you."

"Yes, that's true."

"If we've got twelve hours," the Prisoner says, "then I might as well start with the beginning."

"I've read your files," the Chaplain says. "You don't need to tell me what happened if you don't want to. I know about your robberies, the storage unit, I know what happened. The murders. You don't need to waste any of your time thinking about me. Whatever is good for you."

The Prisoner thinks about this. "I'm not telling you the story of *what* happened," he says slowly. "Everyone knows that. No sense in rehashing it. No, I'm going to tell you *why* it happened. I think that's a better story."

"Sure. Of course."

"I mean, we might as well pass time, right? Better than praying for twelve hours. It's not like my prayers are going to be answered." He laughs almost gleefully and the Chaplain wonders, for a brief instant, about his sanity.

"I do want to hear your story. But a little prayer never hurt anyone."

"We got time for both," the Prisoner says. "All the time in the world."

The Chaplain thinks this is curious. They have the absolute opposite of all the time in the world. The clock is ticking.

"Too bad your chair is so uncomfortable. Too bad I don't have a pillow."

The Chaplain pulls the other chair up across from him and puts his feet upon it. The Prisoner smiles.

"That better now, Chaplain?"

"Yes," he says. "Much better."

The Prisoner faces the ceiling, closes his eyes, and begins. "I had a pretty average childhood," he says. "Normal house. Normal life. Even had those fucking glow-in-the-dark stars on my bedroom ceiling." He laughs. And the Chaplain suddenly pictures his own childhood room. The train set in the corner, the thick pile carpet where, if you dropped a tack or a pin, you'd find it eventually with your bare feet, the door that adjoined his room to Miranda's, where they would knock secret codes back and forth pretending to be spies. He thinks about his childhood – perfectly normal. So what made the Chaplain do what he did to Tracy? What made him take his anger out on her that way? And, more importantly, what made the Prisoner kill? "You know what I mean," the Prisoner continues. "Normal. White-bread sandwiches for lunch. An older brother, Jack. An older sister, Susan. My dad was an asshole but everything was okay for a while. Until my mother left . . ."

In the hours before he was to join the Prisoner, the Chaplain had felt a sense of foreboding. Not the usual foreboding that comes with unfamiliar work, but a general uneasiness, something intangible that came, perhaps, from his seagull dream. He's been dreaming it since he heard. Since they called him and told him he would be spending twelve hours with a murderer. The exact same thing every night. The cabin and the gull. And the arrow. Shot clean through.

The Chaplain figured this was his subconscious. A contemplation of what was to come, of what was unknown. But every morning – and as he came into the prison tonight – it felt as if there was a weight on his chest he couldn't move.

Even now, listening to the Prisoner speak, he can't stop thinking about the seagull, about how helpless he felt watching it fly over the trees. The horror of it. The feeling it gave him. As if he, himself, had an arrow through his body.

The Chaplain woke up from his quick nap, before coming to the prison, chilled even though the temperature was high and the humidity was thick and full. A stormy summer. Wildfires burning uncontrollably. Heat and tornados. The world is slowly melting, overheating. They used to call it global warming and now they just call it the weather. He woke wrapped tightly in his simple sheet. He pulled the comforter up to his neck until his body recovered some warmth. All the way to the prison, he couldn't shake this chill. He drove with his windows down and the hot, thick, smoggy air around him, everyone else sealed up in their permanently air-conditioned cars. The rain poured down. Sheets of it. Lightning flashed in the distance. Then in the Warden's air-conditioned office, and then in the cold reality of death row, the Chaplain still shivered to keep warm.

"Just be careful, Chaplain," the Warden had said in a deep, low voice. Almost a whisper. "You never know what tricks these guys have up their sleeves. He's a murderer, remember. A violent man. He's not just some thief. We wouldn't be executing him if he were just some thief. This is serious stuff. You never know how much this kind of stuff can fuck with you." The Warden rolled his finger through the air around his temple. His eyes widened. "Cuckoo. Cuckoo."

Larry

Larry faces the dark blue wall of his bedroom and then turns and faces the open room. The solar system – Mars, Jupiter, Earth, Venus, etc. – is above his head, dangling from the ceiling by fishing wire, soft Styrofoam balls. When he turns the light out at night, his ceiling shines with glow-in-the-dark stars and planets. His mother is walking back and forth past his open door, carrying laundry to and from the four bedrooms of their house – his sister's, his brother's, his parents', his. She brings the laundry in, fresh-smelling and folded, and places it on his bed where he can reach it.

"You're old enough to put it away by yourself now, Lawrence," she says, and leaves the room. Always moving, his mother, always doing chores. They've got a housekeeper, but his mother never sits still. She has long blonde hair that is down during the day but she puts up during the evening when she goes out with his father, or when they watch the screen together in the living room. In the day, with her hair down, she is loose and free and his smiling mother. At night, when his father is around, her hair is tight like her face, nothing out of place, nothing untoward. *Untoward* is a word his father uses often, and Larry now uses it because it sounds old and funny. How can you move toward something and then undo that? It makes no sense.

The front door bangs open, catches the hallway wall.

"Careful," his mother shouts down the stairs. "You'll put a dent in that wall."

Larry's brother and sister rush in towards the kitchen, throwing hats and coats and scarves and mittens on the hall bench.

"I did not," Susan says. "You always say I did."

"Did too." Even though Larry can't see them, he can tell by the way Jack is speaking that he has been at Susan all the way home. Larry can see in his head the expression on Jack's face – contempt, anger, bitterness. Like their father. His mother says his brother and his father are so alike they are almost twins.

Larry goes downstairs and joins them in the kitchen.

It is sandwiches on white bread – cheese slice, mayonnaise, bologna, pickles, sweet and salty, sliced thin – and fruit salad. It is cold milk (Jack gets chocolate milk because he complains the loudest and, Larry thinks, because he is the meanest) and, later, after they go back to school, a cookie if he's good and quiet and plays in his room.

Jack says, "Mother." He says *Mother* when he's ready to cause chaos, *Mom* when he's pretending to be friendly. "Mother, Susan says she didn't steal my bike lock."

"I didn't," Susan says, her eyes welling. She is nine years old to Jack's seven, but even so, she's afraid of him. She takes a bite of her sandwich and forces it down her throat. "I didn't. I don't know where it is. I've never seen it."

"Never?"

"Well, not since yesterday. Not since we got back from school yesterday."

"It's a special bike lock."

Susan rolls her eyes. "It's a bike lock. It's not special."

"Yes, but it's mine and you stole it because you've always wanted it because it's special. Because it's green and has a key."

"I don't care about a key. I have my own bike lock. It has a key."

"Because it's green."

"Mom," Susan says. "Mom, he's wrong. I didn't steal his bike lock."

"You did."

"I didn't."

"Stop it," their mother says. "Stop arguing. We'll find it later, Jack. I'm sure Susan –"

"You always take her side. She steals things and you don't punish her."

"I don't steal things. What do you mean I steal things?"

"Jack –"

"Wait until Father hears. Wait until I tell him," Jack says, and their mother's face blanches slightly, enough to notice. There is a change in the air. But then the colour comes back into her cheeks and she sighs and opens her mouth to say something.

"The bike lock is in the garage on the floor," Larry says quietly. "I saw it there this morning." And Larry doesn't tell Jack that he stole the bike lock from Jack's bike yesterday evening and took it into his room and played with the key – in and out – and marveled at the shiny greenness of it until he tired of it, and then Larry took it back out to the garage this morning and placed it on the floor to wait for Jack's return from school.

Jack reaches out, quickly, so quickly that Larry doesn't have time to react, and pushes him off his chair onto the floor. He pushes the chair too. The chair comes down upon Larry and his head hits hard on the linoleum, cracks back, and his mouth takes a chair leg and there is blood suddenly on his lips, in his mouth. Larry opens his mouth to cry but no sound comes out. He feels like he's choking on his blood. He spits. Eyes wild. He wants to say, "I'm only five years old," but nothing comes out of his mouth, no sound.

"Oh, you split your lip," his mother says. "Oh dear." She rushes to the sink and wrings out a rag and comes over and places it on Larry's mouth, muffles the sounds he wants to make. "It'll be okay, Lawrence. It's only a split lip. They bleed a lot but it'll be okay."

"You pushed him," Susan says. She glares at Jack. "You pushed him right over. On purpose."

"I'm sure it was an accident," his mother says, crouching by him. "Lawrence was squirming on his chair. He fell."

Jack smiles. "He was squirming," he says. "It just happened."

"You pushed him and you're mean," Susan shouts. "You're a psychopath."

"Susan."

"He is. He's always hurting Larry and he beats up the kids at school and he's just mean." She takes her sandwich and walks out of the kitchen and puts her coat on and leaves the house.

"Don't be late after school, Susan," Mother calls out. "I want to take you to buy new boots."

"Really, Mother," Jack says. "Sometimes I wonder about you. It's like there's nothing up there," Jack sidles up to where Mother is beside Larry and taps her on the temple. "Nothing in your head."

"Jack, I –"

His mother kneels there, holding the rag to Larry's mouth, and looks up at her son. Larry watches her eyes and he doesn't know what to make of it all. He doesn't know where it's all going or where it has been. He doesn't know what he can do about it.

All he knows is that it seems untoward, this day, this accident, this Jack, it seems as if it's going towards something but not quite – it's *un*. Undone. Not toward. But back. Larry's head hurts more than his mouth and later, when he plays in his room by himself, he will vomit and then he will fall asleep and he will not wake up and his mother will take him to the hospital and the doctor will say that he has a concussion. The first of many concussions because of Jack. All the concussions happening before Larry turns seven. A crack on the linoleum floor. A hockey stick to the head. A rock thrown at him. A push off the neighbour's trampoline. His father will rail about the cost of the medicines, the doctor's appointments, for such a simple thing. "He was obviously pretending to sleep," his father will shout. "You could have woken him up without taking him to the hospital. Those doctors don't know anything."

When Susan and Jack are gone the house is quiet again, and Larry's mother continues to put laundry away, to tidy up, to do the lunch dishes. Her hair is still down, for a few more hours, and she whistles, so quietly that Larry, before he falls asleep, can barely hear her, as she moves around the living room and dining room and kitchen. He sits in his room looking at his blue walls, his solar system, his stars. His head aches. He sees white lights. There is a ringing in his ears. He vomits. And then he lies down on his bed and slips into that deep, dark sleep. Like falling into a well. It's black and Larry can't see anything and falls quickly and hard with no escape.

This is how Larry remembers his mother. Before he is seven and she takes Jack and disappears. He remembers her crouching near him holding a rag full of his blood to his mouth. He remembers that look in her eyes when she peers up at Jack – part fear, part pride, part anger. Confusion. He remembers her hair falling into her face while she looks down at him on the floor. It snakes around her head like a veil. She is kind, his mother, and careful. She is quiet and simple. She can whistle for hours and Larry remembers her singing occasionally, or humming while she cooked. His mother paints his room dark blue and helps him make the solar system. She sticks the glow-in-the-dark stars to the ceiling and every night she turns off the lights and she and Larry pause for a moment – him between day and night and sleep, her between day and night and her husband – and they look up at the stars together, and Larry knows that they both marvel at the beauty and simplicity of it all. When he closes his eyes, back when his mother is still around, Larry sees the outline of the stars on his lids, and he falls asleep quickly and solidly.

Most of Larry's childhood after his mother leaves is a blur. Larry's father is never around and no one ever explains to Larry where Jack has gone. One day he is there, torturing Larry, knocking him around, smashing his head on something, and the next day he is gone. And their mother is gone too, and so Larry assumes they went somewhere together. Larry makes up stories – when he is seven and nine and twelve – stories about where they went. At first they are on a trip, then they have gone to jail, and then they are dead. It is easier that way.

Susan says they went to Florida. She says she has always wanted to go to Florida.

"They didn't go to Florida," Larry says. "They went to jail."

"For what?"

"Robbery. Murder. Extortion."

Larry knows that Susan doesn't know what *extortion* means but doesn't want to ask. She is always telling Larry that his vocabulary is bigger than his head. He knows she feels stupid around him. And it isn't that Larry is any smarter than anyone else, it is just that he isn't afraid to try words. To use words he doesn't know. Words he's only heard on the screen. So far, no one has caught him at it. No one who knows the words is listening, and those who listen know nothing.

"I doubt," Susan says, "that Jack murdered anyone. Or Mom. Can you imagine?"

"But where did they go then?"

Susan shrugs. "I don't really care, do you?"

Larry goes to school. Comes home. Goes to school. His life seems endless sometimes. Kids at school bully him. And so does his father.

"You're a wimp."

"Idiot."

"You're such a baby."

"Clean up the house," his father says. "Lazy bastard."

They are in the living room and his father has stumbled in after work, reeking of booze. Larry moves away from him on the couch, turns up the screen. His father kicks him in the shins. "Clean up the fucking house." Always a drinker, his father has hit the bottle hard since his mother left.

Larry stands in order to get away from the kicks, and his father loses his balance and crashes into Larry until they are doing a slow dance, holding onto each other tightly.

"Don't touch me," his father shouts. "Don't touch me." As if Larry is poison.

Larry drops his father, who falls to the floor.

Larry is nine years old. A black eye from the schoolyard. Homework he hasn't done for weeks piled up on the kitchen table. Watching the screen to get a break from thinking about everything. Where is his mother? Where is Jack? Susan, thirteen, off dating yet another boy. His father drunk. Always drunk. Hates his life. Hates his job. Hates his house. Hates his kids. Hates his wife.

The weird thing is, Larry's father never wonders aloud where his wife and son went. He never says, "I wonder where they are," or even "Do you know where they are?" It's as if he knows exactly where they are but doesn't want to tell anyone. Susan has asked him over and over until he screams at her and slaps her. Larry is afraid to ask. Afraid of the punches, yes, but also afraid that his father might tell him the truth, might tell him where they are, and afraid that wherever they are is not the place Larry imagines them. Mostly, he really believes they are alive and well somewhere. Perhaps that's not the case? Larry doesn't want to find out. But then he does want to find out. So he goes back and forth between wanting to ask and shying away from it, and his father comes home each day, drunk and drunker, and takes out his frustrations on Larry and the house and Susan and the housekeeper. She will quit soon, the housekeeper, and then they'll really be in trouble. Susan keeps reminding their father of this, but he doesn't listen. Instead he yells.

"Clean the fucking house," his father says from where he has fallen on the floor.

"How do you work drunk?" Larry whispers, but his father doesn't hear him. He really wants to know. How is it possible to be a businessman, to run his own small business, drunk? All the time.

The housekeeper has been there. She has cleaned. But Larry putters around with a damp cloth and wipes things anyway. He winds the grandfather clock in the hallway as his father lies face down on the living room floor. Larry moves around him, sweeping and dusting. He takes out the vacuum from the cupboard and runs it around his father, wanting to run it over him, to suck him into the bag. Wouldn't that be great, Larry thinks, a vacuum bag full of his father. Like a snake slowly digesting.

There are days that are fine, that are normal. That are quiet. His father comes home directly after work. His sister is cooking. They eat together and talk about their day. Larry even has a friend at school for one year. The only year he ever has a friend. Blake.

Blake meets him at the park after dinner and they swing and kick the ball around and talk about nothing much. For the year that he has Blake, Larry thinks life might actually be good. But then Blake moves and no one else wants to be his friend because he has no mom and his dad is a drunk, because Larry gets mad quickly and easily and he punches people and trips people and steals people's things. Larry can't help himself. He sees something nice and he wants it. He gets headaches and feels angry and he lashes out. Sometimes, Larry thinks that maybe he is Jack. Maybe Jack didn't really leave, maybe Jack didn't even exist. Because when Larry punches and hits and kicks, when he steals, he feels like he's Jack. He is his brother.

Larry's father, Rick Gallo, owns a clock and watch repair shop: Gallo's Precision Repair. Over on Kingdom Street. When he is ten years old, Larry works there after school. His father drinks out of a mug, filling from a bottle under the counter, and Larry sweeps the floor and winds the clocks and polishes the front window. Larry flips the sign from *Open* to *Closed* and helps his father down the front steps, makes sure the door is locked behind them, and maneuvers him home down the darkening winter streets.

"Don't touch me," his father always says, stumbling. "Get your hands off me."

The days his father isn't angry he is wildly sad. The days he is crying in the store, Larry sits, ashamed, at the counter and watches. When he is older, Larry takes his father into the back room and locks him in. Deals with the customers himself. Learns to fix watches, repair clocks, stop time. Start it again. Move it fast or slow. But when he is ten, he merely sits on the stool and the customers come in, see Rick Gallo ranting or crying or shouting or laughing just a little too loudly, and they turn and leave the store.

Later, Larry blames his father's drunkenness for what he becomes, who he becomes, what happens to him. And he blames his mother's absence. His violent brother, Jack. He blames his sister. He blames everything on everyone else. It's not his fault, he had no chance, he had no choice, he had nothing.

Susan is pregnant by fourteen. Larry is ten. Their father is forty-three with yellowing eyes and a swollen liver.

"You just got your period," his father wails. "How can you be pregnant? How is this possible?"

"I got my period when I was twelve," Susan says, pouting. "You don't know anything."

The baby comes early, only to live with them in the squalor. Susan, now fifteen, a high school dropout, smoking on the living room couch, folding laundry occasionally, the baby rolled up beside her, crying. Larry can't stand the smell in the room. Smoke mixed with laundry detergent mixed with stale food on the unwashed plates in the kitchen sink mixed with baby shit. There are always flies buzzing around.

"He's your nephew," Susan says. "You can change his diaper."

"Fuck off."

"I can't do everything around here."

"You did enough already," Larry says, pointing at the baby.

"You didn't have to have him. You could have got rid of him."

She smacks him. Larry's face stings.

He smacks her back.

All out war.

Susan is bruised and bleeding. Larry has a black eye and his groin aches.

Their father comes home. Stumbling. Off-balance.

"Clean the fucking house," he shouts. "Stop that kid from crying."

"No one helped me, no one told me anything," Susan shouts.

And yet. And yet. There are still some good days. Even after Blake leaves. Even after Susan's first baby. Even though Larry has no friends. Even though they call him "Larry Fairy." There are days he plays soccer in the old field beside the school and the kids cheer him on and he thinks, just for a minute, that he belongs. There are the girls who like him. Rebecca and Stephanie and Darla. They hang out by the soccer field, their hands on their hips, and they watch him with wide eyes and glossy lips. They smell like peppermint and watermelon and coconut. They wear blue eyeshadow and their eyelashes are so big with mascara that it's like spiders crawling out. Little legs coming out of their eyes. Larry can't stop looking. He fumbles with the soccer ball. Trips on it. Misses the kick. They laugh.

After school, he meets Rebecca behind the shade structure and they kiss. She sprays her mouth with Binaca breath mist ahead of the kiss and so, when Larry locks her lips upon his, he gets an immediate rush of medicinal air and his head feels light.

When Darla comes to his house and sees Susan and the baby and her mess everywhere she breaks up with him. She won't hold his hand anymore and she whispers about him at school and points.

Stephanie, on the other hand, wants him more now. She seems to like the baby. She coos at the baby and he smiles at her and reaches out to grab her finger. Stephanie's hair is long and lank, greasy, but she wears the most eyeshadow and her breasts, if that's what the bumps would be called, are the largest. It isn't until she finally meets Larry's father that she dumps him.

"He's freaky," Stephanie says. "He keeps staring at me."

This is his childhood. Up to ten, eleven years old. A mixture of light and dark – mostly dark – a subtle grey. Things changed slowly, but also rapidly, when his mother left them. Some days good. Mostly bad. His mother and Jack have been gone for three years by the time Larry turns ten. He often forgets what they looked like, what they were like. He lies. He cheats. He steals. Girlfriends come and go. Things he knows he would never have done if his mother had stayed. But he isn't now who he becomes later. So when he tells the Chaplain about this time, Larry's eyes are clear. Nothing is too complicated. It makes sense to him, those years. It doesn't, for a minute, tell him who he is or how he got here. But it gives Larry the idea that, if something had happened differently at the very beginning, he might not be where he is right now.

1:01 a.m.

"Eleven hours left," the Prisoner says.

1:01 a.m. on the digital clock on the wall of the room. The Chaplain stares at it. He has been watching the time count down for almost an hour, ever since they got in this room, the whole time the Prisoner has been talking. Each time the number changes he gets a chill. Feeling death in the room, creeping closer. Feeling the souls of all who have waited here before. The Chaplain isn't sure exactly how many executions have taken place in this prison. But he is sure that whatever the number, it's too many.

While the Prisoner talked, the Chaplain tried to focus. And he did. Most of the time. But occasionally his thoughts rushed through to his own childhood, to his parents – both now dead. To his relationship with Miranda, his sister. A tough little girl, a fighter. Someone who always stuck up for him. An idealistic childhood, he thinks now. Too perfect, almost. But as the Prisoner talked, he remembered that hidden under their happiness was a grain of sadness. As if grief were present before it was even necessary. Even before their mother died when they were teens, there was that lingering sadness. Even before the Chaplain was bullied in school. There was a vein of sadness some days, when he came into the house after school, that seemed to permeate everything – the walls, the floors, the furniture. But his mother or sister or father would smile brightly when they saw him, and that sadness would dissipate but hover. Like dust in the sun. He thinks that maybe there was something in that sadness that caused him to do what he did later to Tracy. Holding in his anger, his pain, something cracked then. There was something hidden from him in his childhood that felt breakable – a childhood that seemed perfect but maybe wasn't. Perhaps that caused him to snap later? To do what he did to the woman he loved?

The Prisoner rolls from lying on the cot into sitting up. He places his feet on the floor and stands quickly. The Chaplain stands too. An instinct – don't be vulnerable. Then the Chaplain stretches. His bones creak. His legs, his hips, his back. All of him is aching. The Chaplain doesn't think he moved once in the hour. He tried to listen carefully, only thinking about himself when the Prisoner paused or broke off mid-speech to think. Not once did he ask a question. He nodded his head occasionally, but even his fingers stayed still, his leg didn't jiggle, he didn't adjust himself on the chair or clear his throat.

Now, of course, he feels like his bones have fused together.

How can he think about his human comforts, though? He is slightly in awe of the fact that his body is still telling him things when his mind is trying to stay in the moment. He wants pure focus, but he aches and needs to move now.

"You get used to it," the Prisoner says.

"What?"

"Sitting in one place in a small room for hours at a time. I used to meditate."

"Really?"

"Yeah." The Prisoner laughs. "Before I was sent to Death Row we had someone come in and teach us yoga and all of us would do it just to see her ass in those pants, but then at the end of each lesson she would make us lie on the mats and she would put quiet music on and then she would talk and we would relax. This was years ago but I still remember that feeling."

"What did she talk about?"

"She would take us through our bodies, from the tips of our toes up to the top of our heads. She would make us aware of each part – 'feel your calves, be aware of your knees' – and move up the body. It was like she was massaging us. You could feel every part right when she said its name. Most of the guys," the Prisoner laughs, "jacked off when she got to the groin, but she had her eyes closed so I don't think she knew."

"Oh."

"So, if you're ever stuck in a position, if you can just imagine those parts, think about what is hurting and focus on it, you'll work through the pain. Believe me."

"I'll try it." The Chaplain starts to sit down. To listen more. But the Prisoner is up and walking around the room now. The COs peer in the window – they are always at the window but the Chaplain has forgotten them, and now they peer in at the two men in the small room. Suddenly he is aware of the size of the room, how small it is. He can smell the Prisoner's body odour, he can smell his own odours – the garlic in the sauce he had on his spaghetti last night in his small apartment by himself, the smell of his deodorant, the slight odour of his slip-on dress shoes, leather and sweat. Being aware of the smells makes him extremely hungry and a little nauseous. He wonders again what the Prisoner ordered for his last meal, and he wonders what time he asked for it. The two cups of coffee are roiling in his stomach.

The Warden said that this prisoner was violent, but the Chaplain feels no anger coming off him. Yet. Not since they bumped into each other in the hall earlier. And he knows the feeling of anger. The smell of anger. He can sense it immediately from the other prisoners when he speaks with them. He can feel it build in himself sometimes too. In fact, the Chaplain feels he's a bit of an expert when it comes to anger these days. But there is nothing here. Maybe as the time creeps by, the Prisoner will become frantic and angry and mean?

He is intelligent sounding. He speaks well. He didn't have the usual upbringing. The Chaplain has counseled enough prisoners to know that, in general, they all have the same backstory. Physical and sexual abuse, drug addiction, alcoholism, extreme poverty, usually teenage mothers, no fathers. This prisoner had a mother up until he was seven. He lived in a nice house. His father had a business. Yes, the father was an alcoholic and there was obvious neglect and emotional abuse, but it's not the same story he hears every day. The Prisoner never starved. He had clean clothes and boots and coats. He had his own bedroom. He went to school. He may not have had many friends, but he wasn't a loner in the true sense of the word. The Prisoner's file – read quickly before meeting him – mentions some anger issues at school, early on, but nothing he was called out for. He spent no more time at the principal's office in elementary school than anyone else. A scrap here or there, a scuffle. He once had a girl's purse in his backpack, so there was some theft in the early days. The concussions are a factor, sure, but there is nothing tangible from the beginning that shouts, "Death Row." Nothing that calls out his eventual future, or, rather, the end of his future. The Prisoner has no more future and, in the beginning, at least, there is nothing that indicates that this was the way his life would turn out.

But was there any indication that the Chaplain would eventually beat his girlfriend almost to death?

"Do you want to pray?" the Prisoner asks.

"Sorry?" the Chaplain says.

"For me? Or for yourself? For the fact that your back aches?" The Prisoner says this with a smile on his face. He is standing close to the door, looking out at the five corrections officers. One officer has his face close to the window, and it looks for a minute as if he and the Prisoner are kissing.

"Do you want to pray?" the Chaplain says. "Do you want me to pray for you?"

"Nah." The Prisoner knocks on the window at the COs. He waves.

"What do you want?" CO4 unlocks the door and pops his head and upper body into the room.

"Just wanted to say hi," the Prisoner says.

The CO scowls. Looks at the Chaplain. "You okay, Father?"

"I'm not a priest. I'm just a chaplain. And, yes, I'm okay. I'm fine."

"Let me know if you want a break."

"I could use a break," the Prisoner says.

The Chaplain laughs. The Prisoner smiles over at him.

The CO glares at the Prisoner and the Chaplain.

So far, everything the Prisoner has said is what the Chaplain has already read in the files. Nothing new. But it's still fascinating, hearing it come out of his mouth. It's almost as if the Prisoner is reading his own files out loud. It seems rehearsed and planned. Nothing like the gushes of emotion that came from the Chaplain when it was recommended he see a psychologist and confess to how he felt and thought and why he did the things he did when he had no idea, really, why he did anything. But what about the Prisoner's feelings? Where are they as he talks? What is the Prisoner doing here, his last twelve hours, repeating the story of his life? Why is this necessary? The Chaplain thinks that if he only had twelve hours left, he certainly wouldn't be talking about his sister's kids or his uneventful childhood. The Chaplain would, instead, be atoning for his crimes. He would be apologizing or at least asking for forgiveness from God. Wouldn't he? Isn't that what he would be doing? Isn't that what he essentially did after Tracy, even without the death penalty hanging over him?

He's not sure, of course, seeing as he was not in this exact position himself. Facing death. Instead, he was facing only charges, perhaps some jail time, some community service. Maybe if he were facing death he would start with stories of his youth. It's a way to relive memories, he supposes. Say them aloud and you see them in your mind again. Three kids fighting over sandwiches, a mother with long blonde hair, the smell of a father's gin-soaked breath.

The Chaplain thinks of the bullying he got in elementary school. The way his sister used to fight anyone who said anything mean to him, how she was always there to protect him. She's there for her own kids now in the same way. Just last Sunday, at their regular family dinner, Miranda turned on her son, Damian, and smacked him hard across his head.

"What'd you do that for?" Damian howled.

"You're bullying your sister," Miranda said. "I want you to know what it's like to be picked on by someone older than you, by someone twice your size."

Her husband, Richard, laughed in that way Richard has – he crosses his arms and holds his chest as he chuckles, almost as if he thinks the laughter will pop him open, a trait that endeared him to the Chaplain when he married Miranda fifteen years ago. "Smack you right back, he will," Richard said. "You watch out, Miranda. I'm going to have to step in and stop the fight."

The Chaplain knows that Miranda's sense of right and wrong has always been black and white, and that is what he loves most about her. If you bully my brother, Miranda thinks, then I will bully you. Everything has always been this way for her. No alternatives. An eye for an eye.

Miranda is angry at her brother. She is angry that her brother is counseling a man who so deserves his fate. The death penalty makes sense to Miranda. For years she followed this case through appeal after appeal, the hard evidence, the soft evidence, the final admission of guilt. Everyone followed the Prisoner's story. It was compelling news. Terrifying. Gut-wrenching. The Prisoner was the man little children thought was hiding in their closets, behind their doors, under their beds. Why, Miranda thinks, does this man deserve sympathy and an open ear?

"Why would you ever want to listen to what he says?" she said at dinner. "I can't get over it. Why does he get a chaplain in the last hours? What about his victims? They don't get a chaplain now, do they?"

In a sense, Miranda is right. The Chaplain knows this. But he reminds himself that this prisoner is as human as his victims. He deserves a kind ear at the end. Surely, he does. The Chaplain doesn't have to forgive or to understand the Prisoner's deeds, but he can listen and he can hear.

Miranda would have executed this prisoner years ago when he committed the crime and no amount of arguing with her can change her opinion on that.

"It was a completely obvious case," Miranda said, rolling

her wine glass in her hand. "He did it. He even confessed to it. They had so much proof." Miranda watched the trial on the screen religiously. She followed all the news and discussed it at work. She knows more than her brother knows about the case now.

"Shouldn't that be something, then?" the Chaplain had said. "He confessed to it. He obviously feels remorse."

"All murderers probably feel remorse," Miranda countered. "But I bet that won't make their victims come back."

"Do they all confess? I don't know. Are they all remorseful? I don't know."

"Makes no difference, Jim. Listen to yourself."

"But, Miranda, the death penalty has never brought anyone back, nor has it deterred anyone from committing a crime."

"I'm sure it has lifted the weight off the victims' families' shoulders. I'm sure it has dulled their aches."

"Killing another human makes them feel better? Seriously, Miranda. Think about that."

Richard chuckled nervously. Filled up the wine. Poured himself a cup of coffee. Stayed out of it. As he always does. Off on the road tomorrow, he was probably thinking about work. The Chaplain can never figure out what Richard is thinking, but he knows that Richard is more often than not preparing mentally for those long hauls of driving a truck alone, for those stretched distances of silence on the bitterly boring road. For leaving his kids and wife for another week.

"Besides," Miranda said. "You didn't say this guy was remorseful. You just said that he confessed. You can confess to something that you'd still do again in an instant. I confess that I just smacked Damian on the head and it made me sad for a minute, but if he bullies his sister again, I'll just as soon smack him again."

"Mom," Damian hollered. "You can't hit me. That's illegal. Right, Uncle Jim?"

The Chaplain smiles. "You're right."

"Yeah, well. Behave."

"If it made you sad, you shouldn't have done it," Damian said.

"Yeah," his sister said. "Why'd you hit Damian, Mom? You said never to hit."

"Oh, for God's sake," Miranda said. "I didn't hit him, I smacked him. There's a difference."

The Chaplain held up his hand. "Falsely accused?" he said.

"Don't start with that," Miranda said, raising her finger.

"Can I smack him too, Mom?" Daisy raised her hand and hovered near Damian.

"You two! Up to bed. Now. Both of you."

"I'll take them up," Richard said. "Books? Bath? What'll it be?"

"Book," said Damian.

"Bath," said Daisy.

They kissed their uncle and went up with their father to the second floor. The Chaplain filled his wine again and looked at his sister. They stared at each other, listening to the commotion from above – the bath water filling, Damian shouting something down the hall, Daisy thumping in her room, Richard's chuckle.

"Little devils," Miranda said with a smile on her face.

"Yeah, we hate them, don't we? We should execute them."

Miranda threw a fork at her brother and he dove just in time.

The Chaplain thinks of this now, this regular dinner he has with his sister and her husband and her kids. His lovely, crazy, wild niece and nephew. Even if he ever had the opportunity to have his own family, he doesn't really need them – his own kids, a wife – not anymore. Not when he has Miranda's family. He might have had the opportunity once, perhaps, but that is long gone. Who would take him now? Who would trust him now? Even after all he's done to try to right his wrongs. Now the Chaplain spends his time adoring his sister's children. Imagine, he thinks, if they had been the Prisoner's victims?

Miranda is the bully-fighter. She is the holder of right and wrong, black and white. The Chaplain used to be easy to sway, but lately he's been standing up for his convictions. This man in front of him deserves to be treated like a human being. There is no debate. Being here, however, doesn't mean that he believes in the death penalty.

The Warden had said, "Don't let the Prisoner talk you into saving him." The Warden didn't know how right he might be, how prescient those words. The Chaplain's soul, his sister says, is soft.

How strange to think that the next time the Chaplain sees his sister and her kids, the man before him will be dead. Killed by the government. The Chaplain's quiet life – the one he attempted to build after university, after Tracy, after the charges were dropped, through years of his own therapy and counseling, after years of loneliness and anger, through all his studies, before he realized his calling and took his oath – seems to be a little louder now. He's not sure if that's in a bad way or a good way. He knew when he took this job as prison chaplain that he might be called to the last hours of a man about to die. This shouldn't be such a surprise to him. But being here, seeing it, breathing in this room, well . . . it's not what he was ready for.

And it came on so suddenly. Cancer pushed him into it before he was ready.

"Do you think that guy really stabbed himself in the eye

with a pencil?" the Prisoner asks. Both the Chaplain and the Prisoner are still standing. Only feet away from each other. The air is hot and sticky, closed, in this room. Why won't they give them a window, the Chaplain thinks, in their last hours? A breath of fresh air. A spot of sun? A moon? Why green walls?

"Not sure. Seems likely, though."

"Why does it seem likely?"

"Well, because anything is likely in here, don't you think? I've heard some stories."

"I've seen some things," the Prisoner says, a far-off look in his eyes. "You wouldn't even believe."

"I'd believe," the Chaplain says. "I'd definitely believe."

"Yeah, I guess." The Prisoner sits again on his cot. He wiggles his toes in his canvas running shoes. "Before I was on Death Row, I had a roommate who tried to sodomize me with his toothbrush."

"Oh."

"Yeah."

"What happened?"

"He sodomized me. Not only with his toothbrush. Nothing I could do about it. It hurt. Got a few days in the hospital, though."

The Chaplain has no response to this. He knows this, he hears it all the time when counseling the others. But they don't use words like *sodomize*. They say, "bite the pillow," or "butt fuck," or "stir the peanut butter," or "take it up the ass." Never "sodomy." The Prisoner is a stranger in here just by his choice of words. He is different from all the others even if the crimes he committed might seem to fit in.

Not so unlike the Chaplain. He never fit in either. Still doesn't. A prison chaplain who doesn't quote the Bible that often. He tries, but always forgets to comfort with psalms and verses. He forgets to carry the Bible with him. It just doesn't come to him naturally yet. Instead, he goes straight towards what makes him feel the best – consoling. If a prisoner tells him the correctional officers won't let him out in the yard because he's been fighting with his roommate, the Chaplain tends to nod his head in sympathy instead of counseling the prisoner to apologize, to avoid violence, to be humble and forgiving of others as well as himself. It's not as if the Chaplain is not religious – of course he is, he is a prison chaplain – but he doesn't naturally turn towards his religion first for all the answers. Not yet. He knows that will come with time. The Chaplain's religion is, instead, in his soul, deep down, something so natural inside of him. It's not something he feels he has to wear on his sleeve or quote continuously in order to understand. This is probably why he didn't bring his Bible today. He doesn't really need it, does he? Everything he needs is inside of him. His mentor used to roll his eyes at him when he passed by a counseling session in the common room. He would see the Chaplain with his Bible on his lap, unopened, nodding sympathetically to complaining prisoners.

"You might as well have gone into psychiatry," his mentor would say and roll his eyes.

Before this, before his life as a chaplain, he didn't fit into school either. In university, he studied English literature and political science, hoping to eventually apply to law school. Instead, in his final year, just before the incident with Tracy, he became hooked on an elective course on world religion. And after Tracy, he wanted nothing more than to be a minister, or if not a minister, to at least minister to others. He wanted penance. To be forgiven for his sins. Miranda thought he was crazy.

"Just because of Tracy, it doesn't mean you have to be a priest, Jim."

"I'm not going to be a priest, I'll be a minister. United or something. Something like that. And it has nothing to do with Tracy."

"How does this not have anything to do with Tracy? We weren't even religious growing up, for God's sake. You never even went to Sunday school."

"You did."

"Yeah, with my friend. But only because if I memorized a verse from the Bible I'd get candy." Miranda laughed. "And Mom never gave us candy."

"It's not like I'm going to be a different person," the Chaplain said. "I just need something to believe in right now, and I believe in this."

"Sure. Until you meet another woman."

"Miranda. What woman would be crazy enough . . . ?"

"Honestly, Jim, I don't know what to do with you. Do you know what we should do with him, Richard?"

Richard shrugged. He placed an arm around Miranda's shoulders.

"God, Jim. Religion? Being religious is not going to make you feel any better about yourself."

"Why does this matter to you?" the Chaplain said, insulted.

"Because I don't want you to be someone you're not just because of what happened with Tracy."

Tracy and Jim. All through undergrad. They would dive into dorm rooms – hers or his – make love under the overbleached sheets, the scratchy blankets, try hard not to make any noise through paper-thin walls. Groaning and grunting, giggling, grasping. His body was sore, his mind was full. He was in love with this woman, his first true love. Tracy. Hair black and straight. Wonky teeth, a big grin. Beautiful eyes. Tracy hooked him the first day she sat next to him in his course on Thomas

Hardy. She sat down and this smell, she gave off this smell, it sucked him in. Later he found out it was Chanel No. 5, and Tracy soon made the connection that his mother used to wear that perfume. The smell must have been in his memory channels, floating through his head, full of life and love and care.

They were together for three years. He was sure they would graduate and find a house and get married and have children. They would live down the street from Miranda and Richard, and Tracy would talk to Miranda about children and everything else. They would have Christmases together, they would have barbecues. His father had recently died of a heart condition, his mother died when he and Miranda were in high school of breast cancer, and he was looking for a family to fill the gap. It was something he needed desperately.

But Tracy met David and that was the end of it. It was amazing, actually, how fast it happened. She moved out of their apartment within weeks of meeting David and straight into his place. Recently separated from his wife, David was the teaching assistant for their Children's Literature course. People told him later that David was sleeping with everyone, not just Tracy. But not everyone moved in with David, only Tracy.

And so, after his court-appointed therapy, after everything that happened, he burrowed down into religious studies. Religion classes were the only classes that seemed to speak to him then – they made life seem less complicated and more doable. They filled a gap in his body and soul, a gap he didn't realize was there. A black hole, a chasm that opened after Tracy (but which the therapist also quickly linked back to the death of his mother). And he soon graduated, got his master's degree, trained in psychology and pastoral counseling, got ordained, got well and a year ago started here, at the prison, being mentored as a chaplain. He is even certified. He even did that. His mentor's cancer has catapulted him into a position he wouldn't have been put in for another year, but he knows you can't always plan your life, you have to take it as it comes. This experience, what happens in these next hours, will affect him for his life. But these hours will also make him a stronger chaplain, a stronger man of God. And he's grateful for that.

The Prisoner lies down on his cot again, puts his hands behind his head.

"The one good thing about being put in solitary on death row," he says, "is that I didn't have to have a roommate again."

The Chaplain is amazed that the Prisoner never seems to look at the clock. The Chaplain has been watching each number turn. The red digital light is giving him a headache. It's wonderful and strange, too, how the digital clock works, how it's merely a rectangle with a line through the middle and each number fits into that – from one to nine. It's only a matter of one or two red lines coming and going, here for a minute, then gone. A four becomes a five simply by the addition or subtraction of lines.

"My father's clock-and-watch business gave me a start in life. A hand up. Something my friends didn't have. I mean, I learned a trade young. That was good," the Prisoner says, suddenly, and the Chaplain realizes that they are moving back into the story, into the Prisoner's life. "Of course, I never applied it. I never put any of that to good use." The Chaplain takes the chair he was sitting in, pulls it into another position, sits on it and puts his feet up on the second chair. Leans back slightly, tilting. His back aches already and he has hours and hours left. But his physical pain can be overcome. He takes the Prisoner's advice and thinks about his ankles, stretched to tilt him back, he thinks about his calves, his knees, he focuses on each part of his body – quickly, because he doesn't want to be concentrating on himself while the Prisoner talks – and soon he is aware of the fullness and size of his body, of what it contains. He is suddenly unaware of his back problems. The Prisoner is right. This kind of focus does work. The Chaplain's mind turns to the Prisoner's voice, and he knows he can sit here forever.

The Figurine

When Larry is twelve years old, he is caught shoplifting. From his father's store. He justifies this.

"It's not stealing when it's yours," he shouts.

His father smacks him around. "It wasn't your watch," he says. "It was a customer's watch."

Larry sold the watch for a hundred dollars. His first crime. Unfortunately, a stupid crime – he unknowingly sold the watch back to the owner, a local thug, Dwight, the guy who collected protection money from all the businesses in town. A drug dealer. A petty thief.

"I had a watch like this once," Dwight tells Larry. "Some little creep stole it."

Larry swallows hard, nurses his ribs where his father kicked him when he was down. It doesn't matter, though, he needs the money.

For what? He isn't sure. It's just something people need. Money. Lots of it. Supposedly it'll make your life better somehow, Larry is never sure how. And even when he finally has it, he never finds out how money makes his life better, but he does spend most of his life wanting it, needing it, finding it, getting it. Money becomes a surrogate mother. He craves it, collects it, commits crimes for it. He rarely spends it.

Coffee tins.

But that comes later, he tells the Chaplain.

Dwight pays for his own watch. Larry can't figure out why until one day the large, mean man shows up at the store and wants a little help with a job. He needs small fingers, he says, a tiny frame. A kid who can slide through windows, who can look innocent if caught, who has no connection to Dwight.

Larry's first B and E.

"You slide in through there," Dwight whispers.

They are in the dark behind the house. A kitchen window is slightly open. It's a small window; Larry isn't sure he can get in. He is small, but not that small. His bones aren't liquid.

"What about the screen?" he asks.

"I'll cut it. Like this. See." Dwight takes out a box cutter and slices through the screen like butter. The knife is brutally sharp. Larry takes a breath. Swallows.

"You get in. Don't make any noise or I use this on you." Dwight holds up the knife. "Then you open the back door for me. I'll do the rest."

So Larry squeezes through the cut screen of the window. Lands with a tiny thump on the kitchen counter. A cat meows below him and he almost screams. A spoon on the counter rattles. Larry can feel his heart in his throat. The pulse drowns out his hearing. He panics. He can hear it in his head, so loud, beating so wildly, the blood rushing. He swears everyone in the house, sleeping, can hear his heart. He holds his breath. The cat meows again.

"Fucking cat," Dwight whispers from the window. "Get down and open the door."

Larry climbs down from the counter. He can breathe again. So far so good. He goes over to the back door, the cat following, meowing, and he unlocks the lock. Dwight comes in slowly and quietly – for such a big guy he is, well, cat-like. The cat disappears out the door, with a small kick from Dwight. Dwight puts his finger to his mouth. Larry wants to leave but Dwight signals that Larry should come with him. They move together throughout the main floor of the house. The kitchen, the living room, an office, a small bathroom.

There is a moon, perhaps it's full, the Prisoner can't remember now, but everything seems lit up, clear in his mind.

Dwight collects pills and prescription bottles from the bathroom. He takes a laptop computer from the office. He pockets a watch and a ring that were lying on the kitchen counter. In the living room, he takes whatever he can – another computer, a clock, a few odds and ends. Mostly he's there for the pills, he's told Larry, but he might as well fill up with other things too.

Dwight encourages Larry to take something. He mimes putting something in his pocket and he points to Larry.

There is a noise from upstairs. A door opens. A creak of the floor. A *thump, thump* as someone walks down the hall.

Larry makes as if to run but Dwight holds him back. Shoots arrows from his eyes. Stay, his eyes are saying. Don't move.

Another door closes. The sound of water. Then a toilet flush and the same *thump, thump* back down the hall, creak, the door to the bedroom closes. Silence.

Larry is wide-eyed. Terrified.

Dwight shrugs.

Larry pockets a statue that is resting on the fireplace. A small figurine. A young boy, fishing, leaning back on a log. It's delicate, yet heavy. The boy's fishing pole and fishing line are made out of wood and string. The boy's expression is one of contentment. His eyes are half closed. Larry puts it in his coat pocket, careful not to break it. Dwight shakes his head.

"What the fuck are you going to do with that?" Dwight says, later, when they are back at his apartment, pulling everything out of their pockets, out of Dwight's bag. "It's not even worth anything."

Larry shrugs. "I don't know. I just liked it."

"Idiot. You can't even sell it. You should always take something you can sell."

Larry will always remember that first B and E. He will remember the *thump, thump* as those footsteps came down the hall upstairs. He will remember the way the cat meowed at him, looking up at him with wide, glowing eyes as he crouched on the kitchen counter. He will remember the look in Dwight's eyes, an adrenalin coursing through him that Larry realizes later in his life is more addictive than crack or booze. The feel of getting away with it. Dwight was high on it. Later, Larry knows that feeling and can't get away from it either. No matter how hard he tries.

Sometimes, when Larry has squeezed into a window and is standing in a darkened house, he thinks about Jack and what he might be doing. He wonders if Jack is taking care of their mother or if he's left her and gone off on his own. He wonders if Jack is still alive. Jack would be fourteen when Larry is twelve. Hard to believe. The asshole brother of his youth – last time he saw Jack, he was nine and Larry was seven. Susan was eleven. Larry can't imagine Jack being older than he was then. He can't imagine him having to shave or being taller or broader or having a deep voice.

Larry wonders if Jack would be proud of his prowess, proud of the money he is saving. Dwight gives him some, sometimes – after Larry pays off the one hundred dollars he owes Dwight for his watch. They work most nights after Susan and the baby have gone to bed, after his father has passed out on the living room couch. Dwight throws pebbles at Larry's window and he sidles down the drainpipe of his house and goes out into the night. When he is older, Larry merely walks down the stairs and out the front door.

No one ever asks him where he's going.

No one ever asks him what he's doing.

When Dwight shows Larry the gun, things change. The box cutter was one thing. It kept Larry in line, made him aware of Dwight and his power and his need for Larry to be small and quiet and fast. But when Larry is fifteen and Dwight shows up with the gun, things change drastically.

Larry works at the watch store most days after school. He's failing school but doesn't worry about it. Susan's the only one who knows – she screens the calls from the school – and she says nothing to their father. She smacks him on the head, though, and tries to tell him to smarten up, work hard, get a diploma at least. Fucking idiot, she screams. But she is now pregnant with her second child (from two different men) and a high school dropout herself, and so she doesn't have time to take care of Larry and his life and his future. It's surprising, really, that their father lets Susan live at home at nineteen with two kids and no job. Larry knows that it's because their father is usually so shit-faced when he comes home that he doesn't even know who lives there. Baby crap everywhere, toys all around, smelly diapers in the trash cans, Susan with some guy on the couch. Different guys each week. Larry avoids the house as much as possible. Their father pays the bills occasionally, sometimes just throws the money at Susan when she hollers for it, but other than that he leaves them alone. At work every day, Larry and his father toil in silence. His father's hands shake now, so Larry does the small stuff. He uses the magnifying equipment and the small tweezers, and he resets watches and puts new batteries in and winds springs and fiddles with the tiny screws. His father handles the customers when he's not completely soused, and he looks after the grandfather clocks, which are less finicky but which startle him sometimes with their loud bongs. Sometimes he jokes about changing the sign to Gallo and Son's Precision Repair, but then he gets angry and changes his mind and tells Larry to leave him alone and stop touching him and clean the house or the store or whatever flashes into his mind at the time.

It's a fragile affair. Larry balances between it all. He puts on his armour. Begins wearing his pants low, like a gangster. He begins to get tattoos – because Dwight has them – but gets them where his father or Susan won't see – his upper arm, his back, his calf. Larry wears jewellery, mostly stuff he steals, like huge chains, thick gold ropes. He wears a baseball hat backwards and he spits as much as he can, when he can, when he thinks it'll make him look good. He has stopped using words like *untowards*, stopped reading and caring about anything. His running shoes are always untied, and the tongues slap while he walks. The walk of a man with pants falling – shuffle, step. Dwight tells him that all the real men are wearing their pants this way, but it's not until Larry is in jail, later, that he understands why. No belts in jail. Nothing to hold up the saggy pants. They are imitating the fallen.

In prison, he is given an orange jumpsuit.

On death row, he is given a white one with the letters *DR* on the back. No more baggy pants.

"That's another thing," Dwight tells him. "Why the fuck do you go by Larry? It's such a stupid name."

"And Dwight is better?"

"Lawrence?" Dwight laughs. "How about Lawrence?"

Larry's mother used "Lawrence." The sound of that name makes Larry shudder.

Dwight smacks Larry on the head. "Well, at least you can shorten your name. I can't. Fucking what else can I do? D? Dwighty? There's no short for Dwight."

"I guess I could go by another name. I never thought about it."

"Yeah, well, sometimes you need to know things, bro. You need to know why you do things. Don't just do things because that's the way you do them. Do things because you know why you're doing them. Take me, for example. I do things for a reason."

Larry looks up at Dwight. "Like what reason?"

"I steal to make money to buy drugs to sell to make more money to buy drugs to take." Dwight laughs. "Fucking idiot. It's a circle. Goes 'round and 'round." He swirls his finger in the air. "Snake swallowing its tail." Dwight points to a tattoo of a snake on his wrist. The snake's tail is in its mouth.

"Yeah, I guess."

"It's common sense, man."

Larry doesn't know if that's what it is – common sense – but he's comfortable with Dwight after all these years. It's the two of them, three years now, and Dwight hasn't fucked him around once yet. He gets his portion of the proceeds. Always. Dwight may tell him he's stupid all the time, smack him on the head a lot, but Larry knows Dwight trusts him. And Dwight needs him. Even now that Larry is getting bigger and filling out and getting wider and having more and more trouble getting into the small windows. Dwight still needs him because he's always high and Larry is sober and they work well together. Larry wakes him up in the morning when he's slept too late and he tells Dwight when to run.

That's why Dwight gets the gun.

"More options," Dwight says. "More ways of getting into things."

"And hopefully getting out of things. Alive," Larry says. And Dwight smacks him on his head and laughs.

"Fucking idiot, Larry. You're a fucking idiot."

They didn't mean for it to happen the way it did. The gun went off prematurely. Dwight said he knew how to use it. Larry didn't know how to use it. He only knew how to hold it and that was from watching the screen and movies, not from ever handling a gun.

They are in the 24-Hour Variety on White Avenue. Just a few streets over from Gallo's Precision Repair. It is midnight. The *Open All Night* sign flashes in the store window, which is steamed over from the cold rain on the hot pavement. The guy behind the counter is watching his screen. He's got a little screen fixed to the wall, up high, and he leans back on his stool to watch it. He's a big guy, muscular. Larry swallows hard when he sees him. Tattoos on his arm, cryptic symbols, crosses, a mermaid, numbers, fancy italic script.

Dwight enters the store first and shops around. This has been planned out, talked about, discussed, now put into action. He moves up and down the aisles as if searching for something. He has a backpack slung over his shoulder and his hood up. He avoids the surveillance camera. The guy behind the desk gives him a once-over and then goes back to watching the screen. Dwight clears his throat several times when Larry enters the store. Larry goes straight up to the counter.

"Player's," he says.

"You're too young to buy them," the guy behind the counter says, without even looking at Larry. "Fuck off."

Larry says, "Player's, please," and the guy looks at him, stands, looks down on him, and says, "Get the fuck out of my store."

"Hey," Dwight says. "That's not nice. Be nice to the little guy."

"Are you buying something or are you just loitering?"

"Big word from a big guy," Dwight says. "I'm here to rob you."

The guy laughs. Larry blushes bright red. He stands back and lets Dwight in at the counter beside him. Dwight reaches into his back pocket and pulls out the gun. He points it at the guy. "Bang, bang," he says.

"Fuck," the guy says. He backs up. He looks at Dwight and then at Larry. "You in on this?"

"I just wanted cigarettes," Larry says. His voice cracks with excitement. "If you'd just given me the cigarettes. I asked nicely. I said please."

Dwight laughs. "Get the cash," he says, pushing Larry towards the back of the counter.

The guy reaches down slowly, as if they won't notice, and goes for the alarm button. Dwight shakes the gun in his face. "No fucking way. No way. Get your hands up where I can see them."

The guy lifts his hands up and Larry comes around the counter and then all chaos breaks out. The guy's arm – his big, beefy, tattooed arm – comes down on Larry's nose, and Larry's brain goes black. Just for a minute. Like when Jack gave him concussions. Everything turns off. Larry shakes his head to clear his vision and then a gunshot rings out and Dwight is shouting and the guy is slumping down behind the counter. There is blood everywhere. On Larry, on the floor, on the guy, on the counter, on the gun. Even on the ceiling.

"I didn't mean to shoot," Dwight screams. "I didn't mean to shoot. The gun just went off. It went off by itself. I didn't shoot. I didn't pull the trigger. I didn't –"

"Shut up," Larry shouts. "Shut up, shut up, shut up!" Larry's nose aches, his head swims. He grabs the gun from Dwight and pokes at the guy on the floor behind the counter. He is still. But breathing. Larry swears he can see his breath.

Larry looks straight at the surveillance camera in the corner of the store. "Deal with that, Dwight. I'll get the cash."

And Dwight takes the stool, drags it through the blood and over to the camera, climbs up on it and starts bashing the camera with his gloved hands, with a hammer he has in his backpack, with anything he can. He bashes until it's in pieces on the floor.

"These things sometimes go straight into the security place," Dwight says. "Sometimes they feed straight there."

"That one doesn't," Larry says. He is standing over the guy and pulling all the money from the cash register. Larry's vision is clearer and his nose has stopped aching. Some of the money gets blood on it, but there is nothing Larry can do about it. The guy has stopped breathing. "We have one of those at my dad's store. It's just a recorder. Check the back for the recording."

"Oh fuck," Dwight says. "Do you think he's dead? Is he dead?"

"No," Larry lies. "He's just injured. Don't worry."

The money goes into the backpack. Even though Larry doesn't smoke, he grabs a pack of Player's cigarettes. They take one last look at the guy on the floor, the pool of blood thickening under his body. He is face down, which is good, because Larry knows that he would dream about this guy for the rest of his life if he saw his face. His unseeing eyes.

They find the recording in the back and then clear the store, rush out into the night, into the rain, which is pouring down, rush out into the street and away.

Later, Larry counts his money. His bloody half. Dwight is shaking hard. Freaking out. "We fucking killed a man, I know it," Dwight says. He is leaning over the sink in his apartment, trying to wash the blood off his portion of the bills.

"He's just hurt," Larry says over and over, until they see the news and watch it over and over on the screen – *Murdered 24-Hour Variety Man*. Two kids. Ex-wife. Ex-convict. Just released after ten years for drug crimes. Was making good. Got a job. Worked late shift. Murdered. Shot twice in the stomach ("Twice?" Dwight says. "I only shot once. Did you hear more than one shot? I only shot once"), bled out. No suspects.

Eventually the cops think it's drug-related. Think it has nothing to do with robbing the store but more to do with the employee's history. Dwight and Larry breathe a sigh of relief. They laugh about it later. Their first big score. Made $1,034.25. Split in half that's $517.12 each. Enough to buy something big.

But Dwight's hands still shake. Larry has to hold the gun the next time because Dwight's hands shake so much.

And the next time.

And the next.

"We killed a man," he says.

Soon the gun is more Larry's than Dwight's. Soon it has become part of Larry. It fits in his hand like the gloves he wears to hold it. He flashes it around easily and confidently. He doesn't need to shoot it, just show it. There. My gun. They go into the heart of the city and into the suburbs. They rob convenience stores and inconvenient ones. They wear masks and hoods. Sometimes Larry has to shoot to warn, but this is rare. The gun becomes merely an extension of his hand to wave around and cause fear, to get the money. Dwight uses the

money to buy drugs, which he then both takes and sells. Lately
he's taking more than selling. Larry saves his money for now.
He puts it in a coffee tin under a loose floorboard in the attic.
And then another coffee tin, and another and another. When
Larry is seventeen, he will move out of the house with his coffee
tins and his gun. He will move away from Susan and his father
– although he will still work often at Gallo's – a kind of cover
for his extracurricular activities. A way to make sure his father
is still alive.

2:01 a.m.

There is a knock on the door. Corrections Officer 6 enters carrying a tray. On the tray are two coffees, black. Two cookies.

"Thought you'd like a snack." He smirks.

"Fuck," the Prisoner says. "A cookie and coffee? What about milk and cookies? It's like kindergarten."

"If you don't want it . . ." The CO starts to leave.

"Stop."

"You can have both the cookies," the Chaplain says to the Prisoner as he takes the coffee cup from the CO. "I'm not hungry."

Surprisingly, the Prisoner wolfs both cookies down. As if he's starving. He barely chews them. Crumbs all over the bed. Then he slurps at the coffee loudly. "Hot," he says.

The Chaplain is standing again. Stretching his back out. He looks at the clock. 2:03 a.m. Less than ten hours left. He quickly does the math in his head. Six hundred minutes. Thirty-six thousand seconds. That's all there is.

CO6 leaves them with the disposable coffee cups. The Chaplain supposes the Prisoner can't injure himself with them.

And then he wonders if eating the cup would do anything – besides cause upset stomach. But if you had an upset stomach before execution, would they delay the execution? The Chaplain isn't sure how all of this works. He asks the Prisoner.

"They had some guy earlier, a medical guy . . . examiner . . . come in and look at me. See if I was fit to be executed. Kind of funny. He poked and prodded." The Prisoner pauses. "Fit to be killed." Then he pretends to bite the disposable cup.

The Chaplain has so many questions now. Questions he didn't think of asking before. When his mentor got sick and the Warden told him to do this, the Chaplain thought it was about listening, not thinking, but now he knows it's about thinking while you listen. He's hearing the Prisoner's story, and the more he hears, the more questions he has. Yes, he read the files. Yes, he knows what the Prisoner has done. Except for that first murder – the 24-Hour Variety employee. That wasn't in any of the files. Because they weren't caught. There is no record of that. In fact, it could be a lie. Besides, the Prisoner didn't pull the trigger; it was this Dwight who had the gun. But still. It makes the Chaplain feel slightly off-balance that a new crime is coming to light now, with only hours left, as if the Prisoner has saved it for the end. His new confession.

And that makes the Chaplain wonder about all the things the Prisoner has done that he hasn't been charged with. Does this mean that the Prisoner is guiltier than the Chaplain knows? That he deserves execution even more than the government thinks? Or could he be lying about things? But why would someone lie just before their execution? You would think that this is the perfect time to finally tell the whole truth and nothing but.

The Chaplain comes back again and again to the way in which the Prisoner is telling his story. It seems emotionless.

Sure, the Prisoner tries to crack a joke here or there, he tears up slightly when talking about his mother, but in general, he isn't showing much emotion. It's a tale told verbatim, a tale that could very well have been written down, read aloud. Even the way the Prisoner lies on the cot, his feet up, his hands behind his head, as if he has all the time in the world and is getting really comfy. He likes his audience. He likes *an* audience. The Chaplain has the impression he would love it if the lights suddenly dimmed and out there, behind the door, was a crowd. Cheering. Listening. Booing. This is all a theatre for the Prisoner. His life is a stage play. The Chaplain is the fan. He hasn't yet digested his life, taken it in, and this worries the Chaplain. If he is to die soon and feels no remorse, or, if not remorse, something – if he feels nothing – just talks and talks – if that is happening, is this right? What would Miranda think about this? Can a man go to his death never fully understanding what it is he has done?

The Chaplain guesses that this happens all the time.

Heart attacks, aneurysms, car accidents. People die without contemplating their lives all the time.

He sighs.

The Prisoner stops slurping his coffee, he is finished, and begins picking apart his cup. Picks around the rim and puts the pieces into the cup and the cup gets smaller and smaller as he does this. Like a snake eating its tail. Like Dwight's tattoo.

"Wait a minute," the Chaplain says. "Dwight? The Dwight who is in here?"

"Yeah, Dwight Mercer, that's the guy."

"I talked to him a little while ago. Dwight Mercer."

"Yeah. Dwight came in about a year ago."

"But." The Chaplain doesn't know what to say. Dwight wasn't in the files on the murder case that put the Prisoner on death row. He had no idea they were connected.

"He got caught selling drugs. We haven't been hanging together in years. First time I saw him in," the Prisoner pauses, thinks, "eleven years, I'd say, was in prison here about six months ago. They keep us separate – the regulars and death row – but I saw Dwight when I walked past a window one day. He was in the yard, being Dwight. Being the same asshole he always was." The Prisoner laughs. "He was taking bets on something, I swear. Fucking gambler. Always betting on everything. He'd even have you betting, Chaplain. In a second."

"I doubt that." The Chaplain smiles. Although he used to play a monthly game of poker in university with Tracy and another couple, the Chaplain never bet high, got out before he lost anything. He's always been too careful to be a gambler. Tracy would tease him mercilessly, preferring to bet their rent money and take a chance. The Chaplain thinks now that this should have been a sign. Maybe if he'd been more interesting, if he'd taken more chances, Tracy wouldn't have left him.

"He didn't see me. But I saw him. Jesus, he got fat. I heard he was in for drugs. Selling."

"Yes, he is. I spoke to him about two weeks ago." The Chaplain watches the Prisoner for emotion. This man, Dwight Mercer, this man who took the Prisoner as a young child and shaped him into a criminal – you would think that this would warrant some sort of emotion? And it suddenly does.

"Wish I could have said goodbye," the Prisoner says. Quietly. He turns from the Chaplain then. Turns towards the wall. But his voice gives nothing away. "It's fucking small in here, isn't it? I've got to –" he points towards the toilet.

"Sure, yes." The Chaplain knocks on the door. A CO comes in. He tells the CO that the Prisoner needs privacy. The CO takes the two coffee cups, one torn in half, and motions for the

Chaplain to exit the room. Five COs stare through the window in the door at the Prisoner as he relieves himself.

In the outside room, there is air. The Chaplain didn't realize how stifling it was inside the cell, but out here the walls are white, not green, and the lights are brighter, and there is a small window to the outside – although it's pitch black and the Chaplain can't see anything but the night. The air feels cooler in here and cleaner. There are no real smells (although one CO is wearing heavy cologne). The Chaplain sniffs.

"How's it going in there?"

"As good as one could expect," the Chaplain says.

"No trouble?"

"No. No trouble."

The Chaplain glances towards the execution room door. It is open and even though the lights aren't on, the Chaplain can make out the shape of a chair with straps, heavy curtains on one wall. He is suddenly assaulted by a vision of the seagull with the arrow through it flying past him. As if it's right in front of him. He holds the back of a chair for support, wobbles a bit on his legs, and the COs take note of this and lower him into the seat.

"Thank you. I'm just tired, I guess."

"It's hard shit in there," CO7 says. "Take it easy."

The Chaplain swears he can hear the gull crying as it flies past. The arrow straight through the body, top to bottom, almost comical, cartoonish. Why the top to the bottom, too? Wouldn't the arrow be through the chest if shot from below? Or was the bird standing on the shore, feeding, perhaps, and someone snuck up behind it? The Chaplain shakes his head. The toilet flushes from within the cell. The Chaplain stands.

"Take it easy, man," a CO says. "You can stay out here for a bit if you want."

"No. There isn't time," the Chaplain says. He points towards the execution chamber. "There is no time."

"Calm down," CO7 says, in a voice that reminds the Chaplain of his mother or his sister. A voice of reason and strength.

He enters the small cell, which they open for him grudgingly. The Prisoner looks ashamed and the Chaplain realizes it's because of the smell. His stomach is obviously upset. The coffee and cookies didn't help matters. The Chaplain pretends he smells nothing and takes his seat again. The Prisoner paces. Moving the air around.

"So, what did Dwight say?"

"When?"

"When you saw him. Did you tell him you were coming here?"

"No. I found out after I saw Dwight that I would be with you. And I had no idea you two knew each other. I didn't make the connection, even though I've read your file. I should have made a connection. How many people are named Dwight? I'm sorry."

The Prisoner sits on the bed again. He yawns. Stretches. "No problem. It doesn't matter now. Nothing matters now."

"This leads me to ask," the Chaplain says, clearing his throat. "Is anyone coming at noon? Any of your family? Susan? Your father?"

"My father is long gone." The Prisoner stands again. Although he is yawning, he is becoming more and more agitated and fidgety. He cracks his fingers. Stretches again. Yawns. Dogs yawn, the Chaplain thinks, when they are nervous or agitated or excited.

"What about Susan? Your nieces and nephews?"

The Prisoner laughs. He sits again on the cot. "I haven't

spoken to her for a long time. I don't know her kids very well."

"What about," the Chaplain ventures, "Jack? Your mother?"

"My mother is dead and Jack is dead to me," the Prisoner says, loudly now. Angrily. "Jack is dead to me."

"But maybe he should be here, maybe he would –"

"Shut up," the Prisoner says. "Just shut the fuck up about them. They are all dead to me. I don't have any family. And I'm fine with that. Why do you think you're here? If I wanted anyone, I would have asked for them, not you."

The COs knock on the door. "Everyone okay in there?"

"Yeah, yeah, whatever." The Prisoner lies back down on the bed. His hands are shaking. The Chaplain feels alive, electric. The anger swirls in the air. For a minute, he knows he saw the real man. The real Prisoner. Just a flash of him. That intense anger. He's crazy, Miranda would say. But the Chaplain feels that this fearsome part of the Prisoner shows more about real human emotion than it shows about sanity or insanity. He lets his true colours show only in anger. He is only himself when he's angry. The Chaplain himself let his inner feelings come out in anger, feelings he didn't even know he had. Feelings Tracy had no idea about either. This Prisoner has been angry at the world since his mother left (and the Chaplain? Since the minute Tracy betrayed him and told him about David). Since his mother took Jack and left (since Tracy left with David). All the world is the same, the Chaplain thinks. No matter how you cover it – with religion or a prison jumpsuit.

The Chaplain wishes he had had more time with the Prisoner before this day. He wishes he could have researched the Prisoner's life better – a quick skim in the last several days wasn't enough – perhaps he could have found Jack, at least found out what happened to his mother. Brought Jack here. For what? To watch his brother murdered? Strapped to a chair.

Bolts of electricity coursing through him? No, maybe not.

Wouldn't his mentor have looked into all of this anyway? He was with the Prisoner for a long time, years. Surely he would have asked the right questions, helped in some way. Wouldn't he? If there was a family member the Prisoner wanted to see, his mentor would have arranged it.

The Chaplain's mind goes back, suddenly, to the crime scene photos in the Prisoner's file. The gruesome photos. The blood. The hands outstretched. Pleading to be saved. It's impossible for him to imagine the man in front of him creating those bloody messes and doing it without a grain of remorse. With no regret. No guilt. Here he is, ten years later, after his appeals – after all legal avenues have been followed – with no remorse. No tears. No begging for forgiveness. Instead, he wants to recite his story, line by line. Waste his time, his final moments, rehashing his past. Instead, his only emotion comes out when he thinks of Dwight, another criminal, the man who started him down this slippery slope. The Chaplain doesn't understand.

There isn't much he understood until religion. The incident with Tracy made him feel as if he was merely a shell of a man walking around, as if there wasn't anything worthwhile underneath his skin. He hated himself. He wished, sometimes, that Tracy hadn't dropped the charges. He wanted to be punished. The judge making him go into therapy didn't seem enough at the time. Religion, his faith, what he was learning about in school, grounded him. Made him feel real again. But religion isn't helping either the Chaplain or the Prisoner here. The Prisoner doesn't seem open to prayer or contemplation, at least not yet. And why would he be when the end result, in his mind, will be the same.

The Chaplain wishes that he had been religious, that he had believed, on the night Tracy came to tell him about David.

➤———→

"I've fallen in love with him, Jim," Tracy says. Straight out of a made-for-screen movie, or a romance novel. What is Jim to do? "We have so much in common," she says.

In common? What? Children's literature? Her grades?

It's not you, it's me, he wants to shout. He wants to finish her lines for her.

"Three years?" is all he can say. "We've had three years together and now –"

"I'm so sorry, Jim. I'm sorry."

They are standing in the living room of the little flat they have rented for two years, the flat they are happy in. Goldfish in a bowl by the screen. A duvet spread across the futon couch in case Tracy is cold while reading. A coffee table they found in the garbage one night coming home from classes. Kidney-shaped.

He thought they were happy. Weren't they happy?

He looks out the window. It is late. Dark. Winter. There are tracks down the road from the cars that have recently passed in the new-fallen snow. He can see it still coming down. Thick, wet flakes. "What do we do now?" he says. Because what else can he say? What's the next step?

Tracy cries. There are tears. And maybe because of the tears, he snaps. His therapist tells him later that if Tracy had stayed strong, had not cried, he might not have done it. But she did cry. And he did do it. She showed weakness. And he snapped. Although that isn't an excuse. There is no excuse.

First the fishbowl. Shattered on the floor, fish flapping up and down, struggling in the air, frantically flipping under furniture. Tracy crying and shouting. What was she shouting?

The Chaplain now wonders if it's because, after the fishbowl, he turned his head slightly and looked out that front window again, past all the trappings of his life with Tracy, past the idea of their future together, past their past, past the shining snow, and saw the reflection of her crying there, sobbing. He looked out into the dark snow and there he was. David. Standing under the street light, waiting for Tracy. He then took note of her coat – still on. Her boots – tracking snow on the floor. Her hat, still placed upon her head at a jaunty angle. Her mittens, clapping together nervously. A light bulb flicked on over his head. She was leaving immediately. Right now. This instant. Out of his life. No turning back. No debate. No discussion. Three years was nothing to her. She was leaving. With David. There was going to be no wheedling and begging and crying. She had left the Chaplain no release. She had made up her mind already. For good.

First it was the fishbowl. Cracked. Empty. Fish flapping, dying.

Then it was Tracy. Her face. Her head.

Her face.

"You know," the Prisoner says, "I'm glad I don't have anyone coming. Who'd want to come to something like this? I hear your skin burns. I hear they put a hood over your head." Here he stops. The Prisoner stops talking straight after he says "head," as if he has choked on his words. The Chaplain imagines it, the hood. The Prisoner is imagining it, the hood. Over his head. Blacked out. A hot, suffocating hood. But not before you look out and see those you know, you maybe love, those who hate you, looking in at you behind the glass. You are strapped to the chair, electrodes on your temples, your arms, your legs. Attached to wires everywhere.

"I would have chosen lethal injection if I could have," the Prisoner says. "Not the chair."

The Chaplain swallows.

The Prisoner says, contemplatively, "But lethal injection isn't so reliable anymore, and so now it's back to the chair. Even if it's the most inhumane . . ." He clears his throat. "Remember those cartoons you'd watch as a kid? You watched cartoons, right?" The Prisoner looks over at the Chaplain. "Like a normal kid?"

The Chaplain nods. "Yes." He tries to smile. "I was a normal kid."

"Remember when they would get electrocuted?" the Prisoner laughs, hoarsely. "Their arms and legs would go straight out. Their hair would stand up." Silence. And then. "I thought it was funny at the time, didn't you?"

"I did," the Chaplain says. "Once upon a time."

They settle into the quiet again. The Chaplain looks at the clock. 2:32 a.m. This hour has gone even faster, if that's possible. The brief walk into the hall to give the Prisoner privacy made the time race. He was out of here, then back in here. Something the Prisoner will do only once. He will go out, he will go next door to that dark, shady room with the curtains closing off the viewing room, and he will never come back into this room once he leaves.

"When that guy got shot at the 24-Hour Variety," the Prisoner says. "I thought about those cartoons. Weird. I actually thought about the way their arms and hair and legs went straight out in such a funny way. It was like I knew what was eventually going to happen to me. Like I knew I'd get the death penalty. Like I'd seen the future."

"But you didn't shoot him. Dwight did."

"Yeah, I guess," the Prisoner says. He looks away. Shadily. Avoiding eyes. Is his story true? "But it was like I could see the future." He stares straight ahead. "Dwight did do it. But it doesn't really matter, you know. The guy died. That's what matters."

When the Chaplain remembers himself taking that first wild swing at Tracy, when he felt the connect and saw her cheek sag as if the bone had disappeared, he remembers he thought nothing. There wasn't an image in his head. Just white or black or nothingness. Pure emotion. No thought involved. It wasn't until the second swing, the second connect, until David was standing in the living room, shouting, his wet bootprints mixing with Tracy's puddles, with her blood, on the hardwood floor, the fish barely flopping anymore, mouths opening and closing, puckering, gasping for air, Tracy doing the same – it wasn't until that moment that he saw anything, in fact. Because before that he was on autopilot. He was robotic. He swung and hit. Swung again and hit again. Twice. Hard. Tracy hit the floor with the back of her head.

And then there were sirens. And police pulling David off of him.

Could have killed her, they said. One more punch would have killed her.

A broken cheekbone. Shattered. Reconstructive surgery needed. A broken nose. Concussion. He was charged with assault, but then Tracy dropped the charges. She didn't want him to have a permanent record – even after he rearranged her face. This was the Chaplain before he found God. What irony. Hypocrisy. The shame he felt still wells up inside of him. Constantly. His ability to cause harm, to be so intensely angry, to be so self-involved that he didn't know what he was doing – it's something he can't ever get over. One more hit and she might have died. One more hit. Even Miranda, his bully-fighter sister, looked at him differently in those months and years after. Even she was ashamed of him. It took years for her to forgive him for his actions. Years for her to see that it wasn't what happened with Tracy that made him become a chaplain, that made him become a man of God. It was his guilt, the guilt that surrounds him all the time, coats him still, his need to be forgiven. As if covering himself with God is his protection, a layer of goodness disconnecting his evil actions from what could be his true self. It's his penance.

Perhaps if he had been charged? If his life had been changed drastically, a stint in jail, a permanent record? Perhaps then he would feel better?

Does the Prisoner feel better having been caught and punished?

"Tick-tock, tick-tock," the Prisoner mumbles. "I kind of wish it wasn't a digital clock so we could hear it."

"Is time going quickly for you or slowly right now?" the Chaplain asks.

"Neither."

"It's going too quickly for me," the Chaplain confesses. "Every time I look up, it seems a number changes."

"I guess I'm such good company. You don't want the day to be over." The Prisoner looks over at him. The Chaplain is leaning forward on his chair, his elbows on his thighs, his hands clasped together. He is exhausted, mentally drained, physically in pain. His back aches. He can't get comfortable. But all he can really think about is the time and how it's counting down so quickly. It certainly makes him aware of his own life because, if you think about it, everyone's clock is ticking down. Everyone is slowly heading towards death and the end. Not just the Prisoner. *Tick-tock, tick-tock* is right. The Chaplain sighs.

"So," the Chaplain says. "If no one is coming and you don't want anyone there, what do you want me to do?"

The Prisoner shrugs.

"I'd like to be in there with you, if you're okay with that."

Why did the Chaplain say that? What was he thinking? He merely said what came into his head. Quickly. He didn't think.

"No," the Prisoner says. "Seriously, it'd fuck you up. No one should watch someone get electrocuted. I mean, I don't mind that the assholes who put me here are watching – fucking suits, they deserve to have nightmares – but you don't even know me. You shouldn't have to watch."

"Thank you," the Chaplain says, strongly now, "for your concern. But I'd like to be there beside you. I'd like you to be able to look at someone who cares."

"Hood, remember?"

"Oh, yes. Well, at least you'll feel me there. Right? That will be something?" The Chaplain clears his throat. It feels tight. Wait until Miranda hears he's done this. She will kill him.

"Well, if you want," the Prisoner says. "Each to his own. Whatever makes you tick."

The Chaplain shrugs. "I think it will be good for you."

"You think I'll really care at that point?" the Prisoner says. "I think it'll be good for you, though. See your job through to the end and all. Make sure your soul feels good about doing all you can to help. Forgive yourself. All that shit."

"If you don't want me there –"

The Prisoner looks at the Chaplain. "You can stay. Hold my hand." He laughs. "Make us both feel better."

Hold his hand. The Chaplain imagines a bolt of electricity passing between them. He imagines the Prisoner's life ebbing out through his own hand, coursing through the Chaplain's body. A macabre Frankenstein image comes into his mind – the Prisoner's brain in his brain, the Prisoner's soul melded with his. Again, cartoons.

"I'll be there for you," the Chaplain says, and the Prisoner laughs.

Davis Street

"I'll be there for you, man," Dwight says. "I'll be right behind you."

Larry is seventeen years old today and is robbing a bank. Or trying to. Dwight can't figure out exactly how they should do it. Should they go in together or separately? It seems as if all the drugs Dwight is selling and doing are finally affecting his brain. He's upped what he takes since the 24-Hour Variety. His shaking hands – which haven't gone away. His rolling eyes. The fact that he never remembers what they've been talking about. Dwight's too old, in Larry's opinion, to be doing hard drugs. Everyone over twenty seems old. He's pissing Larry off.

"Wake up, man," Larry shouts. They are standing in Dwight's apartment. It's a mess. Roaches scurry on the counter around dirty dishes, more dishes in the sink, leaking faucet, filthy windows, and when you can look out, all you see is bird shit on all the outside windowsills, peeling paint everywhere. A fan on the ceiling going around and around, covered in dust and spiderwebs. A smell Larry can't identify. "You said you were coming in with me, remember. Jesus, Dwight. Which is it? You'll be behind me or you'll come in with me? Get this right, man. You got to get this right."

"Yeah, yeah. Okay. Let me think." Dwight is wearing stained long johns and a T-shirt that says *Northern Church is #1* on it. It's from a church-league baseball team, Little League, and is too small. His large stomach shows at the bottom, and he's cut the sleeves off because his arms are too big. "I'm tired, man. I need to get some sleep. Late night last night. You should've come. All these chicks, man –"

"But we have to go over this together. We have to get it right."

"Larry, chill." Dwight plops down on his ratty couch. "Why do we have to do this now? What about tomorrow?"

"It's my birthday, that's why. Today. I want to give myself a present."

Dwight looks up at Larry. "Your birthday?"

Larry sits down. "Yeah, my birthday."

"Fuck."

Dwight sniffs a bit. Scratches at his crotch. Yawns. Larry watches a roach scurry across the floor towards the kitchen.

"Well, that settles it, then. We rob a bank today. Let's go."

The bank is small. It stands by itself on the outskirts of a strip mall two towns over. It is Tuesday, mid-morning. Not crowded. A few elderly people are lined up waiting for tellers. The ATM machine is around the side of the bank. Anyone taking cash out won't be able to see what is going on inside. There is no security guard. Only three bank tellers. A security camera. A man in an office in the back. Dwight has been watching for two hours. Waiting. Larry has gone to the bank machine once, made sure his face was covered. Sunglasses and hood. Checked out the security camera. Noticed the light wasn't blinking – not working.

"Scoped it out," Larry says, climbing into Dwight's rusted Chevy. "The camera isn't working. They're so fucking stupid. They deserve to be robbed. We're set."

"You sure, man? This gets you time. Lots of time. Especially with the gun. More time with the gun. I know. Frank, you know him, tall guy, star tattoo on his neck? He got twenty years for using a gun."

"I'm sure. I want to do this."

Larry doesn't know why he wants to do this. Convenience stores are too easy, perhaps? His adrenalin highs aren't as high anymore? Except for the first fuck-up, each robbery has been easier than the last. They go in, they show the gun, they take the money, they leave. Boring. Larry shakes his head, readjusts his baseball hat, pulls up his hood. His head hurts. All this thinking.

"Maybe we should go back to doing B and Es," Dwight says. "Get some more prescription drugs. Not just money. Things to sell. I don't know." Dwight rubs at his eyes. "I'm so fucking tired all the time."

"I can do this without you, you know," Larry says. "In fact, why don't I do this without you?"

Dwight looks at him. Looks hard at Larry's face. "No way, man. No. I'm in."

When did this happen? Dwight, the tough guy, is old and tired and getting fat. Larry is taking over now, ordering Dwight around, planning, doing, needing, wanting, working. He's skinny, Larry is, but he's tall and mean and he's growing into himself. Soon he'll be thick and pumped. He's the tough guy now.

"You've changed, you know," Dwight says. "Used to be –"

Larry gets out of the car. Slams the door. Heads across the street and into the bank. Dwight watches him go. Doesn't move to follow. Larry adjusts his hood, his sunglasses on. A gun shoved down his pants, his coat wrapped tight around him.

"Fuck," Dwight says to himself. He waits. Watches. His hands on the key, ready to start the ignition when Larry comes running.

Which he does. So fast he's a blur. Dwight starts the car and Larry jumps in and they peel out across the street and away.

Larry counts the money. "Ten thousand, I think, something around there," Larry shouts. He's freaking out. Giddy. Can't stop talking. "Fucking right on, man. Oh God, that was amazing." He can still hear the alarm ringing in his ears – he got out fast enough, before the cops came. "On the edge, man. Just crazy." Larry shouts out the window of the car, the air cool and wild, flipping his hair, his hood off his head. "Shit," he screams.

The adrenalin. The fear. The excitement. The craziness of it. Larry can't get enough. His coffee tins are full of money he doesn't even want. Dwight is stoned and high all the time, spending more money on drugs than he is stealing. But Larry hoards his money away and uses his gun and goes wild. High on fear. High on the job.

One of Larry's coffee cans holds the figurine from the first B and E, the little boy with the fishing pole. Every so often, Larry pulls it out and looks at it. The pole is broken now, the string trailing down. There is a chip on the boy's hat. But Larry's heart beats fast whenever he looks at it.

Larry's head hurts all the time now. Pulsing headaches. He shakes his head a lot as if trying to get rid of the pain, trying to rattle it out. He hasn't had headaches like this since his first concussion, since Jack pulled the chair out on him and he crashed to the floor. Every concussion, until Jack left, the headaches were intense and wicked, but the pain would eventually stop. And then Jack left and the concussions stopped and the pain ended for good. His head hurt after the 24-Hour Variety murder, when the clerk smashed him and he kind of blacked out, but it went away quickly, like they all do. Until this year. Until he turned seventeen. The headaches are numbing and black and full of fire and ice. Piercing. Larry has to close his eyes when they happen. He can feel the pulsing. He can hear the blood flow through his head. He can feel his heart beat in his temples. Sometimes he blacks out. Sometimes he can't remember anything and wakes up and things around him have changed. As if sleepwalking. As if someone pulled the curtain on his eyes but left his body in the light.

Except when he has the gun and is in the middle of something. Then the headaches stop. Completely. He feels nothing then, a beautiful calm serenity – robbing a bank, sticking up a convenience store guy, breaking and entering, beating up an asshole on the street – nothing. The headaches disappear.

Dwight is high on drugs. Larry is high on adrenalin. Same thing.

Soon Larry is doing everything on his own. He's taken Dwight's Chevy. He's taken Dwight's gun. Occasionally Larry gives Dwight some spending money, keeps him in drugs, but more often than not, Larry forgets about Dwight and carries on in his own way on his own time.

There's a girl. His first serious one. Samantha.

God, there's a girl. A hot girl. She hangs out at Dwight's house – does drugs – but has no interest in the older man. She's interested in Larry and his money, which he starts to throw around. She's interested in his gun and his mysteriousness – he comes and goes, makes money, brings money, supplies Dwight with drug money. She doesn't know what he does and doesn't care. As long as there's no blood on him. As long as he doesn't beat her, like her last boyfriend did. As long as he brings her what she needs and as long as he does what she needs.

Larry can't get over his luck. Samantha is something else. He brings her home to meet Susan and even Susan thinks she's hot. Kids screaming around her, Susan says, "Holy shit, Larry, why does she like you?"

Larry wonders this, but soon forgets to worry about it because he's getting bigger and tougher and angrier and more in control these days. His arms are covered in tattoos. He's lifting weights when he's not busy. He has dropped out of school and doesn't need to work with his dad anymore. But he does. Because if Larry doesn't go into Gallo's Precision Repair every day and open the store, the store will go out of business. Larry's father is passed out behind the counter most days. Doesn't even notice Larry is there.

Just after Larry hooks up with Samantha, he moves out of his house. Away from Susan and her shitload of kids, away from his drunk dad, away from the memories of Jack and his mother. Away, especially, from his dark blue walls and the solar system. The stars on the walls don't glow anymore, anyway. They stopped glowing years ago and are peeling off, half-hanging. Depressing.

Seventeen years old and in a trashy studio apartment above a store on Davis Street. A mattress on the floor. A hot plate. A microwave. A beer fridge. One chair in the corner and a big-ass screen. Alarms and firetrucks and ambulances keeping him awake at night. Bedbugs. Samantha tries to spruce the place up – pictures taped to the walls, venetian blinds, even coasters for the folding table she finds in the garbage and drags over one night.

Years later, Larry realizes that his first apartment is a lot like prison – the room is almost the same size.

"All we need now are chairs," Samantha says. "We could

even have dinner here. Sit on the chairs, at the table. No more eating on the mattress."

"Whatever," Larry says. Now that he has to pay rent, he's scared to spend too much of his coffee tin money. The tins he took from under the floorboards in the attic and brought here to this studio apartment and hid under the floorboards in the closet. Having the money is not about spending it anyway. It's about having it. Larry needs nothing, wants nothing. Just the big-ass screen to watch. A good cellphone or two. Food. Beer. Rent money for the place. Occasionally he buys things for Samantha – necklaces, earrings, wine. Once he bought her flowers, but she laughed at him. Mocked him. Ruined his image for a while. Now he says, "Whatever," and doesn't give her anything much. Enough to keep her interested and coming back, but not enough to make her complacent.

They fuck like rabbits. He's seventeen. She's twenty. She's always high on drugs. He's clean and sober but wants her badly all the time. Two, three times a day sometimes. Whenever he can get it. It's the best time of his life. His headaches dim and taper off. She's on top. Below. Behind. Sucking him off. It's a fucking orgy. His seventeen-year-old brain is going to explode.

Susan is in his apartment when he comes home from work one day. With Samantha. They are curled up on the mattress together doing coke. Sniffing from broken glass. Rolled five-dollar bill.

"What the fuck are you doing here?"

Susan shrugs.

"Where are your kids?"

Susan shrugs. After the third kid, she got her tubes tied – Larry isn't sure if the doctor did it without telling her or if she asked for it. They must have been sick of seeing her in the hospital, another C-section, another drugged out baby – fetal alcohol syndrome or worse. Low birth weights, all of them. Susan smoking up a storm all through pregnancy. Drinking. Drugs.

"Hey, Larry, hey. If she'd stayed," Susan says now. "If she'd stayed with us, do you think we'd be like we are now?"

"Who?" But Larry knows exactly who she is talking about. Their mother. "What are we now, Susan?" Larry asks, leaning back on the folding table. Crossing his arms over his chest. "What do you think we are now?"

"Look around," Susan says and waves her arms expansively. They all turn and watch a bug skitter across the floor.

Samantha laughs lazily. Her breasts are falling out of her tank top. She's wearing his boxer shorts.

"I think we'd be even more fucked if she had stayed." Larry says this but doesn't believe it. He thinks about it. He'd probably be in grade twelve, graduating this year. He'd be working at his father's store (same as he is now), but maybe his father wouldn't be so far gone, maybe he would have kept his drinking in check. He did when she lived with them. Kept it quieter, at least. Maybe his mother would have painted his room over, made it more for a teenager, less for a kid. Got rid of the planets and stars. Unstuck the stars. Susan certainly wouldn't have three kids with three different fathers. She wouldn't be here, on his mattress, next to his girl, doing drugs.

"Get out of here, Susan. You're pissing me off."

Samantha says, "Let her stay, baby. She's tired."

They laugh at him. Drugged out. Lolling on the mattress. Mouths open.

Larry wants to get laid so badly. He is aching. His head hurts. All day he's been dealing with his father's clients – old people with watches and grandfather clocks. Needing batteries or adjusting or rotating or winding. Needing things from him.

Paying him little. Larry wanted to get home, fuck Samantha, maybe order in Chinese. Go to bed early.

He leaves now. Slams the door on his way out. Hears their giggles from the mattress on the floor. Goes to Dwight's. Finds him passed out on his floor. The door open, music blaring. Larry turns off the music, bundles Dwight into his bed, closes his door and leaves. Where to go? Larry finds himself walking past his father's house. A light is on in the front room and Larry can see in. His father is there, eating something from a tray – microwave dinner. He is sitting in front of the screen, which glows throughout the room, the walls blue and flashing. He looks sad and lonely and Larry feels sick a bit. Seeing him from afar like this, not hearing his wrath, not taking his bullying, just seeing him there. An old man. Grey and tired. He knows nothing about him. He almost feels sorry for him. Larry's head aches. When he got the tattoos, his father said nothing to him. When he moved into his own apartment, his father said nothing to him. Didn't tell him not to, didn't ask him to stay, just put his hat on and went to work. Nothing was said between them about any of it. Not even at the store.

Suddenly Larry sees one of Susan's brood looking out the window on the second floor. She waves at Larry, her hair ratty from sleep. He can't remember her name. He waves back and then turns and continues on down the street alone.

3:01 a.m.

"I didn't mean to say 'fuck like rabbits,'" the Prisoner says. "Sorry about that. I get carried away thinking about Sam. She was hot. And it's been a long time." He shakes his head.

"Don't worry about it," the Chaplain says, leaning back in his chair. "I've heard much worse since I've been here."

"Yeah, I bet."

"Can I ask you a question?" the Chaplain says.

The Prisoner shrugs. He rolls to his side on the cot and holds his head up with his hand.

"Why are you telling me all of this?"

"Why not?"

"It's just. I don't know," the Chaplain says. "I wonder what the point of it is."

The Prisoner rolls onto his back again. The Chaplain wishes he could lie on the cot for a bit, wishes the Prisoner would take the chair.

"I have twelve hours. What the fuck else should I talk about?"

"Nine."

"What?"

"Nine hours left."

The Prisoner laughs. "Timekeeper, eh?"

"It's just that it's all you have. Nine hours. I thought you might want to talk about other things. About the crime that got you in here, perhaps, about your remorse, guilt, feelings in general. Maybe you want to talk about what you want done with your body when this is over, if you want to be cremated or buried. What do you want done with your things? Do you have any money you need distributed? A house? Any letters you want to give to anyone? Do you –"

"Shut up," the Prisoner says coldly. "Can't you just shut up?"

The Chaplain immediately shuts up. He wants to say sorry but knows that if he utters a single word, the Prisoner will snap. He can feel it in the air. The Prisoner is tense. An animal about to attack. Nine hours.

The Prisoner gets up from the cot and walks over to the toilet. The Chaplain cringes when he passes, expecting to get punched. He pisses in it without once glancing over at the Chaplain, who turns from him to give him some privacy. The Chaplain breathes a sigh of relief. When he is done, the Prisoner returns to the cot.

"Don't you have to go?"

The Chaplain realizes yes, he does have to go. He doesn't want to leave the Prisoner for even a minute, though. Steeling himself, he walks up to the toilet and stands there, awkwardly, trying to urinate. The Prisoner laughs. The flow comes. He's fine.

"No way you can be self-conscious in this hellhole," the Prisoner says. "You get used to it quickly. Guys always watching."

The Chaplain washes his hands – no soap – uses a paper towel to dry them, sits back in his chair.

"I'm sorry about what I said –"

"I said shut up. Just cause I'm joking with you doesn't mean you haven't made me mad."

"Sorry."

The Prisoner sighs.

A knock on the door. CO6 pops his head in.

"You want your last meal now?"

"Now? It's only three, right? Is it three? Not now," the Prisoner says.

"I don't know. I just thought you might be getting hungry."

"I could use another cookie. You want a cookie, Chaplain?"

The Chaplain nods. CO6 leaves the room and comes back with four cookies. The Prisoner wolfs down two and the Chaplain nibbles at his.

"These are good cookies."

"Yes, I guess." The Chaplain thinks about cookies. About Miranda's cookies. She learned all her baking from their mother and used to spend weekends as a teenager cooking the best chocolate chip cookies he has ever tasted. Until their mother got sick, she would bake with Miranda, and the Chaplain would pass by the kitchen hearing them laughing and whispering and talking. They were friends before mother and daughter. Comrades. He wanted that. With his father. Or his mother. Or even Miranda. But no one in the house talked to him like Miranda and his mother talked. They were close. Identical, his father would say, snapping back his newspaper, sitting in the big chair by the fire. Like twins. Exactly what the Prisoner's mother said about Jack and his father.

And then their mother got sick. Breast cancer. A year of radiation and chemotherapy didn't work. She died. The Chaplain was fourteen years old, in grade nine; Miranda was sixteen and in grade eleven. Just getting her driver's licence. Dating the boy next door. Going to school dances. Braces came off a year earlier. It devastated her, their mother's death. Miranda was never the same. Formed a shell around herself, never to be hurt again, no one could touch her.

Until Richard, of course.

When their mother died, Miranda began seeing the world in black and white, right or wrong. No other shades. No grey.

The therapist told the Chaplain that when his mother died, he kept his anger about being deserted by her deep inside, so deep that it didn't come out until he hit Tracy.

"Bullshit," he had said to her. "That's ridiculous. My mother didn't desert me. She died."

After all, his relationship with his sister had become stronger after their mother died – he wasn't a woman-hater. He would never hit a woman, he thought. He loved women and respected them. In fact, his sister was his best friend – his only friend – no matter how much they argued. He had never hit anyone before, male or female. There was nothing inside of the Chaplain, no anger, that had to come out on Tracy. It just happened. You can't explain it easily, he thinks, and that's what makes it so hard to understand or accept or admit.

The Chaplain eats his cookie and notices the Prisoner staring at the other one in his hand. He gives it over – "You take it, I'm not really that hungry." The Prisoner eats it quickly, as if he's starving to death. The Chaplain imagines that facing death, he probably wouldn't be hungry, but some people deal with tragedy and anxiety by eating a lot. He's not one of those people. In fact, he'd probably vomit if he ate nine hours before he was going to be electrocuted. The thought of this actually makes the cookie come up in his throat, a bit of wet bile. He coughs. Swallows.

"You'd think they could have given us cookies like this here." The Prisoner motions his head back down the hall, towards where they came from, where they walked when the sound of the other prisoners shouting was all around them. "Why didn't we ever get cookies like this? We got those stale ones that are hard. Oatmeal. No chocolate chips. These are way better. I could eat a million of these ones. They remind me of my mom's cookies. They're even a little chewy." The Prisoner goes quiet.

Time is moving towards the Prisoner fast. He eats his cookies. Tells his tale. Lies on the cot. Wouldn't the Chaplain pace the floor anxiously? Wouldn't he pray? Wouldn't he cry? Wring his hands? What would he be doing? He knows his heartbeat would be elevated, his hands would shake.

The Chaplain sighs.

"Bored?"

"No, sorry. Tired, I guess. It's odd how a human body gets used to sleeping at specific times. I took a nap before I got here. I shouldn't be tired."

"I'm not really tired. I'm not really anything. I don't feel anything." The Prisoner stares at the ceiling. The Chaplain stares at the tattoos on the Prisoner's arms, really looks at them. "Except a weight. On my shoulders. Ever since I knew the date, I've felt this heavy weight right here." He rubs his shoulders. "They tell me I'm clinically depressed but that's bullshit. I feel fine. Just empty. Empty and a weight. Here. On my shoulders."

"You have the right to be depressed," the Chaplain says. "I would be, I think."

"Yeah, I guess. It's more a lack of energy, really. Not depression. I'm not sad. I'm tired. I sleep all the time."

The Chaplain focuses on the Prisoner's tattoos. A blurred mess of lines. The Prisoner has a thin line of barbed wire tattooed around his neck and a large cross tattooed on the inside of one ankle, which the Chaplain can see because his pants have ridden up and his socks are short.

"Tell me about your tattoos."

"What's to tell?"

"What do they mean? Do they mean anything? When did you get them? Why did you get them?"

"Aren't you full of questions today."

The Chaplain sees the name *Samantha* etched into the Prisoner's bicep. He also sees *Becky* and *Mayve*. And *Susan*. There is a *Susan* there on his arm. His sister? This means something.

"They don't mean anything. Just bored."

"You got tattoos because you were bored?" The Chaplain smiles. "I watch my screen or do puzzles."

"You should try getting tattoos. Much more fun." The Prisoner laughs.

Miranda has a tattoo on her back. Up by her left shoulder, on what she calls her wing. It says *Veritas. Truth* in Latin. Something the Chaplain supposes he is trying to get at here – the truth. The odd thing is, Miranda doesn't want the truth, really, if you think about it. She condemned this man without ever even meeting him, without knowing anything about him. She knows his crime (everyone knows his crime) but will not forgive. She does not seek the truth.

How rapidly Miranda accepted the death penalty.

The Chaplain will have to remember to tell Miranda at dinner about how her tattoo is reflective of what he's doing, not what she's doing. Getting at the truth. It's a good angle and he might just win their recent death-penalty arguments. No one, in his opinion, deserves to be executed. But no one especially deserves to be executed alone, without the ability to talk to a man of God before they die. He's in a Catch-22. He's here for the man, but he's also working for the government that will soon kill him. The Chaplain can't win. But he can win something small from Miranda. Veritas. Truth.

It occurs to him suddenly that maybe that's what the

Prisoner is trying to do. He is attempting to speak the truth. Or his version of the truth. If he lays it all out before the Chaplain, before God, before himself, maybe the Prisoner will understand the answers to his own questions. Maybe he will figure it all out. So, even though his recitation isn't really believable as a confession, it is, in a sense, a baring of his soul. He is reciting his life for the Chaplain to hear, for someone to understand him, for someone to take away the truth about it all.

Maybe?

The Chaplain's not sure. It still seems odd that the Prisoner is speaking as if what he says, in these last hours, doesn't really matter, isn't going to change things. He doesn't seem to be making the connections or even placing any blame. He isn't confessing and he isn't asking for forgiveness. It's merely, "This is my life. Listen. Then you can kill me."

Clinical depression makes sense. Emotionless. Vacant. Nothing.

This experience, so far, isn't anything like what the Chaplain imagined. He imagined thrown furniture, screaming, crying, begging, pleading, anger, remorse, fear. He imagined telephone calls to loved ones, last-minute appeals, rooms full of people rushing about. He imagined high emotion, not the story of a life and cookies and quiet talk.

"Tattoos are pretty easy, actually," the Prisoner says, admiring his arms. He traces his fingers up and down some of the lines. "They use this drill thing, it sounds like a dentist's drill, and it moves a needle up and down really fast. Depending on where you go. Some places have faster needles than others." He traces a tattoo that was obviously not from a professional. It is jagged, wobbly, the lines uneven. "And in prison, it's different, of course." The image on this tattoo isn't even clear. "But most of these I got on the outside."

"The ink is in the needle, right?"

"Yeah. The needle presses the ink into your skin with each puncture. But I'm talking really fast puncture marks – like fifty or maybe even a thousand punctures a minute. I don't know. Maybe even more. Depends on the machine, I guess, and the quality of the shop. Like I said. Doesn't go deep. But it spreads out."

The Chaplain says, "Any you regret?"

"Fuck, man," the Prisoner looks at him. "There are always tattoos you regret. Always. I've never met anyone who doesn't regret at least one tattoo."

"Becky? Mayve? Samantha?"

The Prisoner looks at those names. He touches them. Covers them up with his hand.

"Weird to think they'll still be there, in my skin, when I'm dead. Until my skin rots off. Do tattoos burn quicker? Does the ink burn?"

"During cremation?"

"Whatever. I don't know. Rot. Burn. I don't know."

"Shouldn't you know what you want done? Don't you want to know now? Shouldn't we talk about this?"

"I don't know, man. I don't want to talk about it. What does it matter to me? I'll be dead."

The Chaplain takes note of the Prisoner's position. He is sitting up, tracing the lines on his arms, covering some with his hands, tracing again, every muscle in his body tense, as if he's going to run. His neck bulges muscle. Because he is lean, every vein and ligament is stretched and visible. If the Prisoner doesn't tell the Chaplain what he wants done with his body, the prison will cremate him and bury the urn in the plot out back. If no one claims him, he will be placed with the other unclaimed souls.

The Prisoner stands quickly and stretches. The Chaplain sits up straight in his chair.

"Don't fuck with me," the Prisoner says, looking at the Chaplain. His voice is low. Quiet. "I didn't ask you to be here to fuck with me. If I don't want to talk about some things, you got to respect that."

"Yes, sure. It's just that one of my jobs is to find out what your wishes are."

The Prisoner laughs. "My wishes? My wishes? Jesus, man."

"What to do with –"

"I know what the fuck you mean, Chaplain." This is a growl. "I just don't know what I want."

The Chaplain feels shaky. His back aches from sitting straight up like this, his legs are tensed to run towards the door. The air is thick in here.

"It's just," the Prisoner paces in front of him. Two guards look into the room through the window in the door. "If I think about it, then I can't breathe."

The Chaplain says nothing.

"Every time my mind goes anywhere near the next bit, anywhere near what will happen, if I think of any detail of it, I stop breathing."

Panic attack, the Chaplain thinks. The room is right next door. Right there. Beside them. Five, ten, fifteen steps away.

"I want to go to my punishment, to my death, breathing." The Prisoner barks out a laugh. "Breathing."

"I can understand that," the Chaplain says quietly. "I understand."

"And I want," the Prisoner stops pacing and looks straight at him. His eyes are sad and red, his skin sallow, his cheeks thin. "I want to tell you how I got to where I am now. Is that too much to ask? That you listen to that and you take it with you after everything is done?"

"It's not. Not too much. No." The Chaplain is ashamed. He looks away from the Prisoner and down to the dirty floor. "I'm –"

"Sorry, yes, I know. I heard you before."

The Prisoner sits back down on the bed. "I fucked up, I guess," he says. He runs his fingers through his hair. "I really fucked up. But at the time, when I was in it, when I was doing the things I did, it felt like the right thing to do."

"The murders?"

"No, fuck, no." The Prisoner glares at him. "Not the fucking murders, but the B and Es, the robberies, the money. I felt like I was doing something I was good at, you know?"

The Chaplain has never been particularly good at anything. Adequate, he guesses. And he tries. He isn't even very good at being a chaplain. He was a crummy, boring boyfriend, a half-assed student – he tends not to pay attention when studying, thinks about things that have nothing to do with what is at hand. Wonders what the point of all of it is. He wasn't a very good son – when did he ever play catch with his father? – or isn't even a very good brother or uncle now. He eats dinner every Sunday at Miranda and Richard's place, and he has never once offered to bring anything or put the kids to bed for them or do the dishes. Every day he wakes up in his rented apartment and he drives his car to the convenience store and he buys a coffee. He never tips the guy behind the counter. Every day he drives into the prison with intention, good intention, and every day he leaves thinking he has accomplished nothing. The men talk to him. They confess and cry and feel better for having seen him, but, in the long run, what good did the Chaplain ever really do? Did he make them better people? No. Did he find out the truth about them? No. And, even more, does doing this even help him find out his own truth? Something he would love to know. Who he is and what he is good at.

The point of religion for the Chaplain was to make a difference. Has he done that?

Miranda would say he's good at listening. "Jesus, Jim, I talk and talk and you smile at me there, lazy-like, and say nothing. Don't you have anything to say? Sometimes I think that you might not be listening. Like it's all an act. Maybe you've been fooling me. I don't know."

His faith is sometimes lacking. In small ways. Because the Chaplain doesn't believe in himself, it puts weight on his faith. If you can't believe in yourself as a man, how can you believe in God? Each man has his own God and that God is fashioned after each man – but if the man does not like himself, does not have faith in himself, then what kind of God has he fashioned? One that questions everything? One that lacks conviction?

But, no, that's not right. The Chaplain does believe in his God. It happens, though, that his God is very different from the God others see and hear and feel. His God. Who is his God, and what is he doing here in this cell with this man who committed such horrific crimes against those people? This man who isn't showing much remorse and merely wants to talk and talk and talk – about himself, narcissistic – until he dies. In a building where there are people who are willingly going to kill this man, something the Chaplain is wholly, completely against.

The room spins and he watches it spin, and he crosses his arms across his chest and leans back in his chair and tells himself to listen, to pay attention. His job here, what he needs to do, is to listen. That's it. Nothing more. Listen.

Stop, the Chaplain thinks, stop trying to figure yourself out.

Asthma

Dwight is in the hospital. Car accident, drugged up, split head and sore neck. Samantha was in the car with Dwight but is unharmed.

"Where were you going?" Larry asks, leaning back on the mattress in the apartment. Samantha's hair is tangled over the pillow, dirty and sour-smelling. Her drug problem is getting worse, and Larry feels as out of control around her as she must feel doing the drugs. She hasn't washed or eaten in days. He wants to be with her, to fuck her, but can't stand that vacant look in her eyes anymore, can't stand the dirtiness, the stench of her body. She is beginning to disgust him. That look reminds him, oddly, of his mother. When she whistled and hummed as she did the laundry or dishes, he would catch her eyes, try to get her attention, and those eyes would be empty. No soul. Larry had forgotten about that until now. It hadn't occurred to him that his mother was unhappy when he was a child. Children never notice adults in that way. But he had noticed her eyes, he had waved his arms in front of her face, said, "Mom, Mom, are you listening?" He had known deep in his young mind that she wasn't all there. She was gone already. Before she even left.

Samantha sits up, track marks up and down her naked arms, her breasts hanging flat against her chest. Larry is twenty years old now and Samantha looks older than her twenty-three years. Three years together and Larry thinks that, yes, it's time this was over. They aren't doing each other any favours.

"Dwight's an asshole," Samantha says. "We were buying drugs. He crashed before we got them. He was so high. You got any drugs?"

Larry shakes his head.

"He left me with nothing. I got nothing." Samantha starts to cry.

Larry leaves her in the apartment, crying, and never goes back. All she wanted him for was the drug money anyway. Larry anticipates the withdrawal she will have until Dwight gets out of the hospital to get her more drugs. He wants no part of this withdrawal, he wants no part of her anymore, and so he leaves. He thought he loved her once, when he was seventeen and feeling good about getting out of the house, but now she's only a burden. She's a mess. She, like Dwight, stops Larry from going forward, moving ahead, getting on with life. Larry takes his coffee cans of money and leaves her everything else – the card table, the mattress on the floor, the rent to pay. He finds an apartment eight blocks over and moves in the same day he signs the lease. He pays with money from the coffee tins. It is clean and freshly painted. It has two rooms: a living room/kitchen area and a bedroom. The bathroom has a tub and a shower. There are no more bugs. Larry feels as if he's made it. He's come up in the world. He's a new man.

Larry meets Becky through Susan. She is Susan's hairdresser and comes to the house – his father's house – once in awhile to do Susan's hair when she can't get a sitter for the brats. Under-the-table pay. Becky doesn't have to share this money with the salon she works for. They drink and smoke as Becky highlights Susan's hair, and the kids scream and shout and push each other around the house. Larry's father has taken to his room. Every so often he comes down the stairs and heads out of the house to check on the store, but Larry is in control of everything now and opens when he wants, closes when he wants. Never normal hours. He's losing customers but he doesn't care anymore. At the beginning, when he wants, Larry advertises a bit on the radio, and once he buys billboard space, but his half-assed attempts to keep the business going don't work. The store gradually loses all of its customers and stays closed now more than it stays open. So his father disappears to his bedroom more and more, and Larry finds other ways to make money. In the kitchen one night, Becky doing Susan's hair, Larry there, drinking beer, swatting kids who run by, watching Becky move, her hips sway, her breasts full:

"So how's the shop?" Susan asks.

Larry shrugs.

Becky says, "You own a shop? Right on."

"No, I –" but then Larry thinks yes, I do own a shop. "Yeah, well, it's going out of business."

Susan looks over, the smoke from her cigarette getting in her eyes. "What the fuck? What are you talking about?"

"No one replaces batteries or gets watches fixed these days. Watches are so cheap you can just buy another. And grandfather clocks? No one even knows what they are. Ours hasn't worked for a long time." Larry motions towards the grandfather clock in the hallway. Susan looks over at it as if she's just noticed that it hasn't made a sound in years.

"What am I going to do for money?" Susan stubs out her

cigarette and pats at a drip of bleach sliding down her temple. Becky uses a stained towel to wipe her hands. She takes a drag of her cigarette. "Did you think about that? If you go out of business, who's going to pay for me and the kids? And Dad? Who's going to take care of him? He needs some money, you know."

"I got it," Larry says. "Don't worry. I can handle it."

Susan doesn't worry because Larry does take care of it. And he takes care of Becky in the front seat of her car when she offers to drive him home. He pushes into her in the front seat, pushes as far into her as he can get, the seat tilted back as far as it can go. His knees feel broken by the small space, and she groans and her heels smack down again and again and again on the dashboard. The car steams up.

It's a series of girls after that – women – some older than him, some younger. Samantha, Becky, Mayve, Ruth, Mali, Dakota, Lee-Ann. Larry makes no connection with any of them. After Samantha, he feels nothing. Just sex and company. Occasionally someone to buy something for – because Larry likes to spoil the girls he's with. He likes to share. Later, in prison, when he has their names carved on his skin, he does so only to keep track of his history. Not for any feelings towards them.

It's a series of crimes after that too. Proud of what he's getting away with. Because he does get away with it. Never gets caught.

Larry is twenty-four years old. His sister, Susan, is twenty-eight.

"It's my smarts," he tells Susan one day, tapping his temple with one finger. "I should've stayed in school. Maybe I would have graduated."

Susan snorts. "Yeah, you and me both."

"Do you ever," Larry says, sitting back at the kitchen table, Susan beside him, stirring her coffee, looking haggard and old having just been to the police station to pick up her child who was caught driving underage and drunk, "Do you ever wonder where Mom is? If they're out there, Mom and Jack, and they know what we're doing and who we are and what has happened in our lives, but they are maybe too afraid to come say hi?"

"You're kidding me, right?" Susan takes a sip of her coffee. A slurp. It's a horrible sound and makes Larry angry. Like she's doing it to mock him. She slurps again. "Mom and Jack together. Nope. And sorry? Give me a break. I think they are both dead. Jack probably killed Mom. Or, hey, what about this," Susan uses her hands to punctuate her points. "What about Mom's remarried and has new kids and she dumped Jack off right after she left us, dumped him somewhere and he was found and someone else raised him. That would serve him right. He was always such an asshole."

"He was nine, Susan, when they left. I think he knew his address and his name. Besides, the police would have brought him home. Or something." Larry pauses. Thinks. "You are right, though, he was an asshole."

Larry and Susan turn then towards a sound they hear behind them. Their father, leaning against the kitchen doorframe, a bottle of vodka dangling from his hand. "She's dead," he says. "Your mother is dead. Don't you know that?"

Larry never finds out the details from his father because after his father says this, his face collapses and he falls to the ground. He collapses on the floor, smashing the vodka bottle and his head. After a few minutes staring at him, Susan calls an ambulance.

"How would we know that?" Susan asks. "He never told us anything."

A stroke. Permanent brain damage. Liver damage. He is fed by tubes, kept alive by machines; there is nothing behind his eyes. Left to die, slowly and alone. Susan and Larry visit once or twice. Susan cries a little, but Larry can tell she doesn't mean it. She keeps checking her cellphone. It's not as if he was a good father in any sense of the word. He barely provided for them, gave no moral or emotional support. Did not love them in any way. "Don't touch me," he always shouted. Susan shrugs. Larry clears his throat. The last time Larry visits, he goes alone. He is wildly drunk and he stumbles over and pulls the plugs out of the wall and listens to all the machines that are attached to his father stop before he runs out of the room. Trying to help? Trying to end it all? He staggers down the hall of the hospital suddenly feeling calm and good and when the nurses and doctors whip past him, rushing into his father's room to re-plug the machines, Larry smiles a little to himself and keeps on walking.

Plugged back in, his father lasts one more month and then dies. With no one beside him. A washed-up, alcoholic man. Father of three. Grandfather of three. Husband to no one.

Larry must find their mother, or at least prove that she is dead. Otherwise, Susan and Larry get nothing. Their father's will states that their mother gets everything, and the lawyers tell the siblings that this means the store, the house, any savings their father had (which is none, only debts that their mother must pay). Without a death certificate, the lawyer says, they get nothing.

On the road, driving for two days, Larry follows the lead. The lawyer's fee, the detective's fee, the gas for the car, the hotels – Larry is fed up with it all. He uses his gun on the gas station attendant eight hours out. He doesn't harm him, but the fear in the man's eyes when Larry threatens to shoot up the gas tanks if the guy calls the police – waves his arms around like a gangster – stays with him as he drives off down the highway. That fear keeps him going, keeps his headache at bay, as he continues on towards his mother's grave.

She was two days from them. All this time. Larry pulls up to the gates of the cemetery. He knows nothing about her life after she left them, but he knows she died recently, and she had taken a new name. Larry gets out of the car. The heat and dust of the day threaten to choke him. He walks through the gates and follows the map the detective gave him until he comes upon her grave. A simple stone, her name, her dates, separated only by a dash. Nothing else. No *In loving memory* or *Cherished by her family* or *Beautiful mother* or anything. Just her name and her dates. As if she died loved by no one. This satisfies Larry but also makes him extremely sad and angry and frustrated and mean. He wants to kill her himself. He wants to dig her up and spread her bones around, destroy her. He wants to hold her. To hug her.

He would have loved her.

He would have cherished her.

He would have mourned her.

Larry kneels in front of her stone and leans his forehead on it. It is cold and hard. Nothing like the mother he remembers. But what does he remember? Glow-in-the-dark stars. Blonde hair in a bun or loose around her face. The fear on her face when his father got home. He was so young. So naïve. So innocent. And she left him alone.

Larry walks back to his car, drives to the closest bar and begins twenty hours of binge drinking until he finds himself face down in his own vomit, somehow on the sidewalk back at his father's house. He doesn't know how he got there. A day later, he is with Susan and the lawyer. Their mother is dead. It is proven. So the lawyer divides the proceeds of their father's will, after debts have been paid, between Susan, Larry and Jack.

"Jack?" Susan asks. "What the fuck." She stands up and looks down at Larry, at the lawyer. They are seated at the desk in the lawyer's office. All dark wood and red leather. In a storefront office of a strip mall, the sun beating in on them through the large windows to the street.

"Jack," Larry says. "Of course."

Six months later, Larry is holding up another bank.

"Put the money here," he shouts. "Stop staring." He is wearing a mask and a hood. He is fast and serious. The teller is panicking, he can see her breathing become raspy and uncontrolled. "Look," he says calmly, "do as I say and you won't get hurt."

"I can't –" she stops breathing. Her eyes go wide and she holds her hands to her throat. "I can't," she mouths. Larry can read her lips.

"Fuck." He grabs over the counter at the till but can only reach a few bills. "Calm down."

Her face is turning chalky white, her eyes are wider than he's ever seen eyes go before, her lips are blue.

"She has asthma, help her," the bank manager says. He is standing off to the side, his arms in the air. "Help her."

Larry looks around at all the people in the bank – two older women; a security guard on his stomach on the floor in front of him, arms outstretched; a small boy clutching his mother's hand; the teller, not breathing; the bank manager. He looks at them all for a second too long. He does nothing. Just looks at them. He can feel the tension in the air, the electric current moving through them all. The two old women begin to cry. The teller collapses behind the counter.

"Jesus Christ," Larry screams. "Get up, get up."

The bank manager moves towards her, just slightly, a small

movement, but Larry's nerves are strung tight, his finger on the trigger. His head begins to pound, and he shoots. He means to only stop the man, not kill him, but the man moves quickly and the bullet hits the man's chest instead of his shoulder, and Larry knows it's fatal as soon as he sees the expression in the man's eyes. Larry sees the light go out. The man crumples to the floor and the stain of blood moves in a sudden pattern, pulsing, out of his shirt. The smell of blood – fishy and metallic – fills the air.

The two old women scream.

"I didn't mean to do that," Larry shouts. "I didn't mean to shoot."

"You killed him," the boy says, cowering into his mother's skirt. "You killed him."

"Shhh," she cautions, holding him tight. "Shhh."

The security guard lifts his head from the floor and stares straight into Larry's sunglassed eyes, as if trying to memorize exactly what shade they are behind the frames, inside the mask.

Larry looks down over the counter and sees that the bank teller is still. She isn't clutching at her throat anymore, she isn't turning blue, she is completely still. Dead.

Two dead. Five hundred dollars in small bills.

"God damn," Larry says. And leaves the bank.

He drives four cars (all stolen – take one, leave one, keep going) until he is back in town with his small amount of money, his gun, and images behind his eyes that won't go away no matter how many times he tries to justify them. I didn't mean to shoot. I meant to shoot his shoulder. He moved. If he'd just stayed still. It was his fault. I tried to calm her down. I didn't know she had asthma. It was her fault. Not mine. The boy in his mother's skirt, staring up at him. "You killed him." The screaming women. The security guard's stare. "Shhhh. Shhh . . ."

4:01 a.m.

"But I don't understand." The Chaplain is standing now. He's been pacing for half an hour, listening. "I don't understand. You aren't here because of that. I didn't even know about that. It's not in your file. That, the bank, has nothing to do with what they found in the storage unit, the murders –"

"You need to listen, man," the Prisoner says. "Stop talking and listen. Stop trying to figure everything out the way you want it to be figured out."

"But you almost killed your father and you killed a bank manager and a bank teller. You were there when a convenience store clerk was shot –"

"I didn't kill them. I mean that I didn't intend to kill them. It was their fault. Seriously, man, shut up." The Prisoner stands up quickly, really close to the Chaplain, stops the Chaplain's pacing with his body and says, "You need to listen and stop talking, stop saying anything, stop trying to figure it out and fit it into your own little fucking file. After I'm gone you can say what you want. You can think what you want. Right now, you need to just listen. Got it?"

"Everything okay in here?" The corrections officers are there, suddenly, all five of them, inside the cell. The Chaplain realizes again how small this place really is. They are all almost touching. Every time someone comes into this space, the room's claustrophobic feeling becomes forefront. He feels like he can't breathe. The COs use their large bulk to push between the Chaplain and the Prisoner and a baton comes out quickly and is held in one of the CO's meaty hands.

"He won't shut up," the Prisoner shouts at the Chaplain over the COs. "He asks too many fucking questions."

"Isn't that his job, asshole?" CO7 responds.

"His job is to listen. To listen," the Prisoner shouts.

The Prisoner has suddenly changed after these short four hours of talk. The calm that was present only minutes ago has now completely disappeared, and there is a frantic look in his eyes. This couldn't have happened so quickly. Why hadn't the Chaplain seen this before? Why does it take five huge COs in the room for him to see this? The Prisoner's voice had been calm as he was telling his story, but his body was telling the Chaplain everything he needed to know. The Prisoner is beginning to panic. He's as tight as a rubber band right now. Ready to snap.

"Calm down," a CO says. "Just take it easy."

"He won't shut up," the Prisoner says, quietly now. "He won't shut up. He doesn't understand."

The COs look at the Chaplain. He shrugs. What can he say? He doesn't understand. The Prisoner is absolutely right.

"Let's go." The COs lead the Chaplain out of the cell. "Take a break."

"No. There isn't enough time."

"Just a break. Take a break, Chaplain. Come on. There's still time."

The Prisoner watches the Chaplain being lead out of the room. He wraps his tattooed arms around his chest and holds on tight, as if hugging himself, comforting himself. He looks down at the floor and the Chaplain sees the slump of his shoulders, the sag of his back. The man is in emotional turmoil, pain, and he is running out of time quickly. Guilt. For the bank murders. For the final murders. He's done so much, this man, to harm the world. Of course he feels he deserves to die.

"I need to stay in there," the Chaplain says.

"I want you to take a few minutes," CO7 says. "Take a few minutes and breathe. This is shit work, man. Sorry, I didn't mean to swear. It's bad work, and you need to take a minute to decompress."

"Take a look at this, Seven." Another CO points towards the door they've just closed upon the Prisoner. The COs all pile together to look in. The Chaplain stands back, waiting his turn. He is shaking slightly, agitated.

"I need to go back in there. You don't understand. We were making progress. I need to be with him."

"He okay?"

"Not sure."

"Should we go back in?"

"How can you be so stupid?" the Chaplain shouts, suddenly, like a kid, leaping behind them. "Let me go back in."

The COs all turn towards him. CO7 shrugs. The Chaplain walks up to the door and looks in at the Prisoner. He is hunched over on the floor, holding himself, rocking back and forth, crying. He is crying. A broken man.

"Open the door."

CO7 opens the door and the Chaplain enters and goes straight to the Prisoner, kneels down in front of him. He reaches out, tentatively, and touches the Prisoner's shoulder. A hand shoots up, and for a minute, the Chaplain thinks the Prisoner is going to knock him out, but then the Prisoner grabs the Chaplain's hand on his shoulder and he holds it tight. Squeezes it. Human touch.

"I have no one," the Prisoner says, so quietly the Chaplain can barely hear him. "I have no one but you."

They stay like this, together, touching by hand, shoulder, the Chaplain on his creaking knees, the Prisoner rocking back and forth. They stay like this for a bit. The next time the Chaplain looks at the clock it is 4:23 a.m.

When he was out in the hall, something was different. The Chaplain couldn't put his finger on it. It isn't until he sees the clock, the time, 4:23 a.m., that he knows what it was. The light. It is coming upon dawn. The light is changing. The window in the COs' hallway will soon be awash with sunlight. It will be light instead of dark. Day instead of night. Morning is coming. And with it, the day. And with that, the Prisoner's execution. The last seven and a half hours of life. He wonders when the rain stopped. He remembers the storm only a few hours ago, how soaked he got getting his coffee. He remembers the smell in the air of the wet pavement steaming. The heat of the summer washing off. The feel of sunshine upon his face. He thinks of rain. Or snow. The Prisoner will have none of this ever again. So the Chaplain holds the Prisoner's hand as he rocks and tries not to think of the pain in his knees as he kneels there on the cold, hard floor of the cell.

Later, they are back up in their positions – the Prisoner on the bed, the Chaplain on his chair. They have been quiet for some time; minutes have passed. The Chaplain is afraid to say anything that will set the Prisoner off again, that will upset him, that will cause emotion. Although he wants to force emotion, he isn't sure if this is the way to do it. He wants the emotion to come from within the Prisoner, not from something the Chaplain says to make him angry.

The Chaplain thinks of Miranda and how, if he were on death row, she would be there for him. His sister. When their parents died, they came together closer than before. They had no one else. It was the natural thing to do. When he was first charged with assault, Miranda was there. When Tracy dropped the charges, Miranda was there. When he was ordained, Miranda attended the ceremony (albeit with a frown on her face, rolling her eyes, making faces at him, pretending to pray to make him laugh). He saw her children when they were newborns, he held them just after Richard did, and he stood for Richard as best man at their wedding ceremony. He also walked Miranda down the aisle – two jobs on the one day. Stood in for their father. If the Chaplain were strapped to a chair, ready to be electrocuted, he knows for certain that he would look out the window into the waiting crowd of lawyers, lawmakers, wardens, and he would see his sister, Miranda. Even though, while speculating, she claimed she wouldn't come, he knows she would be there. He would see Richard too. Just before the hood came down.

So where is Susan, the Prisoner's sister? Why isn't she coming to be there for him, to be the last face he looks at before he dies? To be family? The Chaplain can't remember what he read in the files about Susan – she didn't seem important when he was cramming. He focused more on the crime the Prisoner is on death row for. And he doesn't want to ask the Prisoner about her.

"You got any advice, Chaplain?" the Prisoner finally asks.

"What do you mean?"

"I don't know. Advice. You guys always give advice."

"We 'guys'?"

"Men of God."

"Oh, religious advice?" The Chaplain sits up straighter, tries to stop slumping. He rubs his eyes.

"I don't know. Just advice. Any kind of advice."

"Seems to me," he says, "that you don't need advice now."

"True." The Prisoner laughs. "I could've used your advice ten years ago when I committed the crime, right?"

"I think you could have used advice from the very beginning. From the day you met Dwight or from the day you stole the watch from your father's shop."

"Wasn't really surrounded by advice-givers," the Prisoner says.

"I give my niece and nephew advice all the time," the Chaplain says. "And if I think about it, it doesn't help at all. Advice is probably overrated. I think that maybe a kid will do what a kid wants to do and will hopefully learn from the consequences. And from example. Someone telling you to do something or not to do something won't make you learn, right?"

"No one ever give you good advice, Chaplain?" The Prisoner rolls onto his side, fetal position, his hands tucked between his thighs. He looks over at the Chaplain, his eyes red from crying.

"I guess my father and mother did. My sister did. But sometimes I'd listen and sometimes I wouldn't and it didn't seem to matter either way. One way or another, I learned from my behaviour. Or from their behaviour around me."

"Maybe that's what's wrong with me, then? I never learned from my behaviour."

"Yes, maybe. I don't know."

"I got better, though."

"Sorry?" The Chaplain notes that the COs are moving out in the hallway. He can see the light from the outside window being blocked and then coming full into the cell over and over. "I don't understand. You got better at what?"

"I got better at the stuff I was good at. So I did learn. I just didn't learn the right things."

"You seem awfully proud of your crimes," the Chaplain says.

The Prisoner sits up. "Yeah, well, fuck. I was good at what I did."

"Until you killed people."

"That was a mistake. That should never have happened."

Settle down, the Chaplain thinks. The COs are looking into the cell again. He waves them off. It's a volatile situation here now, with time running out. As if suddenly a pulley was tightened and the Prisoner's nerves stretched to the breaking point. He's brushed aside the final murders, thinking now only of the bank ones – the ones that happened "by accident." The Prisoner will eventually get to the final murders, the Chaplain is sure of it. He will talk about them before he dies. *And I will forgive him. I will forgive him. No matter what Miranda thinks of me being here.*

"Do the victims' families have a chaplain visiting with them?" Miranda asked last Sunday night. Two bottles of wine in. The candles burning low. Pot roast on the counter, sticking to the pan. Richard upstairs with the kids – he and Miranda could hear water running and laughter and footsteps rushing back and forth down the hallway. "Who's helping them, Jim?"

And who helped the victims themselves, as they were murdered senselessly? Who helped them? Who listened to their fears, their worries, their remorse, their goodbyes? Who listened to the history of their lives?

No one.

"Tell me about Susan," the Chaplain says, clutching his fists together, popping his knuckles. "Tell me where she is. What happened to her."

Jack

Susan is in the bathroom, has locked herself in with her cell-phone, as her ex-boyfriend tries to kick the door down. Susan calls Larry, who is coming up the front walk now, gun in his jacket pocket.

"Get out of the house," Susan screams. "Get out."

The ex keeps kicking.

"Larry's coming," Susan says. "He'll hurt you. Get out."

"That little fag?" The ex laughs.

And Larry comes up the stairs, two stairs at a time, his leather boots thumping solidly.

"Hey," he says to the ex.

The ex turns and as he does, Larry takes the gun out of his pocket and uses it to knock out the ex's teeth.

The kids are screaming. They have some friends over and there are a shitload of kids in the house. One kid is screaming, "Daddy." Too many exes, too many kids. Larry can't keep them straight. All the exes beat Susan, eventually. They all look the same – big men with bellies and beards. This ex holds onto his mouth, holds onto the blood that is pouring out into his hands.

He starts to holler.

"Too much noise," Larry says. "Keep it down."

Susan opens the latch on the bathroom door. Peeks out. She is still holding her cellphone in her hand. She takes notice of the blood everywhere, of her ex clutching at his mouth, of her kids screaming and running around crazily. She takes note of Larry, standing there, holding the gun limply at his side.

"Oh God," Susan says. "What happened to us?"

Larry sees, down the hall, behind the crazy bleeding ex, his old bedroom, now full of Susan's kids' stuff. He sees the blue walls and the sticky un-glowing stars and dim planets, and suddenly the force of the situation comes full at him like he's been kicked in the stomach. What did happen to them?

Their mother fed them sandwiches at lunch every day. White bread. She did their laundry, tidied their rooms, paid the housekeeper, kept them dry and clean and fed. She smiled at them when they told a joke. Clapped when they learned to walk. Protected them from their angry father.

Susan pushes past the men and her kids and thumps down the stairs and out of the house. The ex makes his way out behind her, holding his mouth. The kids stop screaming and turn on the screen. One kid puts an old sweatshirt on top of the blood stains and steps over it. And Larry turns from his old bedroom, from the images in his mind of his mother folding soft, sweet-smelling laundry, whistling, ruffling his hair, cutting his peanut butter sandwich in half. He turns from this and walks down the stairs and out of the house. Leaves the kids to themselves.

Jack.

This is now all he can think.

Jack.

Jack did this to them. Not his mother, not his alcoholic

father. Not Susan. Jack. His mother left not with Jack but because of him. She was protecting Larry from his brother, protecting Susan. One too many concussions? One too many beatings? That must have been it. Why else would she have taken Jack? It couldn't have been just their father that made her want to leave – he was a drunk all through their marriage. It was Jack. He was too much like their father.

Why didn't Larry realize this earlier?

One thing Larry is good at is getting things done, and now his focus is on Jack. Larry has a gun now. Jack can't scare him anymore.

Larry is twenty-six. He hasn't been caught once. Not even once. Dwight has been in and out of jail. Paroled several times. Samantha is in jail now. Drug charges. Prostitution. Becky, the hairdresser, was slapped on the wrist for selling drugs. Even Susan has seen the system. Her kids get arrested all the time. She herself was in for soliciting prostitution, even though she says she was just asking the guy to pay for a couple drinks, at least, if she was going to fuck him. Who knew he was a plain-clothes cop? And what happened to chivalry, Susan says. What happened to paying for a lady's drink?

But Larry. He has never done time. He has never seen the inside of a jail cell. He has never needed bail money or been inside a courthouse other than to pick up a niece or nephew once in a while.

"I've obviously got the brains in this family," he tells Susan again and again. "I've never been arrested. It's obvious. I should have stayed in school."

She laughs. "If you are considered smart then I'm afraid for this world."

"I don't get caught. Everyone gets caught. I don't."

"That's luck. Not smarts."

Larry takes a drag of Susan's cigarette.

"Get your own smokes, asshole," Susan says.

"I bought you that cigarette."

Larry thinks, later, on death row, that it's a shame the seriousness of his offense outweighed the fact that he was a first-time offender in the eyes of the law. Maybe then he wouldn't have been given the death penalty.

Susan looks down at her hands resting on the kitchen table. Worn, rubbed raw by dishwashing in the diner where she works. No manicure here. No fancy nails. Ripped cuticles, jagged skin bleeding. She clears her throat. "Listen, Larry. I wanted to tell you."

Larry looks at her, his sister. "What?" He can hear something in her voice he's never heard before. Usually she's flippant and annoying. Right now, she seems scared. "Another fucking boyfriend?"

"No. No, not that. I," Susan pauses. Breathes deeply. "Well."

"What?" Larry takes another drag of her cigarette.

"I'm trying to tell you. Stop interrupting."

Larry leans back in his chair.

"I saw Jack."

Larry is closing the store up for the last time. He's locking the door and is going to take the keys over to Mr. Mallone, the guy next door who owns the shoe repair shop and wants to expand. Mr. Mallone gave Larry and Susan a good deal and they've divided the money in three and put Jack's third away, according to advice from the lawyers.

Larry thinks it's kind of funny how much time he's spent with lawyers lately, considering all the crimes he commits. He turns the lock on the door, last time, looks into the glass at the empty store, at his father's drunk ghost slumped at the counter, at the non-existent grandfather clocks and all the tools, now sold, that it took to make them work. The sound of the store will stay with him forever, the ever-present *tick-tock, tick-tock* that made his skin crawl when he was a kid. A countdown of life. Always. No wonder his father drank himself to death. No wonder Larry does the things he does – the constant reminder that time is running out.

"Lawrence." A voice, behind him in the dusk. Larry sees the reflection of a man on the glass of the empty store. He turns.

Jack.

Twenty-eight years old. A slight beard. He's taller than Larry. And wider. Chunky, almost fat. His stomach protrudes. He's missing some teeth, and his hair and beard are reddish-brown, stained looking. His eyes are hollow, drugged. Jack is holding a cigarette in his hand but he doesn't take a drag. Wearing a hunting jacket, camouflage, and army pants with pockets everywhere. Big boots. Biker boots. Larry wouldn't even know him if it weren't for the way Jack said his name. *Lawrence.* The same way he used to say it before he would hurt Larry. He can feel it's Jack, even if he doesn't recognize him.

"Jack."

They look at each other. Awkward. Larry, nervously, glances down at the ground first. The old emotions creep up in him, he can almost feel the concussions, the beatings, on his skin, in his head. Larry remembers what it was like to be four years old to Jack's six. To be seven to Jack's nine. Always one step ahead – two years bigger, better, smarter, meaner, taller, and one step more dangerous.

Jack. His brother.

"So." Jack stares at Larry. "What can I say?"

"Closing the store for good," Larry says, looking up at the

darkened sign that reads *Gallo's Precision Repair* – soon to be replaced by *Mallone's Shoe Shop*. Larry added the money Mr. Mallone gave him to his coffee tins. Lots of them now, quite the collection. Larry feels safe with money. Money takes care of him. And he knows he can always get more. But there is something in Jack's behaviour, in his stance, that makes him suddenly think about his coffee tins and worry. Worry about his safety in general. All the old demons and fears emerge, and Larry's head suddenly aches.

"I hear Dad died," Jack says. No emotion.

"You call him 'Dad,' do you?"

"What else should I call him? He was my fucking dad."

Larry turns and begins to walk away. Jack follows. They say nothing. Larry turns into Mallone's store and hands over the keys to the girl behind the counter. "Enjoy," he says.

"Yeah, we have a shitload of packing and moving to do, and the wall needs to come out, and –" she's snapping gum as she rambles.

"Enjoy." Larry says again and leaves the store. Walks out mid-sentence.

"See you around," the girl calls out expectantly. "Keep in touch, Larry."

"One fuck and they think they own you," Jack says to Larry and laughs. A gruff laugh. A guffaw. Short, sharp. A bark.

Jack walks quickly to keep pace with Larry. He breathes deeply, out of shape. "Let's go get drunk and talk all this over," he says. "Susan tells me I've got some money coming? She says she's told you nothing?"

"Nothing."

"Not like her to keep her mouth shut."

"And what would you know about Susan?"

"That's fair," Jack says. "I remember she was a shithead when she was younger. Always thought she was right."

Larry and Jack walk into Borough Pub. They sit in a booth by the bathroom and order two pitchers of beer. The waitress brings over a bowl of peanuts in shells and Jack begins to crack and eat as if he's starving to death. Larry sips his beer slowly, preferring to stay in the moment, to stay in control. His hands shake slightly. His older brother makes him nervous, brings up all the old fears, the unfairness and hurt and pain of a life with Jack.

Turns out, after another pitcher of beer, that Jack has been just as lucky as Larry. No jail time. Except Jack's crimes aren't like Larry's, they are more violent and meant to cause pain and suffering. Sort of like when he would push Larry down the stairs, or trip him when he wandered past. Jack's crimes are complicated and involve bike gangs and hunting rifles and drugs and knives. They involve broken arms and legs and trash barrels dumped into lakes or empty wells. Larry feels good that he's his own man, his own boss, while Jack seems to take direction from others. But it worries him immediately that, no matter if they were brought up by their father or their mother, everyone in this family turned out fucked up and a criminal. There must be something in the blood, Larry thinks. In our veins. Coursing through us. Look at Susan's brats too. It never ends.

"So I left her when I was sixteen," Jack says. "Spent seven years with her. We moved a lot. She was always trying to keep ahead of him."

"He didn't try to find her. I know that."

"Sure he did, asshole. Of course he did. Wanted to kill her, Dad did."

"No."

"Yes. He found us a couple of times. Took it out on her. Bruised her. Beat her. But she never gave in, she never went back."

Larry is astonished. All that time he was growing up without a mother, his father knew where she was. He found her? He beat her? He never told them anything, never even mentioned her.

"Why didn't she come back for me and Susan?"

"She could barely keep it together for me," Jack says. "Let alone take care of you two."

But she picked you, Larry wants to shout. She picked you. Why you?

"She finally settled. Met this guy. Moved in with him. Took his name. Dad stopped coming around, stopped finding her. This guy, Eric, he was big man. Large. Like this," Jack spreads his arms wide. "Fucking kill you if you so much as looked at him. But he kept mom safe from Dad, and he kept her in booze money and nice dresses."

"Eric."

"You a parrot, Lawrence?"

"Don't call me that."

Jack smirks. "Anyway, he died years ago and I was gone so she drank." Jack looks nervous suddenly. Guilty. "I found her at the bottom of her stairs one day. I hadn't visited in about four months. I was busy. She'd been dead a couple of weeks. Her fucking cat was eating her."

Larry swallows his beer hard. It comes up. He coughs.

"Don't puke on me, man." Jack stands up. Wipes the regurgitated beer from the front of his coat. "Jesus."

"Sorry." Larry takes a napkin and mops up the rest of the beer that came out of his mouth. His whistling mother, the one who painted his world blue, died alone at the bottom of her stairs. Drunk. Life sucks, Larry thinks. All the things he'd imagined for her – death even – were nothing compared to the reality of what happened to her. Sure, he wanted her to hurt, wanted her to suffer because she had made him and Susan suffer, but he didn't really expect that that's what would happen. That her life was for nothing. Larry wants to believe that she tried to save him from Jack, but now he isn't so sure. After all, Jack is here now. She saved him from nothing. She gave birth to Susan and to Larry and to Jack, but her life amounted to nothing else. Look at all of them now. Three criminals. Larry swigs back more beer. His glass is empty. He refills. Gets up to take a leak. Stumbles slightly.

"Can't hold your booze, can you? You were always a skinny little guy," Jack laughs. "We must not be related."

"Fuck off." Larry sways towards the bathroom and leans on the wall while pissing into a urinal. When he comes out, Jack is gone and has left him with the bill. Larry wonders if, maybe, he imagined his brother. Maybe the whole thing was a nightmare.

Susan doesn't know where he lives. She knows even less about Jack than Larry does.

"Why do you want to see him again anyway?" she says.

"I want to give him his third of the money and forget about him."

Larry does see Jack again. A month later. He sees him coming out of the same bar they had beers in, as if looking for Larry. Jack takes the money Larry offers him, picks it up at the house, says hey to Susan and her kids. "Jesus, ever heard of birth control? Three kids. You're just like mom," he says. Her face is stricken. This is the last Larry sees of his brother before everything that happens later. Before things get out of control.

5:01 a.m.

"So both Susan and Jack are still alive?"

The Prisoner shrugs. "As far as I know. I haven't been in touch and they haven't been in touch with me."

"I wish I had known all of this. I wish I had been with you before. I could have helped more. I could have brought them here, let you see them. Helped you make amends. You could phone them. I'm sure I could get a phone brought in. Do you want me to ask?"

"What the hell for?" The Prisoner is pacing again. Back and forth. The light from the COs' window is brighter now, infused with sunlight. "Bring them here for what? A party? A death party? Hey, let's celebrate my execution? Eat cake? Bring presents? And what would I talk to them about? You're really fucked, man. For a chaplain, for a guy who's supposed to be smart, you're just fucked."

"I guess. You're right. Yes, I am."

"I tried to frame Jack for the murders – didn't you read the files?"

"But he doesn't know that. It didn't go anywhere. Your

lawyers rejected that appeal. Only you and the lawyers know that."

"It was my last hope," the Prisoner says. "He deserved it."

The Chaplain stands now and paces too. He walks the opposite direction from the Prisoner, both of them crossing each other's path frequently. They pace back and forth like the zoo animals they are. Caged in. Stretching the legs. Getting the blood flowing. The corrections officers look in and shrug. They are only mildly interested in this insanity. Put a man in a box and see what he will do. Put two men in a box and it's only slightly more interesting.

Less than seven hours left. Suddenly, that seems long to the Chaplain. All this time it felt as if time was speeding up and running out, but now seven hours feels like an eternity. Not even halfway through the ordeal. It's torture, making him wait. The Chaplain shakes his head to clear it. They've been doing nothing. Talking, that's it. Listening to the Prisoner talk, occasionally saying something himself. But they haven't really accomplished anything in these five hours together. He realizes that he's getting antsy now. Even though he can leave anytime he wants to, he's feeling confined, chained up, held hostage. And it makes his skin crawl. It makes him shiver. It makes him anxious and confused and frustrated and angry.

Locking already angry men up in little cages, the Chaplain thinks, doesn't do anything but make them angrier. Ah, he's learned something now. Something he can take away from this – prison reform! The Chaplain will gather the troops with the rallying cry – bigger cells, more free-roaming from room to room and floor to floor, more time in the yard. Fresh air. Sunshine. Let the men free. Organic prisoners. He snorts. He laughs out loud. He's going crazy.

"You're weird," the Prisoner says. "Strange."

"Yes, well, no one ever said I was normal."

The Prisoner thinks about this. The Chaplain can see him thinking, see the wheels turning in his mind. If a prison chaplain, an educated man, is not normal, then who is? What is? Maybe the Prisoner is the most normal person in the world. After all, everyone else is conspiring to kill him. Legally. With electricity. With sterilized equipment and laundered hoods. Men will get paid to walk him to the chair, to strap him in, to electrocute him. People will watch him die. What is normal anyway?

There is a knock at the door.

A new CO comes in – one they haven't seen before, a woman – rolling a cart in front of her. She introduces herself.

"I'm CO11," she says, even though they can see her number on her uniform. "I've got your food."

CO11 places the cart in the middle of the room. Again the Chaplain notes how small the room is. The cart takes up a good deal of it. The cart is covered at the top and is draped in a tablecloth at the bottom. The Prisoner makes some comment about hiding under it, wheeling out, escape. Like in the movies. CO11 laughs. "Every prisoner says that," she says. Her teeth are raggedy and yellow. She is older than both the Chaplain and the prisoner. Her hair is dyed orange and thinning at the top, the part grey. The Chaplain notes a large boil or burn on one hand. He feels queasy. CO11 takes the cover off the top of the cart, and there is the Prisoner's last meal.

The Chaplain sits down quickly and solidly. The smells overwhelm him. He feels nauseous, feels the bile coming up his throat. It's a fine meal, but in such a small space, with such a momentous thing, he is completely knocked over. The Prisoner's last meal. This is it. Food.

From the day you are born, you need food, you want food,

you enjoy food, you hate food, you crave and repel and pick at and indulge in and throw out and relish and throw away and throw up food. Life is about food. Without it we die. The Prisoner's last meal. Ever.

"Man up," the Prisoner says, seeing the Chaplain's face. "Chill."

"It's just," the Chaplain begins to tear up. He is going to cry. He can't help himself. A huge part of him wants to run from the room – the part of him that is Jim, the man – but the other part of him, the Chaplain, knows he must stay. The Prisoner needs to see his tears; he does not need to see him run from his feelings.

The Chaplain begins to sob.

"Fuck. You're ruining my meal." The Prisoner plops down on his bed. "It's getting cold. You got to stop crying, man."

"I can't help –"

"Really? Really? You're crying? Now?"

"It's your last –"

CO11 is still holding the cover to the cart. "You want me to put it back to keep it warm?"

"No. Leave it."

CO11 shrugs. She turns and leaves the room. "I'll come back for the tray in a bit."

They won't leave the Prisoner with shoelaces or a pen, but a plastic fork, knife and spoon, that's okay? But then the Chaplain looks carefully through his tears at the meal and notes that there is no cutlery with it. Everything the prisoner ordered can be eaten by hand. A paper plate. A disposable cup. The Chaplain guesses that the Prisoner could whack him on the head with the cart if he really wanted to. If he was strong enough to lift it.

The Chaplain stops crying. As quickly as he started. He

stands, wipes at his eyes with his sleeves. "I'm so sorry, please forgive me. I don't know what came over me. I'm tired. Emotional, I –"

"Can I eat now?"

The Prisoner stands and moves the cart towards himself.

"Do you want a chair?"

"Yeah, hell. Sure." The Prisoner takes a chair, pulls the cart in front of him – a dining table – and sits down to his last meal. The two chairs and the cart make the space crowded. The Chaplain walks over to the bed and sits down on it. It's soft. He leans into it.

"Mind if I sit here while you eat?"

"Lie down. Get some shut-eye," the Prisoner says. He begins to stuff himself. Quickly and methodically. He looks around as he eats, as if wary of someone stealing his meal, and a small sigh of pleasure escapes between bites. He smiles. "This is fucking awesome. You want some?" He points to his food.

"No. Thank you, though. It's your meal."

"There's a lot here. I can share."

"No. That's fine."

The Prisoner looks relieved. "Yeah, I guess you'll be getting other meals." He laughs. "Nothing as good as this, though."

The Chaplain looks at the tray. On it: a huge hamburger, sesame seed bun, tomatoes, lettuce, ketchup, mustard, onion, pickles. French fries smothered in gravy and ketchup. What looks like a vanilla milkshake. With a straw. A little plate of various sushi, dipping sauce. An orange cut like a flower, spread open and beautiful. Mashed potatoes, of course. Butter dripping into a hole in the mound. Salt. Pepper. A chocolate cake – the entire cake. Black forest, it has cherries on it. The Prisoner swallows bite after bite, not caring in what order. He chews the cake, pops in a piece of sushi, bites the burger, cake, fries, potato, back to sushi, etc. The Chaplain watches for a while, and then he leans back into the bed. He lies down. Tries not to close his eyes. Wills himself not to fall asleep, to stay whole and awake, but his eyes are heavy.

"The best is the sushi," the Prisoner says. "I love sushi. I tried it about eleven years ago for the first time. Just before I came in here. Never had it as a kid. Love the stuff. I think it's the wasabi. Fucking hot, man. I love it."

Lying there, listening to the Prisoner talk and hearing him chew with his mouth open, breathing heavy, slurping and sipping, his straw digging at the bottom of his glass, the Chaplain suddenly thinks about the time Tracy took him to that Japanese restaurant on George Street. She blindfolded him. It was snowing. Thick and white and cold, the flakes fell on his face.

"Happy birthday, Jim," she said, taking the blindfold off right in front of the restaurant. Inside, the lights were bright and warm and inviting. Inside, he could see his sister, Miranda, fully pregnant, and her husband, Richard, holding a Sapporo. Laughing. Inside, he could see friends from university, people from his classes. Lots of them. "Surprise," Tracy said and let go of his hand. She opened the door.

The difference between the cold outside and the warm, glowing light inside made the scene unreal. As if he were watching this on a movie screen. Watching his life before him, lit up and warm and cozy. A huge platter of sushi went past the window. Richard's eyes followed it, and then he looked up and out to the dark night and saw Jim standing there. He could see it in Richard's eyes – the delight of seeing his brother-in-law standing outside in the snow.

"Surprise," they all shouted. He went inside, to the party, and ate and drank and laughed and enjoyed the night. A week later, Tracy left him for David. A week later, he was beating her up, arrested, assault charges pending. A week later, he didn't even remember what his life felt like when he looked into the Japanese restaurant on the night of his birthday. How quickly things changed. He didn't know he was capable of physically hurting someone. He spent his entire youth avoiding fights, letting Miranda fight for him. To connect his fist to Tracy's face, it was something unthinkable. And that was the problem. He wasn't thinking, just reacting.

The Chaplain wonders now, is that what happened to the Prisoner? Was it a matter of not thinking and merely reacting? He knows it wasn't premeditated, obviously, but was the Prisoner actually thinking as he picked up the knife, or was it an instinctual, base, animal thing? How else could he have done what he did to those pour souls? How else could a man take lives?

The Chaplain sits up. Rubs his eyes.

"You dozed," the Prisoner says. He is leaning back on his chair, holding his stomach. "My God, I'm so full."

"Was it good?"

"It was fucking brilliant," the Prisoner says. He burps. "I know why they give it to you so early, though."

"Why?"

"I'm probably going to puke." He burps again. A wet one. "They don't want me puking in the hood." The Prisoner lets out a quick, bark-like laugh and then stops and looks at the Chaplain, his eyes wide and afraid. The Chaplain can see the fear creep through them, almost like the lens on a bird's eye – a quick movement, a milky look. He shivers.

"You should take the bed. Lie down."

"No, man, I need to walk. Burn the calories." Again, the Prisoner laughs, but this time quietly. "Don't want to get fat," he whispers, almost to himself.

The Chaplain tries to smile but can't. The air around him is heavy with sadness and fear and aching pain and emotional tension. It smells of food and sweat and gas. Everything is in the air. In the last five hours, he's felt nothing like it. The high and the low. The palpable fear. The adrenalin. The exhaustion. He sighs.

When the Chaplain's fist connected with Tracy's face, he felt elated. Afterwards he knew that he had to find something bigger than himself to live for. Maybe that's what happened to the Prisoner – he had nothing bigger than who he was at the time to concentrate on. Now he certainly has something bigger than himself. Death.

"Six and a half hours left," the Prisoner says.

"Yes."

"Would you mind leaving for a bit? For half an hour or something? Give me some time to myself? Would that be okay?"

"Sure, of course. Yes. No problem." The Chaplain stands. "I can wait out in the room." He signals to the door.

"No, go for a walk. Just for half an hour. Go for a walk outside and tell me what the weather is like when you come back. Can you do that?" The Prisoner is still holding his stomach even though he is standing, walking. He's holding it as if he's in pain.

"Are you okay?"

"I ate too fast," the Prisoner says. "Didn't chew enough, I guess." He laughs. "Figures I'd get indigestion with my last meal. I should have asked for Pepto-Bismol."

"I'll get you some. I'll bring it in."

"Sure, yeah. Thanks." The Prisoner stops and looks at the Chaplain. "When you come back, tell me exactly what the weather is like. I want to be able to feel it, picture it, know it. Okay?"

"Are you sure you want me to go?"

The Prisoner nods. "If only so I can take another shit." He smiles. A toothy grin. A grin that makes the Chaplain suddenly see the boy in him, the boy he once was – loved stars and planets and blue-painted walls. Loved his mother. What happened to all of that when he committed his crimes? What happened to the boy inside of him?

The Chaplain knocks on the door and the COs let him out into the hall. He comes out of the door as if escaping Death itself and feels a huge weight leave his body. The Chaplain feels as if he'll float to the ceiling if he doesn't hold on tight to something. The door frame. The wall. He turns and looks back in at the Prisoner, who is standing there, holding his stomach, smiling slightly, a faraway look in his eyes.

"Taking a break?" CO11 is there, come to collect the cart.

"Yes. A break." The Chaplain leaves the COs then and walks down the hallway, back to where he started five and a half hours ago. He walks fast and hard, his feet scrabbling on the ground, a heavy tread. Through prison doors that clang open when he comes (the COs have called ahead to let him out). Quickly past the cells, past the prisoners' closed doors, and out past the Warden's office as fast as he can. No time for coffee. The Chaplain must describe the weather. He must feel it on his face. He must look straight into it. And he must take this weather back for the Prisoner. Now. Time is running out.

"Hey, Chaplain? What are you doing out?"

It's the Warden, having a smoke in the yard. Five-thirty in the morning.

"Good morning." The Chaplain stops walking fast and stands next to the Warden and looks out at the world around him, at the huge yard, empty of anyone, of anything. No trees. Just yard and fence for as far as he can see. And sky. Wide-open sky. The rain from the night is drying quickly on the ground around him. He can smell it as it evaporates from the earth.

"He let you go? Doesn't need you anymore?"

"No. Just for now. Just a break."

"How's it going?"

"Fine," the Chaplain says. "Fine."

He doesn't want to talk about how he feels, about what he is feeling, experiencing, right now. Someday he will talk about it – in fact, someday, he knows he'll be telling people about these twelve hours at a dinner party or over coffee. He knows it will become a story and not real life, that the Prisoner's predicament will soon be something to remember, not something that is happening right now. But right this instant, he does not want to talk to anyone. Especially not to the Warden.

"How's he doing?"

"I don't want to talk about it. Fine, I guess. He's doing okay, considering." The Chaplain turns from the Warden. "Listen, do you mind if I take some time to myself? I'm a bit tired. I need to refocus."

"Refocus? Shit. Sure, Chaplain. Whatever you need. The inmates will be out in the yard in about an hour."

"I won't be here for very long. Only a few minutes."

"Sure, refocus all you want." The Warden laughs. Shakes his head. "Jesus, refocus. Is that some religious mumbo-jumbo or therapy talk or what?"

The Chaplain turns to walk away but then finds himself turning back. "Warden? Did the Prisoner go through all his appeals? Is there no hope for a stay of execution?"

"He's fired his lawyers, Chaplain. Even if there was hope, there's no one to file a stay, let alone counsel him. The bastard's ready to die. He wants to die."

The Chaplain thinks about this.

"What about his family?"

"What about them? No one has come forward to help him out if that's what you mean."

"He has a sister and a brother. Are they coming?"

"They haven't registered to come watch. Not yet. They always could last minute, I suppose."

The Chaplain pauses. "And the victims' families? Will they be here?"

"I assume so," the Warden says. "If they decide to show up. They know about it. I'd bet a million bucks they'll come. Wouldn't you if that were your kin? Wouldn't you want to see him fry? I sure as heck would."

"Yes, I guess."

The Warden looks confused for a minute. "Aren't you a man of God, Chaplain?" He smiles.

"I mean, no, I wouldn't want to see him die. I just understand what you are saying. I can understand human nature about this, about anger and about loss. The crime was so violent. I get it."

"You bet you get it," the Warden says. His voice has gone low. A bit of a growl to it. "Don't go turning soft on me. Don't let him get to you."

The Chaplain turns and walks away again. He does two laps of the yard, paying close attention to everything around him. To all his senses: touch, taste, smell, sound, sight. He can see the Warden finishing his cigarette, and when he passes close enough by him to hear, he hears the Warden say to himself, "Fuck, refocus? What does that mean?" as he goes back inside the prison walls.

By being here, doing this, is the Chaplain giving the impression that he believes in the death penalty? That he agrees with this? Because he doesn't. Believe in it. He wouldn't want anyone to think that of him. It would be worse than people thinking he committed domestic abuse on a regular basis, which they did think. People. For a while. How, they thought, could someone take even one swing at a woman without ever having done it before? Almost killed her. They thought this before he went into the ministry. Before he gave up his life to serve others. To serve God.

Gave up his life? What is he thinking?

The Chaplain rubs at his eyes with the backs of his hands. They feel raw and exposed. The sun coming up blinds him. He needs to stop. He needs to refocus (fuck the Warden) and get back to the Prisoner. The Chaplain has only been gone for twenty minutes maximum, but to him, it feels as if he's been away from the Prisoner for a lifetime.

When Tracy was a little girl, she had told him, she would think of her pets' experiences through their years. Cat years and dog years. For example, when she left her dog for a day, it would be, in dog years, as if she had left him for a month. When her family went on vacation and her dog stayed in the kennel for two weeks, that would be a year out of his life. Or whatever. The Chaplain doesn't have the math right. But this is what it feels like right now. Every half-hour the Prisoner has left is several years of the life that he might have lived if he hadn't committed the crime. The faster the Chaplain gets back to him, the better.

PART TWO

PART TWO

6:01 a.m.

When the Chaplain re-enters the cell, the smell of vomit hits him. It is strong and sour and vile. The Prisoner is lying on the cot, facing the wall.

"Are you okay?"

"No, yes. No. No." The Prisoner does not turn to talk to the Chaplain. "I ate too much, I think."

"Can I get you anything?"

"Did you get me the Pepto-Bismol?"

"Oh no, I forgot. Oh, I forgot. I'm sorry. I can get some now. I'll get a CO to run for it."

"Don't bother." The Prisoner rolls onto his back and stares at the ceiling. His eyes are bloodshot and puffy. He's been crying. "I think I got everything out anyway. I should feel better in a bit."

The Chaplain sits down on the chair, tries to calm his gag reflex, breathes through his nose. He can see specks of vomit around the toilet and stuck within the bowl. Won't the COs clean up at least? This is inhumane treatment. The Chaplain realizes quickly how strange it is to be thinking this way – inhumane treatment of a man hours before he is to be executed. What is the definition of humane in this scenario? But the vomit. Surely, they could spray some air freshener?

The Chaplain stands and pounds on the door. The COs open up.

"Can you get someone to clean up a bit in here? Can he have some air? He's sick."

"We can't leave our posts." Then, seeing the Chaplain's expression. "Listen, I'll call down to the front and see if they can send up someone to mop or something."

"Thank you. That would be appreciated." He goes back into the room. They seal him in.

"I knew I asked for you for a reason," the Prisoner says weakly. He tries to smile. "Here I thought I was going to get Bible messages thrown at me and instead I get a personal assistant."

"Yes, well. It's not fair what they are doing to you." The Chaplain regrets this as soon as he says it.

The Prisoner looks at him and then slowly sits up. "You don't agree with this? With the death penalty? My chaplain thought it was fair."

"No, I –"

"He never said as much, but I knew that he thought I was getting what I deserved. He was always talking about the murders, talking in detail about them. Almost salivating over them or something. He kept talking about the families and about electrocution and everything. He wanted me to die. I'm pretty sure of it."

"And you wanted him in here with you at the end?"

"To be honest," the Prisoner says, "I was kind of glad when I found out he was sick. To be really honest. I mean, I wanted company – sitting here for twelve hours alone would have been really fucked – and he was all I had."

"Honesty is good."

"You're not like him," he says. "You're not like him at all. In fact, I wouldn't know you were a chaplain if they hadn't told me you were."

He thinks, am I a chaplain?

"I think we should talk more, get our mind off the smell, get back into your story. Don't you?" The Chaplain leans forward, towards the Prisoner.

The Prisoner rolls back onto the cot. Weak. "You never told me about the weather. Fuck, you forget the Pepto-Bismol and you forget the weather."

"I didn't forget the weather," the Chaplain says. "Not at all." And he goes into a full description – the drying rain, the mounting sun, the bleak nature of the yard, the wideness of the sky. He describes the Warden's cigarette smoke, the way the air was humid and thick and the smell of dirt was everywhere. The sun was yellow and foggy, waking up, coming alive. A bird or two chirped. The Chaplain could hear cicadas, loud and electrical sounding, as they met the sun. The Prisoner closes his eyes and listens deeply. He breathes slowly. The Chaplain wonders if he's asleep. Sight, smell, sound, taste, touch, he talks about it all. Paints a picture of the world outside this vomit-covered cell. The Prisoner rests peacefully.

Until the cell door opens and the cleaning staff arrive to spray bleach on the toilet and floor, to flick around a brush in the water, to wipe disinfectant on the sink, to straighten the bed even (they ask the Prisoner to stand), to spray air freshener into the room. The smell of tropical paradise overpowers the smell of vomit and soon the Chaplain can't tell which smell is worse, which smell is making him the most nauseous. The Prisoner smiles at him overtop the staff heads as they bustle around, bumping into each other, into the Prisoner and the Chaplain, the room is so small.

The next minute they're gone. Whipped in fast and whipped out faster. The Chaplain says, "It's like those car washes where a line of kids descends on your car, inside and out, each with their own job. They cover your car and then suddenly they are done. Something cartoonish about it."

The Prisoner laughs. "Yeah. I see that." He sits back on the bed, fanning his face. "I'm not sure I like this smell any better."

The Chaplain sits again. "Me neither."

"Well, you can't say my last couple hours were boring, can you? They've been nothing but a ball of fun. Nothing but excitement. A laugh a minute."

The Chaplain smiles. Leans back. Notices suddenly that his back isn't hurting anymore, that he is, yes, getting used to this. He guesses that a human body can get used to anything eventually.

"Tell me what happened after you gave Jack his portion of the money. After you found out how your mom died. What did you do then?"

The Prisoner lies down again, hands behind his head, watching those imaginary clouds on the ceiling, the ones behind his eyes.

Headaches

Larry finds that his crime spree is more spread out and less focused. One minute he's robbing a store, the next minute he's holding up some guy on the street. He feels a certain anger ever since he saw Jack, ever since he heard about his mother. He sees red now. Walks in a world of deception and pain. His headaches become blinding. He knew his mother had left them, he knew she made a choice – no one forced her to leave them, he knew that – but Larry didn't ever believe she did it without clear reason. Deep down, he wanted to believe that she accidentally walked out of the house and merely couldn't get back in – that she had left her keys, locked herself out, something like that. And he wanted to believe that, maybe, she took Jack by mistake. She meant to take Larry, but she grabbed Jack instead because he was around at the time and Larry wasn't home. Or she took him by design – she took Jack to save Larry from his violence. Why else would she have taken him? He was a bully and an ass-hole. She loved Larry the most. He was sure of that.

Larry's coffee cans are taking up too much space in his apartment. He is nervous having them around him while he sleeps. And so he doesn't often sleep. There is too much money in them and too many girls come in and out of his apartment. And so, one day on the way back from holding up a store, he stops his car on the side of Highway 20, a far way out from the city, with the woods on one side of the road and a strip mall on the other, and he rents a storage unit from the immense Storage Mart located there. Self storage. One of those heated/cooled ones, fifty dollars a month. Large and empty. An orange garage door. When he opens the rolling door and looks inside the vacant space, the guy from the front office watching him, he thinks maybe he'll make it more than just storage. Maybe an office. Set up a desk, a chair, a lamp. Maybe even get a rug for the cold concrete floor. Larry works on this for a while, stacks his coffee cans, buys a laptop. He feels like a man with a job now, even though he doesn't use his computer for anything other than porn. He doesn't even know what he would use it for. Accounting? Keeping track of his coffee cans? Emails? Who would he email? Jack? But now he has a place to go to in the morning, a place to sit and contemplate the future or the past or everything in between. And his coffee cans are safe here. Little did he know then that soon enough he would have a place similar in size on death row.

"What's wrong with you these days?" Susan stops him on the street. She's pushing a few toddlers in a stroller – not hers, she's babysitting for someone else. Larry is pleased to see she's making her own money again. She quit the diner a while ago and has been lolling around on the couch for months. Even though she looks drugged out, stoned, Larry is glad to see her up and moving. Larry is smoking. He stubs his cigarette out on the brick building he is leaning against.

"What do you mean, what's wrong with me? Nothing's wrong with me."

"You never come by the house anymore."

"I give you money, don't I?"

"I didn't mean that. I just mean I never see you anymore and when I do see you, you've got this weird look on your face like you're going to kill someone."

Larry laughs. "Yeah, right."

"No, seriously, are you doing drugs? Man, if you're doing drugs, I'll kill you myself."

"No drugs." Larry shakes his head. "I'm not that stupid."

Susan looks away – she has been caught doing/selling/growing/snorting drugs herself. She has track marks on both arms and her ankles. The only thing she won't touch is meth. Says she can't stand what it does to the jaw. Teeth fall out. Meth-heads, Susan says, are the ugliest fucks in the world. After seeing what meth did to Samantha, Larry would have to agree.

"Come over and hang out sometime," Susan says. "Like old times."

"I'm busy, Susan."

"Busy? Doing what?"

Larry marvels at Susan's inability to figure out what it is he actually does. She seems to think that he made all his money, the money he gives her, the money he lives on, by working in his dad's store. When they sold that, even though she got one-third of the money and it wasn't much, she still seems to think that Larry's better at handling his investments (coffee tins?) than she is, and so it's only natural to her that he still pays for things for her and her kids. Larry finds it hard to believe, some-times, that she's related to him at all. She's a moron. Must be all the drugs she does. Having babies so early didn't help either. Larry swears having kids makes your brain go soft. Dwight just got some chick knocked up and he's all moony now, like some fucking made-for-screen movie on the women's channel. He floats around, acting so big, touching Darla's stomach and making cooing noises. It makes Larry sick. Mostly because it's Dwight, and Dwight used to be so tough, but also because he has no patience for mothers in any form.

Soon Larry's storage unit has lights – a string of white Christmas lights – running around the inside top perimeter. It has a fake oriental carpet in the middle, a stand-up lamp, a glass desk he bought online (his laptop has come in handy). The desk has a keyboard drawer even though he has a laptop, so sometimes he leans back in his desk chair with the laptop balanced on the drawer just because he can. Larry spends hours, at first, watching porn. Then he buys a few things online. Then he thinks about asking his computer all kinds of things, he thinks about researching, and he starts to investigate things he never even knew existed. Like what a bubblegoose is. A down jacket in a bubble pattern. He orders one. Or what a diatomic molecule is. A molecule composed of only two atoms. And then what an atom is, because he has to see the whole thing through. Larry spends hours in his office, worrying, thinking, reading, researching. Too many questions, not enough time. He feels, often, as if he's suddenly gone back to being a child – the child lying on his bed in his solar system room, listening to his mother's whistle as he thinks of questions to ask her later that she will answer and prove, once again, that she knows more than anyone he's ever met. She never even faltered, knew exactly what to say to answer whatever question Larry had. What makes an ant so strong? Why did the vacuum break when it sucked up his toy? Why is grape jelly purple?

Larry forgets to rob places. He forgets to eat sometimes. He doesn't visit Susan or the brats. He holes himself up in the storage unit, the roll-down garage door locking him in, and he works away on his own little world of knowledge, and he remembers his mother and thinks about Jack. His headaches get better for a while.

It's not as if the Internet, his curiosity, stops the adrenalin rush of crime. Larry still craves that like a drug. But having his father's store money and some time on his hands now, having his coffee cans around him and this little space and this world that is in the laptop, means he doesn't get out as often as he used to. When he does, he's all fire and action. Rush in, rob, rush out. Once, he punches some guy who gets in his way, really hard, on the jaw. He crushes the man's jaw with his fist, hears it pop and crack, watches the blood come out of his mouth. Larry feels nothing. Except the pain in his hand.

A hundred and fifty dollars here, there. Whenever he needs it. Convenience stores are the easiest. Maybe that's why they're called convenient? Sometimes there is no money in the till and he just takes food. Cheetos, pop, chocolate bars, milk. It adds up. He spends the money. Gets more. Besides his father's watch store, Larry has never held a real job. Unless you call robbery a job. He wouldn't even know how to put a resume together, although once he researches it on the Internet, he thinks he could do it. There are these great sites that almost do it for you, in fact. If only he could list his crimes. It'd be an impressive resume. Sometimes he wishes he had been caught for something – sometimes he wants people to know what he is capable of, what he can do, who he is. There is a certain talent and charm to being someone who has never been caught. Larry is sure it would look good on a resume.

But is he this? Is this all he is? Larry isn't sure. After seeing Jack, seeing the world he comes from, Larry suddenly isn't as interested in the life of crime he has cultivated. Jack is someone's lackey, that is obvious. He takes orders from someone. You can tell just by looking at him. The way he looks over his shoulder. His tough-guy attitude. His persona. All swagger. People who work on their own don't need that kind of swagger, Larry thinks. In fact, the less swagger you have, the better it is for you, the less likely you'll get caught. And if you have no one to bail you out, you don't want to get caught.

Susan and Jack. Larry wants to rid himself of family. Their parents are gone. What's the point of this, of having family? But Susan keeps pounding on his apartment door, asking for more money, for more of his time, for more of everything. Jack stays out of the picture, doesn't see Larry. But he does occasionally ask Susan to ask Larry for money. Larry finds this out quickly – it's obvious from the way Susan hems and haws when she asks for more. But he hands over the money anyway. Why not? He has a gift, why not share the proceeds. Larry reasons that the more money he gives Jack, the more Jack will stay out of his life. And he is right about this. For now.

In his storage unit, Larry researches crime. He looks into what the perfect crime would be. What can he get away with? Art theft? Bank heist? Diamonds? Drugs? Murder? What is the crime that would set him up for life without having any consequences? How many convenience stores and little strip mall banks can he rob without getting bored? How many purses on the street, ripping out old lady's shoulders? Larry knows to stay away from the drug trade – that, he knows, will get him jailed. Look at Dwight. In and out of jail (and a baby on the way). Diamonds? He'd have to travel for that, which is suspicious. And he'd have to know something about diamonds. Same with art theft. A huge bank heist appeals to him – especially on his own. With no partners. Tunnel in, perhaps? Just Larry in and out of the bank with loads of money. He researches this. Computer hacking appeals to Larry, but he has no idea how money is made from it – or what it is, or if money is involved. Larry is smart but not computer smart.

Larry is at his desk late at night. The rain pours down outside. A fresh spring rain. He's left the storage-unit door open slightly to let in the breeze, and the worms are coming in under the door. When there is a knock on the door, a "Hello?" from a soft voice with an accent, he jumps a foot in his chair and quickly closes his laptop screen. Shuts the naked women inside.

Outside is Mona.

Mona.

He doesn't know this yet, he hasn't met her, but here stands Mona. The first time he sees her. Mother of Bennie and Frankie. Ex-wife of Darren Purcell.

Mona.

She is drenched. Her long hair, black, runs down her back in rivulets. She has brown eyes lined with black. She has dark skin and teeth so white they take Larry by surprise. She stands there with her arms crossed in front of her. Glaring at him. Suspicious.

"Hello," she says. "I'm Mona. I own the Storage Mart."

"Oh." Larry steps back into his room so she can come in out of the rain. She does. She looks around. When he rented the place, a young guy gave him the key. He has never seen anyone else in the front office.

"Are you using this for an office?"

Larry nods.

"That's an interesting idea. Do you sell coffee?"

"Sorry?"

Mona points to all the coffee cans, lids on, lined up in the corner. A small pyramid of coffee cans. All the same brand.

"Yes. No. Well, maybe."

She looks suspiciously at him. "I have to ask," Mona says, "are you selling drugs?"

"What?"

She points to the coffee cans, the desk, the lamp, the laptop. "What are you doing in here? No one has an office at the Storage Mart."

"I'm not sure that's any of your business," Larry says. "Your contract didn't say I had to tell you what I do."

"But our contract is for renting the space as storage, not for living in it."

"I'm not living in it."

"It looks to me as if you are."

"I'm working in it. Not living. I have an apartment. Look, there's no bed here, let alone a toilet. How could I live in here?"

Mona takes this in. Thinks about it. Looks at Larry. Larry already thinks he's falling in love with her, slightly – he feels warm and her eyes are beautiful. It's like they glow from the inside out. Dark brown but specked with gold. She blushes and turns away.

"Okay. Okay. That's okay. You can have your office here."

"Thanks, I guess," Larry says, and he smiles.

She looks at him again, at his tattoos and his baggy jeans and his baseball hat on backwards. At the chains around his neck. She is wearing dress pants and high-heeled shoes. She is wearing a blazer. Straight out of some ad for office workers. Polyester-looking. Larry smiles again.

"My kids," she says. "Boys. Twins. They play around here sometimes on the weekends. I'd appreciate if you kept your door shut? If you're up to no good. They are young and impressionable."

"Up to no good? You have no faith in me." Larry laughs. "Sure, I'll keep the door shut, but you'll have to turn on the air conditioning soon or I'll boil in here."

"It goes on when it's hot," she says. "Not before."

"I could cut out a window?"

"No windows!"

Larry laughs and says, "I'll keep the door shut when I hear your kids around, when I'm up to no good."

"Thank you." Mona turns to leave. "What did you say your name was?"

"Larry. Larry Gallo."

"Thank you, Larry."

"Thank you, Mona, owner of Storage Mart." Larry watches her walk back out into the rain and disappear down the aisle of storage units towards the main office. Her legs are long. Her hips sway. Her hair moves gracefully back and forth.

Mona. She owns the place. She has kids. Must be married. Not that that ever made anyone less interesting to Larry. He sits back down on his chair and opens up his laptop. He closes it again. What's on the screen isn't half as interesting as Mona.

The kids come around the very next day. The sun is out now. Larry opens the door to his office only halfway. He is lazy and ducks under, heading over to the strip mall to pick up a coffee and use the washroom, when they are suddenly standing there. Identical twins. Dark skin like their mother and black hair. Devilish grins on their faces.

"Fuck," Larry says. "Sorry, you scared me."

They laugh delightedly. They are about eight years old and they are riding scooters. Larry backs into his office again, closes his door almost to the ground, but he can still hear them whip up and down the aisles. He sees their shadows flick across the ground where the sun is coming in. They are laughing and calling to each other.

Larry can't get any work done. How can he when they are zooming around out there, when he knows their mother is in the office? How can he when he hears her call out, "Lunch!

153

Bennie! Frankie!" Her voice is strong, her accent exotic.

The boys scooter to her. Larry peeks out of his door, rolls it half open and ducks under. They are gathered around her on the steps leading up to the office. She is handing them something – sandwiches? – and they take these from her and scooter off one-handed. Larry waves. Mona looks at him, shakes her head, and then turns and goes into her office. She reminds him of his mother – that look, the way she shook her head, the sandwiches, the two boys on scooters.

This is the beginning of something, Larry thinks. But he doesn't know what yet. He feels full up when he sees her, satiated, content, drowsy. As if she has put a spell on him. Larry knows she isn't showing any interest in him right now, but he can also feel a spark when she looks at him. Like static. She pretends he's not intriguing, he thinks, but she's interested.

Larry wants to know only one thing about her right now: Where is Mona's husband?

7:01 a.m.

This is it. The beginning of something. Certainly. The end of something too. The Chaplain is standing up straight, alert, staring down at the Prisoner as he lies on the cot, talking. The Prisoner's eyes are closed.

"Them," he says.

"Yes, them." The eyes now open.

"We are there, then. We are at your crime."

"I guess we are." The Prisoner stands and stretches. He avoids the Chaplain's eyes.

"Why you are here. This is it." The Chaplain says this quietly as he backs away from the Prisoner.

The Prisoner sits down on the side of the cot, leans forward and puts his head in his hands. The silence stretches between them.

The Chaplain asks, "How is your stomach feeling?"

"Believe it or not, I'm fucking hungry again." The Prisoner laughs. "I'm empty, man."

"Maybe we can get you more cookies?"

"No, probably shouldn't. I don't want to puke again. It's getting close." The Prisoner shivers. He looks up at the clock. His eyes are red-rimmed. "Past halfway there."

"Yes." More than halfway there. Halfway dead. Halfway electrocuted. Almost there. The Chaplain's hands are shaking. He feels as if he is watching a horror movie and someone is going to jump out at him from behind a closed door. He is on edge. Tense. And extremely tired. Numb. Which is strange, being numb and tense at the same time.

"Do you know what happens to you when you get electrocuted?" the Prisoner asks in a small voice.

The Chaplain sits down, holds his shaking hands together, squeezes them tight. "Tell me."

The Prisoner clears his throat. Stands. Moves around the room as he talks. "I did a lot of research about this when I got the laptop. I don't know why. Maybe I knew this would happen? I don't know. And then I looked into it more in the prison library when I first got here. I had to know how it would happen. Exactly. Like the real details, you know." He pauses in mid-stride. Looks down at his feet, at his hands by his side. Clears his throat again. About to give a speech. "There is a lot of information on electrocution on the computer." He sighs. "Too much information."

Silence. Then: "They'll shave me first. They'll come in here about an hour before and they'll shave me all over – chest, legs, arms, wherever they put the electrodes. Then they'll walk me to the chair and strap me to it with belts." The Prisoner continues to talk as the Chaplain goes through the list in his head, the facts he read online before he came here, the stomach-churning facts. Because he, too, did his research ahead of time: a metal electrode attached to the scalp and forehead over a sponge wet with saline. Not too wet, though, and not too dry – don't want any short-circuits or resistance. Then another electrode, wet with conductive jelly (called Electro-Creme, to be exact. The Chaplain marvels at this – the fact that someone invents a cream that serves this purpose), attached to his shaved leg. They will then place the hood over his head. And the Warden will signal the Executioner, who will pull a handle that connects the power supply. Lights will dim. A jolt of between five hundred and two thousand volts will travel through the Prisoner for about thirty seconds. The body (not the Prisoner anymore but the body, because he will, most likely, be dead) will arch and fill with current and then relax when the current is turned off. A doctor must wait for the body to cool down to see if the heart is still beating. If it is, another jolt, and again, until dead.

The Prisoner will grip the chair and there will be violent thrashing of limbs, perhaps causing dislocation or fractures (it often does). His tissues will swell. There will be defecation, no matter what the Prisoner thinks. Steam or smoke will rise, and there will be the smell of burning.

"I memorized something," the Prisoner says. The Chaplain snaps out of it. Pays careful attention to the Prisoner.

"What was that?"

"Some judge had this description of what happens when you are electrocuted in the chair and I memorized it. Thought that if I said it over and over again to myself, I might be able to handle it. You know. Like when you chant or something and how that chant, what you are actually saying, starts to mean nothing. You know? The yoga woman did that. Those 'oms' or what the fuck, over and over, until you just tuned them out. You didn't even hear them after a while."

"Tell me it. Tell me what you memorized."

"The guy, the judge, said," – and here, the Prisoner, now sitting, leans back and looks up at the ceiling, raises his eyes to the top of the cell but sees beyond it, as if he's reading the words up there, as if he's praying to something. The Chaplain looks up, then looks down, focuses on the Prisoner – "'The prisoner's eyeballs sometimes pop out and rest on his cheeks. The prisoner often defecates, urinates, and vomits blood and drool. The body turns bright red as its temperature rises, and the prisoner's flesh swells and his skin stretches to the point of breaking. Sometimes the prisoner catches fire . . .'" Here he stops. Pauses. Breathes deeply. "'Witnesses hear a loud and sustained sound like bacon frying, and the sickly sweet smell of burning flesh permeates the chamber.'" He stops talking but stares still at the ceiling. His breath evens out slowly.

The Chaplain, leaning forward, collapses back in his chair. He lets out a groan. He can't help himself. His body is shaking. He remembers more facts: the body is hot enough to cause blisters if touched. They must let the body cool before they do an autopsy. There are third-degree burns wherever the electrodes meet the skin. And the one thing that has stuck hard in his mind: The brain appears cooked in most cases.

"God," he says. "My God." His face is wet. He realizes he is crying.

"It doesn't work," the Prisoner says, lying back down, closing his eyes. "No matter how many times I say it, I still feel it, you know? I keep thinking, these are just words. I'm just saying words. And if I say them over and over –" He stops. There is nothing more to say.

"Yes." What can I do? The Chaplain feels panicked. What can I do to save this man? What can I say? It's above and beyond anything he could imagine. Five hours to go and this is what will be happening, this is what they will do – people, ordinary people like the Chaplain, doing their jobs, will cook this man's brain. Because they can. Because it will solve something, the Chaplain is not sure what. It will make the victims' families feel better? It will make common people feel safer? He doesn't know what it will do. The Warden says they can't afford to keep prisoners who are so obviously guilty fed and bathed and clothed and housed. He confessed, after all. Get rid of them, the Warden says. Save the government some money.

What if the Chaplain had killed Tracy? What if, after that second punch, he had punched her again? What if her head had snapped backwards and she had fallen against the mantle of the fireplace. What if her head had split open? The Chaplain knows more than anyone how easily things you don't intend to happen can happen. The Prisoner, though. Three bodies. Intention or no intention, he confessed.

The Chaplain meant to hit Tracy, didn't he? He moved his arm back, balled his fist, meant for fist to connect to face. He wanted to hurt her. After all, he hit twice. He saw David standing in the snow, out under the streetlight, and Tracy was so calm and quiet, and she was saying all those things that you are supposed to say – "It's not you, Jim, it's me" – and the fish were flopping and he reeled back and smashed his hand into her face once, twice, and it felt good. For a minute. Until the blood. Until the screaming. Until David came into the room.

In therapy – anger management – the Chaplain learned that everyone has this same kind of bubbling anger under the surface, that you need to learn how to control it and that most people can control it. People like the Chaplain, however, need to work on controlling it.

"But I never hurt anyone before," he had said.

"It's under there," the therapist had told him. "Always. It will always be there."

As if he had unleashed a kraken into the world. Let loose a monster. Once out, it must be contained. Always. Like alcoholism or drug addiction – the demons must stay down. He never believed in the kind of therapy he had, and after his boring stint in it, he believes even less in its healing power. But he did take this away from the therapist – that everyone has this anger in them. He believes this. Even the eighty-three-year-old woman in the nursing home, pushing her walker. Even the small child in the bath with her sister. Inside of us all is anger and hate and violence. Mixed with our love and kindness. The Prisoner has it in spades. But does that make him any less human? Does that make him deserve his punishment? Or does that make him more human, closer to the reality of being human? A man of emotions that easily rise to the surface.

If only the Chaplain could see the changing sky right now. His need to leave the cell is fierce. The Prisoner lies on the bed, still, eyes closed. Is he sleeping? Does he have time to sleep? No time, no time. No. Time. The Chaplain feels like shouting, or running, or hitting something. His fist against a brick wall, his head against his hand. Anything. He wants to feel – the air, pain – he wants to feel alive.

The information the Chaplain read about electrocution was distant when he didn't know the Prisoner. Now it is tangible. He can feel it, picture it, live it. The agony of it.

Miranda would say, "But he deserves to die."

"We are all going to die, but does anyone deserve to die? By the hand of another?"

"He does. Because he took lives. Brutally. Savagely. He deserves to suffer first. And then die."

His sister, Miranda. What would she think if she were here in this room. If she spent seven hours with this man? Like strangers sitting side-by-side in an airplane as it crashes, the Chaplain feels the need to take the Prisoner's hand and hold on for dear life.

Tinted Windows

He couldn't tell them apart at first. Bennie and Frankie. They looked so alike to Larry. Black hair, brown eyes, dark skin, white teeth like their mother's, devilish grins. And they were always grinning – wide mouths, open all the time. Talking, laughing, grinning, shouting. Back and forth on their scooters, purposefully in front of Larry's office. Why not? No one else was using their storage unit as an office. He was a curiosity to these kids. The man in the storage room, with his laptop and his rug and his glass desk. And his coffee cans. The man with tattoos who occasionally swore when he forgot there were kids around.

Larry comes into the storage unit one day and his cans have moved. He notices immediately. The top layer has shifted.

He stands there and stares at the cans, willing himself to believe that he might have forgotten that he moved them. But, no, he remembers perfectly how they were lined up the night before. He had just robbed another convenience store the next town over and had come back to the storage unit and placed a wad of money in a new can. Larry had lined everything up nicely, carefully, like a surgeon, paying special attention to spacing. And now they are off-centre, off-balance. He is sure of it.

The kids race past on the scooters, hollering.

Who has keys to his room? No one. According to the contract he signed at the front desk on the first day, no one can enter his storage unit without his permission and no one has extra keys.

"We cut it open, physically smash it in, if we need to get in," the young guy behind the counter said. "This is your space. It has nothing to do with us."

Larry believed him at the time, but now he wonders. He goes outside and looks at the door. It doesn't look like it has been forced in any way. There is nothing that indicates a crowbar or screwdriver. Larry has broken into enough houses to know what it looks like if someone picks a lock. There would be scratches on the lock. Nothing there. He looks closely. The boys shoot past on the scooters, singing now. Larry scratches his head. Stands tall and looks out towards the office. It's a bright day, sunny. It's well past noon, Larry slept in. A Saturday. He can see the young guy at the front desk, his feet up, watching the screen. He doesn't see Mona.

Larry goes back into his room and looks around carefully. Takes note of everything. He wouldn't have a clue if money were missing. He never counts it. It doesn't matter to him. What matters to him is that someone was in his space. Someone stepped on his floor, touched his desk, wiped their hands over his laptop. Someone moved his coffee cans. And that someone will figure it out, what he's up to. Cans filled with money can have no explanation other than crime. Larry has never been caught. Because he is careful and smart. Because he doesn't let anyone in. He doesn't let anyone close. He doesn't let anyone know.

"Fuck."

The boys rush past. Back and forth. Laughing.

Larry wants to reach out and grab them. Smash their heads together. Instead, he stands in front of them and they come to a screeching halt on their scooters, Bennie skidding slightly.

"Hey," Larry says.

The boys stare up at him. Mouths open.

"Listen, I was wondering. Have you seen anyone going into my office?"

The boys giggle. They look at each other.

"Bennie. Frankie." Mona is there. She comes down the steps of the office and begins a fast walk towards the three of them. When she reaches Larry, she glares at him. "I told you not to talk to my children."

"I'm just asking them if they've seen anyone in my place. Jesus, someone broke into my place."

"That's not possible."

"Things were moved."

Mona looks around Larry into his storage unit. "Was anything stolen?"

"No. Just moved."

"Maybe," Mona says, pushing her boys away from Larry, "maybe an animal got in and moved things? A mouse? A rat? An animal that likes coffee? No one can go in your room. No one has a key. And I don't see any damage on the door. Unless you didn't lock it, of course."

"I locked it."

"A mouse then?" Mona begins to walk away. "We do have mice. I've seen them." Larry watches her. She is lovely. Her hair flows down her back. Larry is entranced. He is only half-listening to her words. Focusing instead on her mouth, on the small lines around her lips.

"A mouse," he says.

She turns back to him. "No talking to my boys. I told you that already."

"Yeah, whatever."

"I will ask you to leave, Mr. Gallo, if you talk to my boys. I will evict you and your belongings."

Larry nods. Pretends to zip his lips shut. The boys giggle and scurry along in front of their shuffling mother, dragging their scooters behind.

"Into the office," she says. "Come on, you two."

And off they go.

Larry enters his unit again. He pulls the door down, leaving a gap at the bottom for air. He turns on his laptop. He looks at his cans, at where they were and where they moved to. He wonders. Maybe he'll get a mousetrap. It wouldn't hurt to know for sure.

Mona's hair and her legs, her strong ass as she walked away from him. Holding each boy, her arms long and dark and toned. When she is angry, her eyebrows knit together until they are almost touching. A little vein throbs on her temple. Larry sees everything about her, except who she really is.

In the next several days, Larry notices someone following him. He pulls over in the parking lot of the strip mall across from the storage company. The car goes by him quickly, speeds up. He looks at it, doesn't recognize it. A dark sedan, windows tinted. Nothing special. Larry turns his car around and drives home. No use having someone following him to the money, to his office. No one knows where Larry goes – not Dwight or Susan or Jack or Dwight's pregnant girlfriend. No one. Larry likes it that way.

»——

A pretty good bank heist. Larry is in and out in six minutes. With over two thousand dollars. The key, Larry knows, is not to get everything, not to be greedy. Take what you can and get out. Quickly. Don't hurt anyone. He learned his lesson the hard way. Larry targets the small banks, the ones with only a few tellers, one back office, a bank machine. Sometimes he hits the money exchange offices, but then he ends up with all kinds of foreign currency he can't spend. The cheque-cashing places are pretty good too, although they don't have as much in the drawer as the banks.

All of this is starting to bore Larry. He's too good at it. It's not that exciting anymore. And he's running out of places to hit that are close enough to home for a one-day trip but far enough away that no one will recognize him later. Wearing a mask, disguises, is fine, but Larry knows that the way he walks, the way he holds his hands, the way he turns – all of this will give him away eventually. You can't completely disguise who you are any more than you can be invisible. Cameras are catching him – he's seen himself on the screen.

Back in the storage unit. It is late at night.

Footsteps. Larry can hear a shuffling gait. It's subtle, but he is always hyper-aware at night. His door is shut. No one should be here, but Larry hears the footsteps and someone opening a door. The long rolling sound of a storage door as it comes up. Larry thinks the sound is coming from one aisle over, but sound carries here at night and so he can't be sure it's not just next door. He freezes over his keyboard and listens, every sense awake. In the months he's been here, he's seen only four people come to their storage units and that was always in the daytime, never at night. Hauling out old refrigerators and furniture, knick-knacks they've stored for no reason.

He worries about his car, parked outside.

The door rolls down. He can hear it click shut. The footsteps again. Disappearing. Larry has the urge to open his door slightly and peer out, but it's impossible to peer out inconspicuously from a rolling garage door. He really needs an eyehole or something.

These sounds come back over and over in the next several weeks. Someone is making deliveries to their storage unit at night. Larry thinks drugs. Or money. Whichever it is, it has piqued his interest. He isn't the only one taking advantage of these rooms. He wonders if Mona knows what kind of people she rents to or if it's just the young guy at the front desk handing out contracts and keys.

There's the question of Mona – who is she? Why does she own a place like this and is she alone with two children? Or is there someone in her life whom she goes home to? Where does she live? Although she has shown no interest in Larry, he knows there is something there. A spark. Anger. And when there is anger, there is also attraction. You can't be angry at someone you don't care about, can you? Larry suddenly remembers his mother saying something about this, about the fact that even though he said he hated Jack over and over, especially after another concussion, Larry really loved him.

How is it possible to love someone who breaks your head open as often as he can, who escapes with your mother, a woman who leaves you in the clutches of your incapable father, who then comes back and demands attention and money?

Mona, though. She just doesn't know him yet. Whenever he looks at her, his headaches disappear. Whenever he is near her, he can smell her scent. Like an animal, his senses are hyper-alert.

➤———

Daytime. Bennie and Frankie are there. Standing in front of his door when he pulls up in the car. He's hungover. Larry rarely drinks, but last night he tied it on with two women from the bar down the street from his apartment. They insisted he drink sweet drinks with umbrellas and foam, bright in colour, and now he feels sick. He gets out of his car and stretches, tries not to catch the twins' eyes. But they are standing there, staring at him. He looks towards the office but doesn't see Mona.

"What's up?" he whispers. "I'm not supposed to talk to you."

One boy says, "Someone was here looking at your door."

Larry stops short. Moves back from opening his roll-up door. Stares at the boys.

"What?"

"A guy. He knocked."

"What kind of guy? What did he look like?" Larry wonders if Dwight has found out where he's going. Wants to borrow money with the baby here and all. But Dwight doesn't know about this place. No one knows about this place.

The sedan with the darkened windows. Someone following him.

"He was taller than you. He had a beard."

"Red," the other boy shouts. "A red beard, like a pirate."

Larry looks again at the office. Mona will kick him out if she sees him talking to these two. And then he'd have to store his money somewhere else. More importantly, then he wouldn't see Mona anymore.

"What was he wearing?"

"He was smoking. So he was bad. Smoking is really bad."

Larry says, "I smoke."

"Boots," the other boy says. "Big boots. Right?" The boys nod at each other. Confirming.

"Jack." Larry ducks into his room and slams down the door.

He can hear the boys outside for a bit. They are throwing pebbles against the storage doors and the sound agitates Larry. But soon they get bored and move away.

Jack has found him here. In his space. Larry wonders what he wants. Why is Jack following him? Was he the one following in the sedan with tinted windows? What's Jack up to?

"I don't know," Susan says. "Honestly, he hasn't been back for a while. I gave him some money and he took off. I haven't seen him in weeks."

"Weeks?"

"Well, at least a week."

"Why, Susan?"

"Why what?" Susan stubs out her cigarette in the sink. The kitchen is a disaster, dishes piled everywhere. She's out of control. On drugs. Her eyes are glossy and strange. The pupils dilated. Larry looks away.

"Why do you give him your money?"

She laughs. "Because he gives me things I need."

"Drugs."

"Yeah, fuck you. You're so high and mighty, Larry. Just because you don't do drugs. You don't get it. You don't know what I've been through. You just. . . Fuck off." Susan sits down. Her hair is thinning at the part – too many dye jobs or maybe lack of nutrition. Larry suddenly feels sorry for her. He forgets that she, too, was left motherless. She, too, has suffered. But that doesn't make her drug use acceptable. After all, he stayed away from them, why didn't she?

"He's following me," he says. "I'm not sure why."

She barks out a laugh, a cough, and begins to hack. Her lungs are shot. A kid – one of his nephews, Larry assumes – walks past the room and glares at both of them. "Why? Because you have money, asshole. Because he wants your money. He knows where I get it. The money. He knows it comes from you."

"I don't have money."

Another laugh. Another coughing fit. Larry waits. The boy passes by the kitchen again as if he's waiting for them to get out of it and let him in.

"I just give you a bit to help you get by. I'm not rich."

"Get your own dinner, Danny," Susan suddenly shouts. "I fucking have no time to make you dinner so stop staring."

"I don't have any money," Larry says. "You know that."

"Of course you don't." Susan winks.

"Just enough for me to get by, enough to give you for the kids," he repeats.

Susan looks around her as if she doesn't know where she is. "Well, he wants that, then. Anything."

"Tell him to leave me alone, okay? Can you remember that, Susan? Next time he comes, tell him to stay the fuck away from me. Tell him to stop following me, stop bothering me. He's nothing to me."

"He's your brother."

Now it's Larry's turn to laugh. "Yeah, right. My brother."

"You got any money?" Susan shouts as Larry leaves the house. "I need some money."

8:01 a.m.

"Who was it in the other storage unit?" the Chaplain asks. "If someone else was there, maybe –"

"Maybe I didn't do anything? Is that what you're going to say? Maybe I didn't kill –"

"No, that's not what I was going to say. I was going to say that maybe someone saw something differently from how you remember. You know you blacked out that night, your memory isn't perfect. You were stressed, concussed. You were –"

"I never said I didn't do it," the Prisoner says quietly. "I did it. They have proof. I confessed. I was convicted. I will be put to death soon. What don't you get about that?"

The Chaplain leans back on his chair. He had been hunched forward, listening intently. Twice the Prisoner stood and paced the width of the room as he talked. Mostly he lay there on the cot staring at the ceiling, watching the words come out of his mouth and float on the air. Whenever he mentioned Mona, the Chaplain could see his lips tighten into a straight line.

"Your sister? What happened to her?"

"She was like that the last time I saw her," the Prisoner says.

"Even worse. Drugs. A lot of drugs. Jack had her on some pretty bad stuff."

"What about the nieces and nephews? What about this Danny guy?"

"They're old enough now. Or social services has a few of them. I don't know. They were all brats. They want nothing to do with me. I want nothing to do with them." The Prisoner sits up and looks at the clock. "Holy shit, eight a.m. It's eight o'clock. Four hours left." His teeth are bared in an unnatural smile, like a dog about to growl.

"I guess I'm trying to help you," the Chaplain says. "I guess I just want to help you."

"Yeah, well, there's nothing you can do."

"But your sister? Shouldn't she be here?"

"Listen, think about it. Just think about it. She comes down here in four hours, watches me burn, brings her brats, they watch me burn. What good does that do? I won't even see them with my hood on."

"But you will know they are here."

"You don't understand." The Prisoner's jaw is tight. He is grinding his teeth. "It doesn't matter anymore. None of this matters. Family doesn't matter. It never has."

"I wonder if he has family coming. If I were on death row," he asks Miranda at dinner that last Sunday night, "wouldn't you come to be with me?"

"Jim, you don't get it. If you were on death row, you would have done something horrible like this guy did. Something so bad that I don't think I could even forgive you for it. I would come, maybe. I guess I would come. But I wouldn't forgive you. I wouldn't be there to support you. I would just come. Or maybe not. I don't know." Miranda tidies up the dishes. She is well into her fifth glass of red wine. Every time Richard leaves on another long haul, Miranda has too much to drink. As if the hangover the next morning is the appropriate body response for when your husband is gone.

"No, you would come. I know you would. You are my family. I'm your brother. Of course you'd be there to support me."

Miranda waves him off. "I'm not sure supporting is what the family does. Watching, more like."

Richard comes down from upstairs, then; the kids are finally asleep. He takes Miranda by the waist from behind and squeezes her. "You two," he says. "Don't you ever have anything nice to talk about?"

The siblings look at each other. They are combative. They always have been. As children, they would debate across the dining room table, their parents raising their eyebrows at each other, silent communication, on each end. Sometimes they took opposite sides just to make dinner more interesting, not because they really believed in what they were arguing.

"I'd come and watch for you, Jim," Richard says. Then, "If only to see how they do it."

Miranda swats him with a dishtowel and that is enough of that conversation. They move on to the latest news and the kids and Richard's truck and how he can't stand to sleep in the cab but he does anyway to save money, and they talk about the weather and how hot the world has become. They talk about the Chaplain and his work and what they might do this summer, whether their friend Beatrice will invite them up to her cabin. They talk about all of this without touching again on the Prisoner. And then the Chaplain, thinking of Beatrice's cabin in the woods, tells them about his recurring dream, about the seagull with the arrow.

"God," Miranda says. "How many times have you had this dream?"

"Every night since they told me he asked for me to be on death row with him."

"You know what it means, don't you?"

The Chaplain raises his eyebrows. He hasn't thought about what it all means. Not really. He's been disturbed by it and doesn't really want to think about it all. "What?"

"Some guy shooting a seagull with an arrow and not killing it. It kind of suggests wanton killing, or maybe the struggle to survive. The idea of fate. Of having a limited time to live. It's a symbol, sort of, for what you keep trying to tell me about death row. The gull with the arrow straight through it. He keeps flying, doesn't he? Even though he's going to die eventually. Like your prisoner. You're dreaming your life, Jim."

Richard is silent and looks impressed.

The Chaplain laughs. "Your courses in psychology really stuck, didn't they?"

"Piss off," Miranda says. She swats him. "It's true. Think about it."

He leaves that night and goes home to his own apartment, to his night of the crying gull winging over the trees and the kids down by the river or ocean or lake, holding sticks and playing. Even though he now knows what it means, he still dreams it.

"Do you want anything? Need anything?" The Chaplain stands and looks out at the COs. His stomach aches. It could be hunger, of course – he's only had one cookie all night – but he feels sick more than anything. As if catching something or having eaten something rotten. "I think I'll just step out for a minute. Would that be okay with you?"

The Prisoner nods. "Yeah, sure. Grab me more cookies."

The Chaplain nods, knocks on the window. The COs unlock the door and let him out. He breathes. Deeply. Again, the air is fresher in the room with the COs even though it's the same pumped-in air conditioning.

"How's it going in there?" The COs all look at him, expectantly.

"The way you'd expect, I guess. I need to use the washroom." The Chaplain is directed down the corridor and out the door to the visiting area. He goes through three checks before he finds the bathroom. It is empty. He takes a stall, locks it, takes his pants down and then it's as if not only the contents of his bowels but his bowels as well collapse into the toilet. He empties himself. He feels as if his insides are being torn out. Water and crap and a burning sensation. It is as if the bile that is in his stomach, the acid coming up his throat every time he thinks of the next four hours, every time he thinks of the last minutes, that acid is coming out his ass. Burning him.

The Chaplain washes his hands. He looks at himself in the mirror above the sink. Dead eyes. Hollowed out. Black circles. A day's growth of hair on his chin and cheeks. His hair stands up on his head from running his fingers through it. His teeth are yellowing with age and coffee and red wine. Stained. This mortal body, he thinks. We are all going to die. He adjusts his pants, his shirt. Splashes water over his face. Washes his hands again. Leaves. Goes back. To him. To his end.

It seems to the Chaplain as if all of civilization has come to a halt. How can we be a civil society and do this to our members? Running scared and furious.

"How," Miranda echoes in his head, "can he have done that to them?"

The Chaplain wants to believe that it was a mistake, that it wasn't premeditated. That the Prisoner found himself in the wrong place at the wrong time. After all, he doesn't remember parts of the crime. But the Chaplain has seen the files. He has seen the pictures. There is blood on this man's hands. Literally. Lots of blood. And everything he's said so far – his callous holdups, the killing of people during robberies, pulling the plug on his father, the blatant disregard for human life – all of this leads him to believe that, yes, the Prisoner must certainly be guilty of the charges. But does he deserve this punishment? That's the true question. One which lawmakers and politicians have to decide every day. Right or wrong.

Wrong. Of course it's wrong.

There is commotion in the corridor with the COs. Running. Shouting. The Chaplain heads towards it quickly. Picks up his pace. It's CO1 and CO2, they are back. On the 8 a.m. shift after leaving late last night, just after midnight. They are in the cell and the door is wide open. Three other COs, ones he has not seen before, are standing outside looking in.

The Prisoner is on the floor, face down. He is still. CO1 is shouting something over and over. CO2 has backed out into the hallway.

He shouts, "Call the doctor."

"What happened?" The Chaplain rushes in towards the Prisoner.

"Stay back, Chaplain," CO1 says.

"But what happened?"

CO2 says, "He collapsed. He was standing there, looking out at us, but then he turned white and fell over. Hit his head."

"Fainted," the Chaplain says. "He fainted. There's no air in this room. Couldn't they have put him in a room with windows?" He realizes he is shouting this. The COs are looking at him. He kneels next to the Prisoner and carefully rolls him over.

The Prisoner's forehead has an egg-sized lump on it, slowly turning blue.

"Get me some ice."

The Prisoner's eyes open slightly, and he smiles at the Chaplain. There he is, being cradled in the Chaplain's arms, lying on the floor.

"I was hoping it wasn't a dream," he says quietly.

"What?" The Chaplain holds him.

"I was hoping that I had died, that it was that easy, that I wouldn't wake up once I fell to the floor. My whole body felt heavy. I fell. I didn't want to wake up."

Slowly, the Prisoner stands. Ice is brought in and placed with a towel on his forehead. He is given an Aspirin but nothing else. Soon a doctor arrives and looks into the Prisoner's eyes, checks his pulse, feels his neck.

"Wouldn't want me to be sick before you kill me," the Prisoner says.

The doctor has no gallows humour and barely smirks. He gives the Prisoner water and then leaves the room in a hurry.

Again, the Chaplain and the Prisoner are alone in the room. Time has passed. Too much time, according to the Chaplain. Such a waste of time.

"It was slow motion," the Prisoner says.

"What was?"

"When I fell. I could see and feel myself falling, but it was happening really slowly and my body couldn't react to it. It was fucking weird."

"Have you never fainted before?"

The Prisoner shakes his head. "No. Just a lot of concussions, but you go out quickly when you get knocked on the head. There's no slow motion at all." He thinks for a minute. "I hope the chair isn't anything like that," he says. "What if it happens in slow motion? What if I can feel the pain?" He tears up slightly, but then turns away from the Chaplain, faces the wall. The egg on his forehead is dark and mean looking. "What if it takes a long time?"

"I'm sure it won't. I'm sure they won't let it. I won't let it."

"But how can you do anything to help me?"

The Chaplain thinks about this. He can't do anything. Nothing. All he can do is be there. Watch it happen. This is the crux of it, isn't it? The powerlessness of the situation. And, in that, he realizes why they do this, why some people might be for the death penalty – because they want the Prisoner to feel the same powerlessness over his life that he gave his victims. They want the convicted to know what it's like to have absolutely no control over anything. Like the victims, but also like the victims' families. The only control they have is to see him die. To know that he has met the same fate as their loved ones.

"When I was younger," the Chaplain says, "I fainted all the time. I have no idea why. Low blood sugar or maybe anemia or something. Anyway, I would get these feelings, hear a buzzing in my ears, the world would go white. I could still see things, but everything became bleached out suddenly. And I knew I was going to faint. So I would sit down, wherever I was. Just plop down. Sometimes on the sidewalk, or I'd get off my bike and sit on the curb. I would faint. I would keel over for about five minutes and then come to. I remember that slow motion feeling very well. It's almost like falling asleep, when you are half-awake and half-asleep and feel no control over your body, over your mind. You let other forces take control of you then. And you fall asleep."

"It's like falling asleep," the Prisoner echoes quietly.

"Yes. Think of it that way."

"It's just so hot in here. There's no air."

The Chaplain looks around. There is one vent, up high. He stands and walks over to it. He reaches up and feels for air. Nothing.

"These old buildings are hard to cool."

"Saving money, I bet. Why keep me comfortable just to kill me?" A dry laugh. "Hey, did you remember my cookies?"

The Chaplain turns. "Oh, shit."

"No Pepto-Bismol, no cookies. What good are you, man? I'm a dead man, you know. The least you could do is remember my cookies."

Two Aisles Over

There is someone in the storage unit two aisles over. Larry heard a car pull up some nights, again and again. He has seen a light under the door. He sneaks out at night, attempting to discover who it is, but finds nothing out. He gets a quick look at the car but it's not familiar. A nondescript four-door. Kids' stuff in the back. Garbage. Old pop cans, crumpled takeout bags. A few boards, some tools.

And Jack is following him.

Twice Larry sees Jack's sedan in the rear-view mirror. Twice he pulls over, hoping to confront his older brother, but Jack drives past and when Larry tries to chase him down, Jack takes off and disappears.

No one, or no mouse, has been in his office lately. He's caught nothing with his traps. The cans haven't moved. The door stays shut. Mona comes and goes from the office in the daytime and her boys scooter up and down the aisles of the storage facility, laughing and talking and shouting and wiping out. Larry tries to ignore them, but he can't take his eyes off Mona. She is always alone, there seems to be no partner, no husband, no one but Mona and the young guy behind the front desk who reads magazines or watches the screen and picks his zits all day, feet up on the counter. The neon *Storage Mart* sign buzzes and crackles above him. Mona has a back office and she rarely comes out. Bookkeeping. Whatever she is doing. Larry is fascinated. He spends more and more time at his office. Day and night. He hangs a poster on the wall with tape. A black-and-white Eiffel Tower. He vacuums his rug with a vacuum borrowed from the guy at the front desk. He wipes his glass desk clean, tidying up the fingerprints. He researches things on his laptop and he watches Mona and sometimes catches her watching him, and he tries to figure out who is renting the storage unit two aisles over.

Summer turns to fall. The twins have a party in the front office. There are balloons and a cake and lots of kids running up and down the aisles for the day in the rain. Larry props his door open slightly in order to get some fresh air. The worms come under the door escaping the rain. Larry's coffee cans are dwindling. He's lost the urge to do anything but sit in his office. The adrenalin rush isn't there anymore, he feels nothing good or bad when he comes back with money. Even though he has half of what he had before, he figures he has enough to last a while. Besides, whenever he needs money, he can always get some.

At night, if he isn't in his apartment watching the screen, he is in the office. Occasionally he hears a car start or a door shut. Coming from the mysterious other tenant. Sometimes, the car parked there drives away and then comes back. Occasionally he hears uneven footsteps, as if someone is limping, and no car. He listens to all the sounds and can't figure out what this guy is doing. He only comes at night. No one else in this whole huge place goes into the storage units. Just Larry and the guy two aisles over. And Larry knows it's a man because when he stands outside and listens, he can hear him cough and clear his throat.

One day, towards dusk, there is a knock on Larry's rolled-up door. He stiffens at his desk, quickly turns off his laptop, puts it in the drawer in the desk. Rubs his hands over his eyes and stands. He rolls up the door all the way.

"Jack."

"Lawrence."

"Don't call me that. What are you doing here?"

"Just thought I'd visit." Jack starts to walk into the storage unit. Larry sees him take note of the coffee cans lining the wall.

Larry pushes him out. Rolls shut the door behind them. "Listen," he says. "I don't want you here. Stop following me."

Jack laughs. He looks out into the darkening day, down the aisle and into the woods behind the storage facility. He smiles at Larry. "I'm just visiting, man. Take it easy."

A flash of headlights down where Jack looked. Larry sees it. Jack holds his hand up, signaling to a car near the edge of the wood. A sedan.

"Who'd you bring here?" Larry asks.

"Just a friend picking me up." Jack nods towards Larry's door. "What are you doing in there, Lawrence?"

"Nothing. It's my office. Nothing." Larry's arms are crossed over his chest. All the little boy fear of his older brother is still there, inside of him, even though he's now the same size as Jack – if not lighter and tougher. His head starts to ache, anticipating a head injury. His hands are shaking. "We don't see you for years and then you come back and bother us."

"Bother? I'm helping Susan."

"Helping her? Feeding her drugs?"

"She seems to like it." Jack laughs.

The flash of headlights again. Larry can't make out who is

in the car. The windows are caught in the late sun.

Suddenly the door opens at the front office and Mona comes out. She walks out on the steps and turns to put her key in the lock but instead stops and stretches tall. Stiff from sitting at her desk. Both Jack and Larry watch her. Larry watches the arch of her back, the flow of her hair, her arms high and long, stretched to the dying sun. She turns then and sees them standing there in the aisle. A look of fear crosses her face. She locks the office door quickly and walks away. To her car. A fast pace.

"Nice," Jack says. "I could use some of that."

"Fucking leave her alone," Larry says. "Just get out of here, Jack."

Jack looks closely at Larry. There is an anger in his eyes that is uncontrollable. Larry backs up. "You like her, don't you?" Jack pokes Larry in the chest. Larry moves back even farther. "You fucking like her. Little Lawrence has a girlfriend."

"Get out of here, Jack." Larry tries to keep his voice steady. The lights flash again.

Jack turns and begins to walk away. Easy-like. Larry watches him go. His face is hot, his heart beating madly. How can one man, one brother, make him feel this way? Larry has been strong, courageous, top of his game for years. And then his brother comes back and takes over. Makes him weak again. A child. A scared little boy.

"Fuck." Larry hits his hand hard on the roll-up door.

Later, he notices a dent on the door the size of his hand.

There is a strange noise coming from the storage unit two aisles over. The noise stops and starts. A howling or groaning or crying. Larry walks over, quietly, to see what's up.

It is snowing lightly. In the snow he can see a set of footprints. The left footprint heavier by far than the right, sunk right into the snow. The right foot dragging slightly. Someone was limping or taking care of one foot more than the other. That shuffling, uneven walk he heard before.

No noise then. Nothing. The groaning has stopped suddenly. Whoever is in there knows he is standing outside.

Larry puts his ear to the door. Still nothing. He goes back to his office. Sits. Waits.

The next day he sees Mona standing on the steps of the office. She is smoking. He has never seen her smoke before. Didn't her kids say smoking is bad? She looks furious and doesn't even glance his way when he smiles and says hello.

Larry can't help but stare. He stands there in front of his rolled-up door and looks her up and down, looks her over. It's not only a sexual thing, but something else as well. It's as if he wants to consume her, draw her into himself. The way she stands. The anger leaking out of her. He knows nothing about this Mona but also feels as if he's known her his entire life.

Days later, Mona is knocking on his door. Larry rolls it up and stares at her. She stares back.

"Why do you keep staring at me?" she says. "You shouldn't be around always staring at me. People will get the wrong idea. Every day I see you looking at me. It unnerves me. It makes me uncomfortable. Do you get it?" She pokes him on his chest. Her touch is electric. "Stop staring at me." Then she turns on her booted heels and walks back towards the office. Larry watches her go.

People? What people? There is no one around but the guy behind the desk, and he notices nothing.

Larry thinks, finally, that he is in love. Even though she has the weird kids who have taken to pulling each other around in the snow on flattened cardboard boxes as if they are sleds. They pull each other, taking turns, until the cardboard becomes so damp it disintegrates. Then they shout and laugh and talk. They pull. Mona calls them into the office for lunch. Larry listens and occasionally watches. He watches Mona, who comes and goes. He takes note of her clothing, of the way she moves, of the changes in her hairstyles. She stares back at him. Sometimes she says hello. Sometimes she tells him to go away. Sometimes she flips her hair and ignores him. Sometimes she doesn't say anything and acts as if he is invisible.

And then, finally, it is spring again and Larry's money is almost gone. He hasn't visited Susan in months. Jack hasn't been back. No more cars in the woods flashing their headlights. No more sedans following him. The groaning, crying sounds aren't as constant in the other aisle. Mona comes and goes.

It has been raining all night and is cool, but there is the smell of growth all around from the woods. Larry has spent the season trying to understand Mona and has almost given up, but not quite. She is cold and hot. Some days talking to him for minutes, other days walking away quickly. When he has a T-shirt on, she spends an inordinate amount of time staring at his tattoos as if they could tell her something about him. As if she is reading him. He knows nothing about her. She knows little about him. It's a frustrating dance, and Larry spends nights at the bars with women he can understand. He buys them drinks, they take him home. He fucks them.

This Mona and her kids. Larry has never been so consumed.

The rain has stopped and Larry pulls open his rolling door and looks out into the aisle. And there she is. A spring dress, a heavy sweater, her feet in boots. No stockings or tights. She comes down the office steps towards him. He is about to say something but Mona walks purposefully into his storage unit and turns and shuts the roll-up door behind her. Slams it down hard. The light is dim inside even with his stand-up lamp and white Christmas lights.

Larry opens his mouth. Mona glares at him. He closes his mouth. Watches her. She's like a wild animal and he doesn't want to frighten her. He is careful not to move.

It's a seduction that is more angry than beautiful. She says, "Is this what you want? You are always looking at me. Is this what you want?" She throws her arms in the air. Her hair is wild and whips around when she moves. She is fierce and wild and furious. Mona comes at him like a murderer. She bites and pulls at his skin and scratches him with her long fingernails. Her body is lovely and brown and Larry doesn't care if he is bleeding from his lip, doesn't care that she has bitten him over and over. She says nothing. Not a sound comes out of her. Not a groan, a whimper, a cry. Larry works hard to keep his mouth covered with hers or just plain closed, to not give in to the sounds he wants to make. He wants to shout or scream.

When they are done, Mona laughs at the rug burns on their bodies. She sits up and smiles. A lovely smile. She shivers. It's cold on the floor. She looks at the tattoos on his chest, asks him to turn over and looks at the ones on his back. Larry can't figure her out. If he wants to touch her, she won't let him, but she can run her hands all over his body. He doesn't care. Or he cares too much. Larry isn't sure about all these feelings he has, these feelings of closeness. Never before has he felt close to anyone. Except his mother. His whistling mother, fixing his sandwich and milk. His mother, who walked out and left him.

This is the first time. Mona says nothing and leaves.

Then it happens again. Days later.

And again.

And again.

Each time, she comes at him as if she wants to tear his heart out. As if she wants to gouge his eyes, as if she wants to eat him. Each time, he is sore and covered in scratches and bites and a heady scent of anger. Larry has no idea what makes her this way. He doesn't ask. He says nothing. If he says something, he knows she won't come again.

Again he hears that groan coming from the storage unit two aisles over. It is late at night and Larry is resting at his desk, feet up, looking at porn on the laptop. Again he sneaks over, tries to see what's up, see if he can even ask the guy to stop making the noise, it's annoying, but the sound ceases the minute he comes near the door. Is he hurt? Is he sad? Is he angry? Is he turned on? Larry can't tell. And now the noise has stopped.

And there is nothing.

9:01 a.m.

They will shave him first. And wash him. They will wash him of his sins. Or so the Chaplain imagines. He is hazy, confused. Sad. Tired, of course. The Prisoner asks them if he can shave his face, if he can at least go to hell without a day's growth. They will not let him. Of course they won't. They can't leave a condemned man with a razor. And they don't have time to shave him themselves. Why would they? Who has time for a dead man?

The Chaplain isn't sure why the Prisoner didn't shave before, when he had his shower. But that was almost ten hours ago.

"Not even an electric one?" the Prisoner says, scratching his cheeks. "Jesus, man. I'm itchy."

"Won't be for long," a CO jokes.

It isn't funny.

They shave patches on his arms, his legs. They give him soap and a washcloth and stand by while he washes his armpits and face in the small sink. A warm towel, fresh from the laundry.

"That's nice," the Prisoner says as he holds it up to his face and sniffs. "It's the small things, you know. They make all the difference." He laughs wildly.

The Chaplain watches this, his bowels churning. Concerned. Why did he agree to this? Why is he here? He attacked his girlfriend once and somehow this led him to become a prison chaplain, which led him here, to the final three hours of a man's life. Right now, this moment, he can't see the connections.

The Chaplain has comforted the sick at hospital beds. He has held hands as a life left a body. But he never thought he would be sitting by a man who will be purposefully killed. A man who is at the prime of his life – in his early forties – healthy, not a thing wrong with him. The Chaplain wishes now that the Prisoner was as violent as the Warden joked he was. Not laughing crazily. He wishes that the Prisoner would rage and swear and spit and rant. Go violently. The Chaplain wants to see criminal insanity in his eyes. As if that would make a difference at the end. Killing a monster, in the long run, is no better than killing a man.

Is it?

The Chaplain recalls the photos of the crime scene. He imagines the families of these three people. He imagines the lives they could have led. Graduations. Weddings. Children. Grandchildren. Gone in an instant. He imagines the final minutes, the pain they suffered, the fear, the confusion. The Chaplain imagines the blood, how warm it was, how much of it there was, how it would have smelled like rust or metal or fish. How sticky. Everywhere.

But still. Trading one murder for another?

"One murder for three," Miranda says in his mind.

The Chaplain turns to the Prisoner and sees a fairly handsome man, boyish in features, slender but muscular. He sees a man covered in tattoos, with a smile that is quick and softens his face. Hair that sticks up because he runs his hands through it constantly. The Prisoner's cuticles are bloody from picking anxiously as he waits. His jaw is muscular from gritting his teeth. This is a fairly intelligent human being, one who is able to spin a good tale, one who knows right from wrong. But his crime wasn't an accident. It was purposeful. And violent. And horrific.

"We'll come get you at about 11:30," CO1 says to the prisoner. "Are you going with him?" He looks at the Chaplain.

"Yes, yes I am." The Chaplain looks at the Prisoner. The Prisoner nods.

"You aware of what's going to happen? You clear with it?" CO1 asks.

"Yes," the Prisoner says, and his voice cracks.

"I won't go over it then?"

The Chaplain wishes he would go over it, walk them through it, give them a practice run. Prepare him even more for what is about to come.

The Prisoner shakes his head. "No, I don't need to hear it again."

The COs leave, taking soap, towel, razor with them. The room suddenly feels large. The Chaplain sits back in his chair, the Prisoner lies back down on the cot.

"I really should walk around," he says. "I mean, it's the last couple hours I'll ever walk. After that, I'm always lying down." Again his voice cracks. He is crying now.

The Chaplain wants to go to him, but by the way the Prisoner is holding himself, fetal position turned towards the wall, he knows to leave him alone. He says nothing. Lets the Prisoner cry it out. He waits. The Prisoner is shaking. After a while, the Prisoner stops crying, blows his nose on his arm, wipes his eyes, rolls onto his back and resumes staring up at the ceiling. His eyes are puffy and ringed red. They are wet. The Chaplain watches him.

"Do you want some time to yourself now?" the Chaplain asks. "Do you want me to leave?"

"No." This is definitive. "No. Stay here. Don't leave."

"We could pray."

"I don't know."

"What do you think your chaplain would have done at this point?"

"Prayed." The Prisoner laughs. "Yeah, he'd have been praying all this time. Twelve fucking hours of prayer."

"I guess I've failed you then," the Chaplain says, smiling.

The Prisoner looks at him. Smiles back. "Yeah, well, you kept forgetting to get me things, like cookies, Pepto-Bismol, so, yeah, you failed me. But in the prayer department, you've done well. Not like a prayer is going to save me now. A cookie, however . . ."

The Chaplain laughs. "I could try and get you one now?"

"I'm not hungry anymore. Thanks, though."

The Chaplain leans back on his chair. "So you were in love with her, then?"

The Prisoner stares at the ceiling, willing it to have the answers. His jaw tightens. His eyes water. "Yes, I was."

Silence.

"She was wild, man. Just fucking crazy. Always came at me angry. And those kids . . ." Again, his voice cracks. "But there was a spark, you know, something there. I couldn't get enough of her. And I think she loved me too. We didn't talk about it, didn't say anything, but you know how you can feel it, that warmth . . ."

"Then why –"

"I don't know. I don't know why." The Prisoner studies the shaved spots on his arms. He runs his fingers over them as if petting himself, comforting himself. He breaks down. "I don't want to die, man. I don't want to die." Shaking, he lies there staring at the ceiling, his eyes running tears. The Chaplain stands and heads towards him, but the Prisoner retreats within himself, moves away quickly and puts his hand out. "Don't come close. Don't touch me."

The Chaplain returns to his chair.

The Prisoner calms himself again. Lies there quietly for a while. Then, "You know what I loved the most about my mother?"

"What?"

"She never touched me. She never touched any of us. Not me. Not Susan, Jack. Not even my father."

"She never hugged you? Kissed you?"

"No. She let us have our space. We never sat on her lap. We never even held her hand. It was weird, I know. It sounds weird now. But it was nice. We had our space apart. We were ourselves and no one was hanging on."

"I'm not sure that's a good thing," the Chaplain says. "People need human touch. Children especially."

"She sometimes ruffled my hair," the Prisoner says. He puts his hand up to his hair. "My father hated to be touched. He would say 'Don't touch me!' all the time. He would shout if you reached for his hand or even bumped him in the fucking hallway. He never wanted anyone to touch him. Maybe my mother learned from that. Learned not to touch anyone."

"I'm not sure –"

"The point is," the Prisoner says, "the point is that Mona didn't like me to touch her. She would touch me, yeah, but she never let me touch her. And I think maybe that reminded me of my mom. It reminded me that my mom never touched us and so maybe, like Mona, she didn't want to be touched herself. And maybe my dad caused that, you know. I mean, if someone

191

was always shouting, 'Don't touch me!' at you, you'd learn soon not to touch, wouldn't you?"

"So that's why you –"

"No. Fucking listen. Just listen. That's not why. That's not why."

"Sorry."

"I'm just saying that maybe that's why I fell for her, you know. That's why she was different. She was like my mom."

"Yes, I can see that. I can see that the similarities to your mother would affect you. After all, Mona had two boys. Your mother had two boys."

"She didn't fucking leave, though. Mona never left those kids." The Prisoner punches the wall with his fist. The Chaplain stiffens. "Why did she leave us?"

"I'm not sure. No one can be sure. There was obviously something wrong. It's not often women leave their children."

"But she took *him*. She took Jack."

The Chaplain nods. Yes, she took the Prisoner's brother. She chose Jack instead. His whole life mourning her and hating his brother.

And Tracy chose David and the Chaplain has spent years hating himself for it.

The smallest choices affect everything, he thinks.

"The thing is," the Prisoner says, "the thing is that I spent my whole life mad at Jack for this. But it wasn't really his fault. Sure, he's an asshole, but he was a kid. He was only nine. And he missed out on having siblings. Susan and I had each other. Jack had no one. But our mother." He pauses. Thinks. "I guess I've come to that," he says. "Finally. Jack was all alone and me and Susan had each other. And I feel kind of bad about that. It just, well, it explains a lot about him."

"Do you think Jack forgives you for what you've done?"

The Prisoner laughs. "What does Jack need to forgive me for? This has nothing to do with him. I should be forgiving him for all the fucking concussions. Maybe if he didn't give me all those concussions, I wouldn't have blacked out. I wouldn't have killed –"

"I'm just saying that maybe you should say goodbye to him. Call him. I can get you a phone."

"You won't let it go, will you? How many times do I have to tell you that I don't want to see anyone I know at my fucking execution? I don't want to see anyone. Not Susan. Not Jack. Not Susan's brats. I came into this world alone. I'm going out alone. This isn't about them. It's about me. Me. I'm the one facing this. I'm the one doing this."

"I –"

"You've got a one-track mind, you know. Has anyone told you that? You're like some kid poking something over and over and over with a stick no matter how many times his mom tells him to stop. You won't let it go. Dead animal. Dead animal. Poke, poke."

The Chaplain smiles slightly. His sister used to say the same thing to him. He will tell her of this coincidence at their dinner next Sunday night. He will tell her this over red wine and steak, and Richard will be on his way home from the long haul, and the kids will be excited and wild. And when he tells Miranda about this, the Prisoner, this man in front of him now, will be dead.

"What if," the Prisoner says, looking at his shaved spots, "what if it grows a little stubble in three hours? That could happen, couldn't it? And then stuff won't stick? And maybe it won't work? Or the hair will catch fire?"

"Doubt it," the Chaplain says. "Hair can't grow that quickly." And then he stops and realizes what he said. Not that quickly.

The execution is coming fast and furious. Twelve noon. No time to grow hair.

In the silence, the Chaplain can hear the prisoners now. In the yard around the death chamber. In their cells. He can hear them like he would hear a hive of bees. Not really a sound, more like a feeling. Feeling them in your body. Humming and buzzing. The prisoners are awake now, all around, off and about their days. They are talking and shouting and screaming. The Chaplain can feel it around him. It's life. Even if it's meaningless life – waiting out their sentences – it's still life. If this were any other day, the Chaplain would be arriving at the prison, checking in with the Warden, attending a few meetings – maybe talking about behaviour issues or who needs help, some counselling – then out into the common rooms and a group therapy session or two. Sometimes one-on-one visiting. Sometimes meeting with the prisoner's families. A few hours in the chapel. At the end of the day, he would be climbing into his car and driving back to his apartment. He would watch his screen a bit and make something with noodles or rice for dinner. Eat. Read later. A glass of Scotch before bed. Maybe write a bit. Then bed. Over and over, his days are like this. Until today. And until now, he has always hoped he was doing something worthwhile. Listening when no one else listens. Hearing them. Helping them. Even if most days, driving home, he felt like he might not be making a difference – he always had hope.

Now he wonders, What good is all of this? Again and again, the Chaplain sees reoffenders. Back again. Second, third, fourth time. It seems that on the outside, no one listens to these men. So they use fists and crime to solve that problem and he, once again, hears them out. Tries to help. Gives them occasional words of wisdom. Shows them there is a power higher than themselves. That if they only had faith, patience, hope, if they were only kind to others . . .

Now what, though?

"We are the same, you and I," the Chaplain says, suddenly, to the Prisoner.

"What's that?" The Prisoner rolls over on his side and looks at him.

How do you get a man to confess, to ask forgiveness, to tell the story of his crime? You share your own failings.

"I became a prison chaplain because a judge recommended that I do something to atone for my sins. She told me to go to therapy. And my therapist agreed with the judge."

The Prisoner laughs. "A judge told you to become a chaplain? Your therapist? Your sins? Fuck. And this makes you the same as me?"

The Chaplain is startled. He is confessing. "They didn't say that exactly, my therapist, the judge – that I should be a prison chaplain – but they both mentioned that I needed a higher purpose, that I needed to give back to society. I was taking religion courses at university. It seemed the right choice."

"Yeah, that makes sense." The Prisoner rolls his eyes. "You couldn't think of any other job you'd rather have? Garbage man is giving back. Keeping the streets clean. Christ, anything would be better than this. Hanging out with a bunch of assholes all day. Reading the Bible."

The Chaplain pauses. He stands. "I beat up my girlfriend," he says. "I was charged with assault, but she dropped the charges. I did therapy. Anger management stuff."

"Holy shit." The Prisoner sits up. "I've known you all this time and you just tell me this?" He laughs. "And here I thought we were close." He smiles. Pauses. "I didn't think you guys were allowed to have girlfriends."

"The point is . . . the point is not what I did."

"Sure it is. That's the whole point. What. You. Did. That's my point. That's why I'm here. What. I. Did."

"The point is that you and I, we are alike. We have both felt anger, intense anger. And we have been punished for that anger."

"Seems that your punishment is a little easier though, doesn't it? You weren't charged." The Prisoner is leaning with his elbows on his knees. "You're going home tonight. With no record." He is looking at the floor. Suddenly he looks up into the Chaplain's eyes. "Why'd you do it?" he asks. "Why'd you hit your girlfriend?"

And the Chaplain thinks about this. Hard. He knows why he hit Tracy – because of David. Because he was humiliated and hurt and she took their lives, what he thought was their lives, their future, and she turned it all on a dime. Suddenly they weren't Jim and Tracy anymore, and he was alone. Without warning. Or if there was warning, he wasn't paying attention. He hurt her because she hurt him. And the only way he could think of hurting her was to be physical. It was fast. Easy. Simple as that. But he doesn't say all of this. Instead he says what he really feels now, what he knows to be true:

"I hit her because it felt good at the time."

The Prisoner stares hard. It feels to the Chaplain as if the Prisoner is taking the Chaplain's soul into his soul, swallowing him. The room is small and spins. There is silence all around them now, the Prisoner and the Chaplain. Silence that is over-whelming.

"What I did," the Prisoner finally speaks. Clearly, slowly. "What I did did not feel good at all."

Coffee Cans

Mona has an ex-husband. She tells Larry nothing about him, just that he's crazy, that she keeps away from him. That she hasn't seen him in a couple of months.

Larry figures that something bad is going on when he sees Mona on the phone in the summer on the steps leading up to the office. She is crying and waving her arms around hysterically. Larry can see the twins the next aisle over, and they are standing completely still and staring at their mother. The look on their faces tells Larry that this happens often. Mona is shrill and furious, she smashes her hand down on the railing and almost throws her phone away but then sees Larry watching her, looks down the aisle at her kids and sees them staring, and turns on her heels and goes back into the office. The boys scooter off.

She won't talk to him about it. No matter what he asks her, how he phrases his questions, she tells him to shut up, stop bothering her, leave her alone.

"None of your business," Mona says. "This has nothing to do with you."

But the more he falls in love with Mona, the more this has everything to do with him. The calls are more frequent now. The man haunts her, screams at her on her phone and is beginning to demand visits with the twins. He takes the twins away for the weekend. Mona must let him. Larry has never seen him. One weekend the boys are with Mona. One weekend they do not come to the Storage Mart and the aisles echo, empty without their noisy play.

Larry catches Mona crying occasionally.

He benefits from her anger as she comes at him in his storage-unit office. But this lovemaking isn't what he wants. Her frustrations taken out on him.

One day she sits up and looks at him. Naked. Her hair falling down her back, sweat on her temples.

"What's in the coffee cans?" Mona asks. This is the only thing she has ever asked him about himself and it makes Larry feel unbalanced. Naked beside her, he is off-guard.

"Money," he says. He can't help himself.

And she laughs. Dresses. Leaves.

He isn't sure if she believes him.

But that is all that is ever said about the cans.

Larry studies his cuts and bruises then. His bite marks. Sometimes she is more dangerous than other times. Today she was almost gentle. He wonders if she might be feeling something for him. There is no way he can tell.

That night he visits Susan. It has been almost a year since he last saw her, and the change in her, in the house, in her kids, takes Larry by surprise.

"What the fuck?" Larry kicks the door open wide enough to slide through. The hallway is full of things. Garbage, shoes, coats, backpacks, boxes, flats of pop and cases of beer both empty and full. Larry enters the kitchen and Susan is sitting at the table, the table they sat at years ago when their mother fed them their sandwiches at lunch. When Jack pushed Larry off the chair because of the bike lock. Larry can't believe the change that has taken place. Susan's face is skeletal; her jaw hangs open as if it's on a rusty hinge. She is yellow in colour and her eyes are so bloodshot Larry can't see the brown of the irises. Susan's hair is lank and greasy and falls over her face. Unwashed. She smells horrible. Her nails are long and her cuticles are bleeding and her hands move back and forth on their own, across the top of the table. She is actually drooling. She has meth face. Cavernous mouth, no teeth.

"Holy shit, Susan. What happened to you?"

"You got money?" Susan blinks up at Larry.

A few of Susan's kids, and some kids Larry doesn't recognize, walk through the kitchen and head out the back door into the night. Larry takes note of their gang colours. One of the oldest boys is holding a knife. All of them are smoking.

"Meth," Larry says. "You said you'd never do meth."

"Jack," Susan says. "He gives me stuff. I do what he gives me. Do you have money? Can you give me some stuff?"

Larry wants more than anything to turn and leave and never come back. This isn't his problem. She's too far gone. There's nothing he can do. And why should he? Who the hell cares? It's not like they are close. They have nothing in common. He's a go-getter, she's a lazy bitch. Larry wants to smack her around. How dare she do this to him. To herself. To her kids.

Larry roots around in the cupboards for coffee. He finds instant and puts the kettle on.

Susan looks up from the table. "You got money?"

"Jesus, Susan."

The milk in the fridge is thick and lumpy.

He tries to sober her up. This is what he eventually tells anyone who asks – the judges, the caseworkers, the correction officers – when they attempt to use her as a character witness. He does try. But she doesn't want his help, only his money. Larry leaves her then, to Jack, to her life. There is nothing else he can do. There is really nothing else he wants to do if he's honest with himself. Like his mother did to him and Susan many years ago, he turns his back on her. And gives up.

Larry doesn't know why it happens this night. Ten years in his cell, alone, and he still hasn't figured it out. He doesn't understand it. Why this night? For several years he thought it had something to do with his concussions. Blacking out. Rage. Seeing Susan over the top, maybe that triggered something? He isn't sure.

Why this night?

This night, Larry catches Jack picking the lock on his roll-up door at the storage facility. It is late, dark, wet, raining. A hot summer rain, it doesn't cool him off. Larry, terrified, approaches Jack from behind and grabs his arm and takes him down into the mud. He wishes he had his gun. Jack is surprised but slippery and tough. They wrestle and fight. Throw punches.

"What did you do to Susan?" Larry screams.

Jack laughs. He laughs and hits and scrabbles for footing in the mud.

Jack comes out worse for wear because he is drugged out and sloppy. But he manages to hit Larry hard on the head and it feels to Larry as if his brain explodes. He can feel his brain move slightly, as if it has shifted. Another concussion, perhaps, or an old one come back.

He is dizzy, disoriented.

There is a car in the distance, by the woods, and Larry sees the flash of headlights. A signal. Who is waiting for Jack? Susan?

"What the fuck do you want from me?" Larry shouts, holding his head, as Jack takes off, covered in mud, holding his ribs. Jack's nose is swollen and bleeding, and his cheek has been ripped by a pebble in the mud. Larry wipes himself off and tries to stand, breathing heavily, wobbly. There is blood from a cut on his eyebrow. It leaks into his eyes, mixes with the rain. He watches Jack get into the distant car. The car sits there in the dark; it doesn't move. Larry's eyes go in and out of focus. He can't see, everything is fuzzy.

And then the car starts up, lights on, moves off down the road past the strip mall, past the woods. Slowly, like Jack has all the time in the world.

Jack must know about his money.

Jack must also know that Larry will move his money, so he will come back. Soon.

Tonight. This night.

Why this night? Why suddenly is everything happening?

Larry rolls open his door and looks around. His coffee cans are all lined up nicely. His desk is clean except for the laptop and the figurine of the boy fishing, leaning on a log. Larry hasn't committed any burglaries in months; he has lived off his coffee cans, the amount dwindling rapidly. Since he began seeing Mona, he's done nothing but surf the Internet and drink at bars and eat and sleep and think of Mona. Larry pauses in his thoughts and hears that groaning coming from the storage unit the next aisle over. It's late. It's raining. Who the hell is groaning? Sighing? Crying? And why? What are they doing?

He swipes at his eyes as if clearing them, but then realizes the fog is in his head. His vision is wavering, as if he's looking through black liquid.

Larry has no time to contemplate all of this – Jack, the groaning asshole, his money. Mona. He has to move, get moving, get going. He has to get rid of his money. Hide it away. Keep it safe from Jack. His head aches. He is shaky, worried about Jack, afraid for his life, his money.

The groaning continues.

Larry grabs a coffee can, two cans, three cans, as many as he can hold. He looks around. What will he do with them? Where will he put them? In his car first and then move them into his apartment? Or a bank? He stops, laughs slightly. A bank. That's funny. Open an account with the money he stole from banks. Larry makes one quick trip to his car, just where he left it when he saw Jack, down the aisle, hidden slightly, and he makes sure to take note of everything around him. Pay attention. In case Jack sneaks up on him. His vision is clouding but he doesn't see any other cars. He hears nothing. No car engines. The groaning has stopped.

Jack was out of it, might even forget to come back, might go home to nurse his wounds. High on meth, Larry supposes. Maybe he'll come back another time? Larry may have that – some time. Or he may not. He wants to sleep but knows he can't. He may never wake up if he goes to sleep now. This must be another concussion. His brain feels loose. Jingling in his skull. A piercing ache.

He dumps the cans in his car and heads back to his open storage unit to get more. For some reason it doesn't occur to him to move the car closer.

And then, on this night, on this particular night, just when she shouldn't be, Mona is there. What is she doing there at night? She is never at the Storage Mart at night. She is standing inside his unit, by his desk. She is wet, her long hair dripping down her back. As if she's been out in the rain for hours. She is looking at his coffee cans, holding one in her hand, staring at the money inside.

"What are you doing here?" Larry asks. "It's late."

"I forgot my purse in the office so I came back," she says. Her voice is flat. "I saw your door open." She stares at the coffee can in her hand. "Where did you get all of this money? What are you? What do you do? What happened to your face?" Her hands, Larry notices, are shaking. "I thought you were joking about money in the cans. I thought –"

"I have to go. Now," Larry says. "What are you doing here? Where are the boys?"

"The kids are waiting in the car. I saw your door open. What happened to you? What happened to your face?"

"I'll tell you later. I have to leave. Now."

"Larry, I'm calling the police. I don't know what you are doing in here, but I know it's not legal and I want nothing to do with it." Mona reaches for her cellphone and Larry comes at her. He twists her arm and grabs the phone. Doesn't she know how important time is right now? "No," she shouts. "Stop. Give me back my phone."

"Listen, you just have to let me go now. I'll explain later."

"No." She is furious. She tries to grab for the phone and Larry pushes her. Mona lands on her knees on the rug. Her eyes suddenly shift and she is looking behind him, outside the unit, into the aisle. Suddenly she gasps and drops the coffee tin she is still holding. Money spews out. Her hand goes to her mouth. "No."

Larry turns. He sees nothing. There is no one there.

"What?"

"I thought I saw someone."

"I'll be back. Just wait here and we can figure this out together. Just wait. I'm sorry –"

He takes the coffee cans and rushes out of the storage shelter and down towards his car. His eyes aren't working anymore – it's as if he is wearing sunglasses in the night. Everything is dark. Shadows, shapes. The pounding in his head is a noise now. Sloshing. He can hear it all around him. Blood rushing around his brain. A black world. A quick white world. He's dizzy and stumbles and falls. Time seems to pass fast and then slowly.

Larry rights himself and heads back to the storage unit. He walks like a drunk man, swaying, weaving. He doesn't see that the boys are there until after. He didn't see them go in. He saw nothing. Larry's mind is a mess of misfiring wires. He remembers nothing more than this – going towards his storage unit for one more haul of coffee cans. Hearing Mona shouting, "No." At him? To him? Feeling angry. He remembers feeling incredibly angry. At Jack? At Mona? How dare she threaten him. How dare she try to call the police. How dare she look in his coffee tins. He wants her but she wants nothing to do with him. He is furious. And then nothing. He remembers nothing.

But when he regains consciousness he sees them. The boys. Mona.

He is lying on his stomach in the entranceway to his storage unit, to his office, in the mud.

Everything has ended so quickly. Twenty minutes since his fight with Jack. In and out of the storage unit with his cans – waking, falling, drifting. Larry isn't in control of his body, his eyes. He rolls onto his back. He can see nothing until he sees everything.

So much blood.

Larry retches. Vomits. Blacks out again.

Comes to. Sees it again. And again.

So much blood. Thick and black. The smell like fish and rust, metallic and sour. Everything is sticky, covered in blood.

He is covered in blood.

His blood?

Their blood?

Larry can't get the picture of them lying there, splayed, out of his mind. He sees it over and over and over, it is burned across his mind. Ten years it's been there behind his lids when he closes his eyes at night.

Mona is over by the desk. Still on her knees where he left her, but now she has sunken down, almost sitting cross-legged, her legs at an awkward angle under her skirt. As if broken. She looks like a doll, skewed angles, limbs twisted. She is leaning slightly on the desk. Her eyes are open and staring right at him. Her mouth is wide, caught in the midst of a scream. There is blood in her hair, on her blouse, in her hands. She holds her hands out, placed upright on her twisted thighs, and there is blood pooled into them. As if she's keeping a cup of blood for each of her sons.

The boys are lumped together just near the entrance to the storage unit. One on top of the other. Frankie. Bennie. Larry is not sure which is which. There are gashes through their arms, legs, torsos, heads. Thick gashes. Their eyes are closed but their hands reach out towards their mother. Reach out to defend themselves. Blood everywhere. Larry is covered in it.

This is what the jury focuses on. The twins. The innocents. Multiple stab wounds. Larry heard nothing but "No."

They focus on Larry's head injuries, the multiple concussions which, surely, must have led to this kind of intense anger – the fact that he was concussed that night, barely conscious. She was going to call the police on him. She threatened him. The children came in while he was killing her – of course he killed them too.

These are such violent deaths. It amazes Larry that they took so little time. The autopsy states that they did not fight back. Mona did not fight back. One minute they are there, the next minute they are dead.

Larry tells the judge, "I didn't mean to kill them. I don't remember much. I don't remember anything."

10:01 a.m.

"I did it," the Prisoner tells the Chaplain. "I killed Mona and her two sons. She was going to take my money. She was there to steal my money and so I killed her. The kids got in the way. It's obvious. All the police reports say this. It doesn't matter that I can't remember it. I was covered in her blood."

"This makes no sense to me," the Chaplain says. He is standing, pacing. "After your whole story. After everything I know about you now. This makes no sense."

"You read the files. I had years of concussions from Jack. And that night. I don't remember anything. But when I came to, they were dead. I did it. There was no one else there."

The mood in the cell is anxious, thick, worried. The Chaplain can feel it in the stifling air. The Prisoner is avoiding eye contact, looking everywhere but at the Chaplain. "Why would you kill Mona? You were falling in love with her. Just because she found your coffee cans? For money? This makes no sense. You didn't care about the money. You said so yourself. And why suddenly like that? She hadn't called the police yet. You could have talked her out of it easily. And why the boys?

And when did you get a knife in your hand? You were carrying the cans to the car, you were hurt, you didn't have a knife. This makes absolutely no sense."

"She got in the way. I always carried a knife."

"But not *the* knife. They never found *the* knife. This is not possible. You are protecting him, aren't you? Jack. It was Jack. He came back. He did it. You saw him do it."

"They caught me. Get over it. They caught me with blood on my hands."

"But you didn't do it. They never found the knife. I know you didn't do it. It makes absolutely no sense. The whole story you've told me doesn't lead to this. It doesn't . . . It was Jack, wasn't it? Why are you protecting him? Why would you even want to protect him after what he did to Susan, to you?"

"Everything I did in my life led up to this moment," the Prisoner says quietly. "My mother left me and I became this. I murdered that bank manager and the teller." He holds his hands out wide, Jesus on the cross. He is standing by the cot. And suddenly he looks larger, more ominous, frightening rather than frightened.

The Chaplain stands at the door. "Officers," he shouts, rattling the door. "Officers. Let me out."

But the Prisoner is fast and he corners the Chaplain up against the door before the COs can get into the cell. He holds the Chaplain's neck between his two strong hands and squeezes so hard that the Chaplain feels as if his windpipe will collapse. The bump on the Prisoner's head, the bruise purple and black, looks to him as if it's pulsing.

"I fucking killed them, don't you say I didn't. Do you know how many years this has been argued back and fucking forth, appealed back and forth? I'm sick of it. I killed them. All three of them. Because they wanted my money. Because my mother left me. Because Jack was taken, she took Jack, to protect me, don't you see –" the Prisoner lets go and sinks to the floor, sobbing.

The COs break through and wrench the Prisoner up and hold him down on the cot on his stomach. They bind his arms, his wrists with ties.

"What the hell is going on in here?" CO2 asks. "You got two more hours, asshole, and then you're dead. So stop acting like a tough man. Act like a man going to his death. Act remorseful maybe. Or something. Jesus."

The Chaplain rubs his neck. Another CO guides him out into the hallway, where he perches on the edge of a chair.

"You okay?"

The Chaplain nods. Catches his breath. "He's not guilty," he says. "He didn't do it."

"What are you talking about? Hey, listen to this." The COs gather around him.

The Chaplain tells them what he thinks. He says, "I think it was his brother, Jack, who killed the woman and her children. I think Jack came back to the storage place and knifed them and the Prisoner took the blame. Maybe he took the blame because he was afraid of Jack. Or maybe because he had blacked out and just didn't remember anything. I don't know, I don't get it, it doesn't make any logical sense, but he didn't do it." The Chaplain relates the story quickly but the COs shake their heads, look confused, look sympathetically at him. "Why aren't you doing anything? We have to stop the process."

One of the COs is on the phone.

"The Warden's coming down."

"Yes," the Chaplain says. "Good. We have enough time to stop this thing."

There is silence as the COs stare at him. All he can see is a pack of blue uniforms with numbers on them. Inside his cell, the Prisoner, his hands bound together, lies quietly on his cot.

The Warden arrives quickly. Blusters in smelling like cigarette smoke and warm sweat. Smelling like the outside, like life. He is red-faced and angry.

"What the hell did I tell you, Chaplain? What did I say? I said, 'Don't let him get under your skin,' didn't I? Isn't that what I said?" He shakes his head around. Waves his arms in the air. "I knew this would happen. I told your mentor that you're too young, too inexperienced. I knew he'd manipulate you. But, no, he said you were fine, that you'd do your job. Jesus Christ, Chaplain. All you had to do was listen."

"I listened," the Chaplain says. "I listened. In fact, you didn't listen. No one listened. He didn't do it. He didn't manipulate me. He says he did it. I'm the one, I think he didn't do it." The Chaplain pauses and takes a deep breath. Slows down his talking, tries to sound calm. "Listen, Warden, you have to listen."

The Warden sits on a chair facing the Chaplain. He puts his hands on the Chaplain's knees. The Chaplain's shoulders curl inward, protecting his chest. He holds both his hands together in his lap.

"Do you know how hard it is to get the death penalty?" the Warden begins. "Do you have any idea how hard it is for us to get a prisoner this far? How many hurdles we have to jump? How many lawyers and judges and politicians? You can be damn sure, Chaplain, that when we get to where we are now, with –" here he pauses and looks at his watch – "with two fucking hours to go, you can be absolutely sure that every, and I mean every, avenue has been explored. There have been appeals up the yingyang. Hell, there are even picketers out there right now. Join them if you want. But there is no way in the world that this asshole didn't kill those three innocent people.

He fucking sliced them up – didn't you look at the files? – he was brutal. Supposedly," the Warden pauses and looks down at the ground as if summoning the strength to say this, "supposedly one of those boys was still breathing. He was breathing, alive, when the police got there. Imagine him lying under his brother all night, stabbed numerous times. Imagine the pain he suffered. For what? To eventually die when they finally got there to save him?"

The Warden stands quickly and starts pacing the hallway. The COs watch him. Then they look through the Prisoner's door. Then they watch the Warden. Like a tennis game.

"It doesn't make sense," the Chaplain says quietly. "Why would he kill her? He loved her. He didn't really care about the money. And his brother was trying to get the money for drugs. He fought his brother right before Mona came in. What about that? That's how he got the concussion. He was blacked out when they got there. He had to go to the hospital. They never found a knife. He remembers nothing. Jack must have come back, seen Mona there holding the money and killed her, killed her kids. Just because there was blood on the Prisoner doesn't make him guilty. Did anyone find his brother, Jack, and see if he was covered in blood?"

The Warden stops walking and stares straight at the Chaplain.

"Every fucking avenue was explored." The Warden runs his hands over his bald head. "He says he killed them. He says he did it." He starts pacing again. "Why the hell am I even justifying your questions with answers? This isn't up to you, Chaplain. And it's not up to me. It's done. He's been a dead man for weeks now."

"But –" The Chaplain stands. "There must be something we can –"

"Look." The Warden stares up at the taller man. "Look, I'm going to take you off this now. You go home. Get some rest. It'll all be over shortly. You're finished with this, okay? Nothing more. Go home."

"No. No, I'm not going home."

"The guy tried to strangle you."

"I am not going home. I promised I would be here for him. I'm going to be here for him."

"Jesus Christ, man. You're not in control right now. You're no help to anyone. You're overtired and you've been manipulated by a murderer and a thief."

"I am. I am help to him. To the Prisoner. He has no one else. Only me."

The Warden thinks about this for a while. He looks again at his watch. "It is ten-fifteen. They are coming for him at eleven-thirty."

"I want to be with him. Please."

The Warden holds a finger up, as if testing the air. Then he opens the cell, goes in, shuts the cell door behind him. Ten minutes pass. The Warden comes out carrying the ties that bound the Prisoner.

"He says you can stay," the Warden says. "But, Jesus, Chaplain, if you cause any more trouble, if you upset him in any way, you're out of here. And after this is done, I want you in my office."

The Warden blusters out of the hallway the same way he came in – fast-paced and furious.

The Chaplain sits back down on the chair and puts his head in his hands.

"You going back in?" CO1 asks.

"Yes. Do me a favour, would you?"

"Sure, yeah, what do you want?"

"Will you get me my Bible?"

CO1 is wide-eyed. "You been in there for almost eleven hours and you didn't think to bring your Bible? I thought you were a Chaplain."

The Chaplain runs his hands through his hair. He shrugs. "Not a very good one, I guess."

"Aren't you a man of God? What the hell have you been talking about then? If you didn't even have a Bible with you?"

"We," the Chaplain sighs, "are all men of God." He stands and enters the cell again. CO1 puts a call in for someone to deliver the Chaplain's Bible. "He says it's on his desk," CO1 says. "How the hell would I know why he wants it now?"

Into the cell. The Prisoner is standing against the far wall by the toilet. He has just flushed. He is standing there, every muscle in his body alert. The Chaplain takes note of this and tries to enter casually, sit down, remain relaxed.

"Look," the Chaplain says. "I just –"

"If you say it one more time, I will kill you." The Prisoner's voice is low, violent, wild. He is a bundle of nerves. "I've got no time left to hear how sorry you are."

No time left.

CO1 enters the cell with the Bible. He hands it to the Chaplain. He leaves.

"What's that?" the Prisoner asks.

The Chaplain opens the Bible. Flips through it. Finds his place. "I think it's time," he says. He signals with his head to the cot. "I think it's time I did my job properly." The Prisoner walks slowly towards the cot and sits down.

He begins. His voice is monotone and soothing. Quiet.

"Psalm 51:1–12."

He clears his throat. The Prisoner looks at him without any interest. With a look of pure disdain.

"'O loving and kind God, have mercy. Have pity upon me and take away the awful stain of my transgressions. Oh, wash me, cleanse me from this guilt. Let me be pure again. For I admit my shameful deed – it haunts me day and night. It is against you and you alone I sinned and did this terrible thing. You saw it all, and your sentence against me is just. . . . Create in me a new, clean heart, O God, filled with clean thoughts and right desires. Don't toss me aside, banished forever from your presence. Don't take Your Holy Spirit from me. Restore to me again the joy of your salvation, and make me willing to obey you.'"

The Prisoner almost laughs. "Fuck," he says quietly.

The Chaplain pauses. Shuffles the Bible around, looking for something else.

"John 1," he reads. "'This is the message we have heard from him and declare to you: God is light; in him there is no darkness at all. If we claim to have fellowship with him yet walk in the darkness, we lie and do not live by the truth. But if we walk in the light, as he is in the light, we have fellowship with one another, and the blood of Jesus, his Son, purifies us from all sin. If we claim to be without sin, we deceive ourselves and the truth is not in us. If we confess our sins, he is faithful and just and will forgive us our sins and purify us from all unrighteousness. If we claim we have not sinned, we make him out to be a liar and his word has no place in our lives.'"

The Prisoner stares at him. Not impressed, the Chaplain thinks. Of course not. After all, the Prisoner has confessed. In the Chaplain's Bible, there are pieces of folded paper, some of which fall to the floor. He reaches for the papers. He opens one. "This is a Tibetan prayer," he says. The Prisoner suddenly looks interested. "From the fourteenth century." He begins, "'When my time has come and impermanence and death have caught up with me, When the breath ceases, and the body and mind go their separate ways, May I not experience delusion, attachment, and clinging, But remain in the natural state of ultimate reality.'"

"That's not bad," the Prisoner says. "I like that one. What was it? 'The natural state of ultimate reality.'" He lies back on his cot, slowly relaxing his body. "Let's hear more."

"From Martin Luther King Jr.'s *Eulogy for the Martyred Children* in 1963," the Chaplain reads. "'Now I say to you in conclusion, life is hard, at times as hard as crucible steel. It has its bleak and difficult moments. Like the ever-flowing waters of the river, life has its moments of drought and its moments of flood. Like the ever-changing cycle of the seasons, life has the soothing warmth of its summers and the piercing chill of its winters. And if one will hold on, he will discover that God walks with him, and that God is able to lift you from the fatigue of despair to the buoyancy of hope, and transform dark and desolate valleys into sunlit paths of inner peace.'"

The Chaplain is standing now, waving his arms, reading from the papers in his hands. His Bible is down on the floor beside him. When his voice stops, he realizes his position and once again sits down.

"You got more?" the Prisoner asks.

"I've got a lot more. From school. University." The Chaplain pulls out more paper, stretches it out, smooths it on his lap. All his paper is thin from being handled over time. His Bible, on the other hand, crinkles with stiffness, with neglect. "Here's a good one: Norse mythology – 'Fearlessness is better than a faint heart for any man who puts his nose out of doors. The length of my life and the day of my death were fated long ago.'"

"That's good," the Prisoner says. "That's right. Fated. Give me more."

"Sayings of the Buddha," he reads. "'I am of the nature to grow old. There is no way to escape growing old. I am of the nature to have ill health. There is no way to escape having ill health. I am of the nature to die. There is no way to escape death. All that is dear to me and everyone I love are of the nature to change. There is no way to escape being separated from them. My actions are my only true belongings. I cannot escape the consequences of my actions. My actions are the ground on which I stand.'"

"Well," says the Prisoner, "that's not very helpful considering I'm not sick or old." He laughs slightly. Looks at the clock. It is 10:53 a.m. "This is good, though. I appreciate this."

The Chaplain reads, "This is a Catholic prayer for the dying: 'God of all Creation, Be with us now and at the hour of our death. Shelter us from harms' way and lead us on the path to eternal life. Receive our life, all that we are, and everything we do. May the Angel of Mercy stay near us this day and always.'"

"Amen," the Prisoner says. The Chaplain isn't sure if he's being sarcastic.

"Okay, how about Psalm 23? You've heard this one. Psalm of David."

"Go ahead, though. Even if I have heard it before."

"'The Lord is my shepherd; I shall not want'?"

The Prisoner nods.

The Chaplain continues, "'He maketh me to lie down in green pastures: he leadeth me beside the still waters. He restoreth my soul: he leadeth me in the paths of righteousness for his name's sake. Yea, though I walk through the valley of the shadow of death; I will fear no evil: for thou *art* with me; thy rod and thy staff they comfort me. Thou preparest a table before me in the presence of mine enemies: thou anointest my head with oil; my cup runneth over. Surely goodness and mercy shall follow me all the days of my life: and I will dwell in the house of the Lord for ever.'"

The Prisoner is still. Thoughtful.

"I sort of see why you studied religion," he says. "They all have a lot to say."

"True," the Chaplain says. He notes that the COs are all looking into the room, staring into the window. They can't hear the two men in the cell, but they sense something is calmer, more peaceful now. They sense something – the Chaplain can feel it too. The electric energy in the air has settled.

The Prisoner stands and stretches. Then he kneels in front of the cot, places his hands together in prayer, and begins to speak: "Our Father who art in heaven, hallowed be thy name. Thy kingdom come. Thy will be done on earth as it is in heaven. Give us this day our daily bread, and forgive us our trespasses, as we forgive those who trespass against us, and lead us not into temptation, but deliver us from evil. For thine is the kingdom, and the power, and the glory, for ever and ever. Amen."

Like a small child with bowed head and slumped back, like a child right before bed, before lights out, before the glow-in-the-dark stars grow dim on his blue wall, the Prisoner prays.

And then the Prisoner and the Chaplain are silent, both thinking their own thoughts.

Scum

Larry doesn't remember anything until he is woken by the shouting.

By the time the guy at the front desk comes in for his early morning shift, by the time he walks into the office but turns and looks down the aisle and sees, strangely, that Larry Gallo's door is open, the light inside shining out, by the time he realizes that Mona's car is there but Mona is not in the office, by the time he walks towards Larry's storage unit – every step anxious because something is in the air, he can feel it, he can smell it, he can taste it – by this time, the blood has hardened into a sticky mass on the victims, on the floor, on the walls, and Larry is passed out beside it all.

And the guy at the front desk begins to shout.

Larry tries to get up. He slips slightly, he bends at the waist, dry heaves, stumbles down onto the floor again. The front desk clerk is still shouting but Larry can't make out the words. "Help," or "Hell," or just a long line of shouting nonsense, with no words, no sense attached to it. Larry falls again and again backing out of the shelter, trying to get away.

Then nothing. He must have passed out again.

Then suddenly there are lights and sirens and an ambulance. Other people shouting and touching him – carefully, as if they think that he, too, has been stabbed. There are police who are asking so many questions he can't formulate answers, he can't talk, he has nothing to say. The coffee tins are opened, the bodies are suddenly gone, although Larry knows now that they would have been photographed and catalogued for hours. Larry is ignored and then scrutinized. The desk clerk won't stop shouting. They tell him to shut up, to calm down; he's given oxygen or something, Larry can't figure it out, and then the clerk is sent back to the office, a cop holding onto his shoulders, comforting him, guiding him.

Larry is taken away, in the police car. Nobody is holding his shoulders, no one is comforting him. Once they discover that the blood isn't his, he is forced into the car, pushed ungracefully in, and driven upright to the hospital – slumping down every so often, tugged up again and again.

"Help me," Larry hears himself say.

"Scum," a cop whispers. "You scumbag."

And then everything is over. And everything begins.

11:01 a.m.

He walks towards the execution chamber, the Chaplain by his side. This tall man who has spent the last twelve hours of his life with him. His mind is scattered and crazed. Dead man, he thinks. Jesus Christ. God. Help me. Part of the Prisoner wants to grab the Chaplain's hand and hold on tight, part of him wants to just stop walking and make the COs drag him. His head hurts, the lump on his forehead from his fall pulses. His legs are liquid, rubbery, wobbly.

That's not the way it happened, he thinks.

The Prisoner remembers now. He remembers everything so clearly.

Who says you don't see your life flash in front of you right before you die? For several days now, he has remembered. Everything. He has the scene before him now. That piece of the night that was missing, as if cut away from his brain with a knife. It's back. That piece.

He wanted to tell his story to someone. That's what he thought. He thought if he invited the Chaplain in, no matter which chaplain it was, and told him his story, then he would be free of everything. The burden would be off him. But then he started from the beginning, and now it's the end. And still he didn't say anything, he didn't tell the whole story. He didn't tell the right story.

Jack came back, that night, to the storage unit. Larry was stumbling, dazed, coming back again, once more, to load more of his cans in his car. Mona had asked Larry too many questions, he had pushed her, he had grabbed her phone and he had brushed her off. She was shouting at him. Larry had just delivered six more cans in his arms, balanced precariously, to his car. "We'll figure it out. Just fucking shut up," was the last thing he screamed at her then. Dizzy, disoriented, he was coming back from the car. Hearing her shout "No," he looked towards the open storage unit. He saw a figure, Jack, come from the dark and go quickly into the light and disappear inside. And then he saw the boys, Frankie and Bennie, holding hands, crying, shouting something, running in behind the figure. As if to protect their mother. Larry now remembers thinking *Fucking Jack*, but he didn't move forward. He could barely move. His body, his head ached. Everything was confusing. As if all the concussions over the years added up to this final one. He didn't head towards them fast because he was going to pass out, because he thought that if he could just get his head straight, he would sneak back in and take Jack out without him realizing Larry was coming. He would be stealthy and sneak up on the scene – Jack was probably threatening Frankie and Bennie, maybe knocking concussions into those two wild, scootering kids, holding Mona hostage, waiting for Larry. Larry's head was on fire and he wasn't thinking clearly; he needed a few more minutes to figure it all out. He would come in and knock Jack out and then he and Mona and the kids would leave with his money. They would leave as a family, the four of them, with his coffee cans. A family. Into the wet, dark, hot night.

"Are you okay?" the Chaplain asks.

The Prisoner shakes his head. Then nods his head. Shrugs. He isn't sure. "I'm walking, aren't I? Walking forward. Am I walking?"

The Chaplain looks down at the ground. Sees all the feet moving towards the death chamber. The COs', the Prisoner's, his own.

"Yes, I guess you are."

Larry went back to his car and reached into the trunk, put his head down for a minute to get his tire iron, planning to knock Jack out, and then he collapsed. For only a minute. But that must have been when Jack took off. When Larry wasn't looking. Because Jack wasn't in the storage unit when he finally got there. Larry forgot the tire iron and went back unarmed.

The scene that met him. He couldn't have anticipated it. There was nothing that prepared him for it. Not the 24-Hour Variety guy or the bank manager or the dead teller.

He was always so afraid of his brother. But this, *this* was why. Look what he did. Look what he was capable of.

Larry had no excuse. He was covered in blood. He had blacked out at the scene. So groggy he couldn't talk. Memory loss. He didn't remember anything – he didn't fully remember Jack being there, his figure in the darkness, until a few days ago. The police built up a good case. And as he got better, as his brain cleared over the years, he realized that even though he has never thought he was capable of doing this, this was just payment for his life of crime. Because if Mona was dead, if his mother was dead, Larry had nothing left to live for. And only days ago, when he finally remembered fully what happened that night, it was far too late to change his fate. He was ready to be executed for his other crimes. He was ready to pay and let Jack be free.

But now? Is he sure of this now? Is he ready to pay?

11:31 a.m. The COs stop in front of the door to the execution chamber. The Prisoner begins to shake. His whole body is shaking, he can't stop it. Every organ in his body seems to shrink, his eyes tear over.

"Oh God, oh God," he cries.

"Be strong," the Chaplain says. The Prisoner looks at him, his companion, this man he has spent almost twelve hours with – he looks at him through his tears. The Chaplain looks at the Prisoner. There are tears in his eyes too. His hand is shaking; the Bible he carries rustles softly, all those little prayers from other religions wave in the wind created.

The door is opened and the chair stands in the middle of the room. A bright room. Empty but for the chair. Green walls. Green trim. In one wall, a window, open curtains, and the Prisoner sees people out there. Figures. Many people. They are there to watch him die. He loses control of his body and urinates. He can feel the stream of warmth carry down his legs. The Prisoner shuffles in, pulled slightly by the guards, who quietly and considerately avoid stepping in his puddle, avoid drawing attention to it. The Chaplain is right behind him. The Prisoner can hear him breathing heavily, choking slightly and silently on his breath. As if he can't catch it. As if he has run a million miles, not walked next door.

Besides his mother, Mona was the only person the Prisoner had ever loved and he wasn't sure why. He wasn't sure why he loved either of them. The two women who had the most effect on his whole life. Neither treated him particularly well. He wasn't even sure they loved him back. And then he was covered in their blood. Mona was brutally murdered by his brother and so was his mother, in a sense. Murdered by neglect, perhaps.

At the Prisoner's early trials, brain injury statistics were brought into play. Intense anger. Football players killing their wives. Documented evidence. After all, Mona was calling the police. The Prisoner was running with his money. It seemed to make sense at first. The Prisoner didn't know what to believe. The Prisoner didn't know what he was capable of. Before his memory came back.

The Prisoner turns to the Chaplain. His eyes move wildly in his head. The lump on his forehead pulses. The people out there. They look in at him. The COs sit him on the chair. The Prisoner can't bend his knees to sit, he can't seem to do it, and CO1 physically bends his knees for him and straps him in. Tight straps. They take his breath away. The COs move quickly, efficiently, giving him no time to struggle or escape. They have been trained well. There is no hesitation. They are kind and gentle as they apply the straps. Tough but fair.

Blacked out. Taken to the hospital. His memory was gone for such a long time. He must have killed Mona and the kids. They all told him he did it, didn't they? They had proof. Fingerprints, blood, money in coffee tins, and the Prisoner was battered up as if she had tried to fight him off. There were the marks around her wrist where he had twisted her arm, trying to take her cellphone away. There were her hairs on his rug, his sperm, her vaginal juices. It all added up.

And then it was too late. The blood. His vomit. His storage unit. The coffee cans. His confession – of course, his confession. What more could he do? For some time, the Prisoner couldn't remember any of it. And then he remembered a little bit and a little bit more. But a couple days ago, by the time he remembered Jack, the figure disappearing into the storage unit, it was too late. He was sure no one would listen to him. Of course he would blame someone else, they would have said, he got the death penalty. Anything to avoid execution.

The Prisoner realized that this penalty, this death, was what he deserved anyway. For all his other crimes. For loving Mona. For loving his mother. For his father. Susan. Her kids. For the bank murders, the 24-Hour Variety man, the B and Es. Atoning for all of his sins. Every single one of them.

11:45 a.m.

When the Prisoner looks up again, after they have strapped him in, after the electrodes are placed on his arms and legs and chest and temples, when he looks up and tries to catch the eye of the Chaplain, tries to focus on this man who actually believes in him, the Chaplain is looking away. He is looking out the window, to all the people out there. The Prisoner follows his gaze.

There is the Warden. There is a politician or two.

And there is Jack.

Hulking, larger even than the Prisoner remembers. He has come to watch. All these years, Jack has never been in touch, never visited him in prison, never seen him, and now he's here to watch his brother die for the crimes he himself committed. Susan sits beside him, crying. She is thin, a meth-head, her mouth caved in, her eyes like marbles in her skeletal sockets, her hair limp and lifeless. Susan's hands move as she twists and twists a Kleenex. She avoids looking at the Prisoner and, instead, her head moves back and forth, watching everyone else in the room. Jack, though, is looking straight at him, right into his eyes, and the Prisoner's mind goes blank. He tries to feel something, anything, but there is nothing inside of him anymore as he waits, strapped to the chair. Just animal fear. Accelerated heart rate. He can feel his pulse in his neck.

"Larry," the Chaplain says. "Is there any last thing you'd like to say to me?" He is leaning in close, his breath twelve-hours foul upon the Prisoner's face.

This is the first time the Chaplain has used his name, and the feeling he gets when he hears it is close to ecstasy. He is Larry Gallo. He is not the Prisoner.

"Say it again," Larry says. "Say my name."

"Larry. You are Larry Gallo."

"Thank you," whispers Larry. "For listening to me."

"Is that it? That's all you want to say?" The Chaplain is looking panicked.

Larry looks out again at the people watching him. He scans the room. "Fucking vultures," he says under his breath. "What good will sorry do?" he whispers to the Chaplain.

"Are you sorry?"

Larry smiles. And then he sees someone he doesn't recognize. A figure in the back row, a man. He seems familiar and Larry tries to remember. A fellow prisoner, maybe? Someone from his drug days? But then it comes to him. The same eyes as Frankie and Bennie. The same mouth. The way he tilts his head as the twins did when they looked at Larry – as if curious, but really only tilting to hear better, to focus the world their own way. Mona's ex-husband. Father of the boys. Sitting directly behind Jack.

Larry looks back and forth between Jack and the twins' father. Back and forth, trying to figure it out.

Mona's ex never came to court. He never appeared at any of the appeals or in any of the papers. Disappeared, they said, divorced from Mona and not necessarily involved. A history of domestic abuse and so only had supervised visits with his kids and a social worker. Didn't want anything to do with her death, or his children's death. Wanted to be left alone to mourn. Larry had practically forgotten him.

A small smile. The man smiles at Larry. Slightly. Lopsided. Crazed. A smile. As if he knows something Larry does not. He is staring straight into Larry's eyes.

Larry struggles at the straps. Mona's ex-husband stands and turns and walks down an aisle and towards an open door. Away from him. Away from his death. Larry watches him go. The final insult. The man turns and walks away. Turns his back on Larry. He has a slight limp, an uneven gait. A mourning father. An angry ex-husband on the phone berating Mona. Making her cry and scream. A man with a noticeable limp. One foot heavier than the other. The left heavier than the right.

Footprints in the snow. In front of the storage unit one aisle over. Groaning, crying, sighing.

11:58 a.m.

The hood is placed on his head. The lights go out for Larry. He cries and moans.

"Stay still," the COs say. And they begin to leave the room.

"You can't stay in here," they tell the Chaplain.

"I was told I can stay with him –"

"No, you must wait with the others. No one can stay in here."

"I'm sorry, Larry," the Chaplain says. He touches Larry's arm, then the top of his head. The last human touch Larry will feel. The only touch his mother ever gave – the top of his head. She would ruffle his hair with her long fingers. "I'm so sorry, Larry. I will be right outside. I will not take my eyes off of you. Remember that. Know that." And he leaves the room. He forgets to bless Larry. He forgets to say a prayer.

Larry can't say anything. Frozen in fear. The hood over his

face, suffocating him. The electric current will start soon. It will course through his body, killing him. He can't stop shaking. Every part of his body shakes and twitches. If he weren't strapped down, he would shake across the room.

The footsteps leave the room. The door closes. Under the black hood, Larry relives the night of the murders. He relives turning towards the storage unit, his arms full of coffee tins full of money, his head aching, his eyes clouded with pain, his vision foggy, and seeing the figure go from the dark of the aisle into the light of the room with the twin boys racing in behind him, running quickly as if they knew whomever it was. The figure going from dark into light.

Limping slightly. The left foot heavier than the right.

12:01 p.m.

The Dream

December 12, six months after the execution. It's freezing out-side, and yet, I still wake from the dream drenched in sweat. I can't rid myself of it. The damned seagull with the arrow through its body, crying wildly over the trees. The father heads into the cabin to refill his drink, and the crying sound gets louder and everyone pauses after the gull flies past. Every night.

Now I'm hearing the seagull in the daytime, wherever I go. Miranda thinks I should see someone.

"A chaplain, perhaps?"

"I'm thinking a therapist," Miranda sneers. "Not funny."

"I don't need to see anyone."

Miranda sits on the blue sofa in my new apartment above a convenience store on Main at Bleeker. Every time I go down to Mr. Lee's Variety to get a carton of milk, a bag of apples, a chocolate bar, I think about Larry. I can imagine Mr. Lee him-self being robbed – late dark nights, winter here, Mr. Lee perched at his counter watching the screen above the cigarette rack. Not really paying attention to who comes and goes from his store. I sometimes want to warn him, shout, "Watch out, someone will rob you," but instead I buy milk, chocolate, say goodnight and head back up to my one-bedroom apartment above. Mr. Lee can take care of himself. I have too much going on in my own life now to worry about things I can't control.

"It's not a scary dream, it's just annoying at this point."

"It started right before the execution, Jim, there's got to be more to it than you think. I thought it would disappear once everything was over, but it hasn't. Sometimes talking to someone –"

"You're telling me this?"

Miranda smiles. "I guess you know what you're doing."

"Sometimes, sister, talking to someone doesn't help. Did you ever consider that? Maybe, sometimes, we should all just shut up."

"That's the spirit," Miranda says. She smirks.

"Talking doesn't help, Miranda. Why do you think I gave up?"

"You didn't give up on talking, believe me," Miranda says. "I'd know if you had. Blah blah blah." She laughs.

"Religion isn't about talking, though, is it? It's about listening. I wasn't a good listener."

"Oh, God, Jim. You're the best listener." Miranda stands and walks over to the window. "Do you know what I think? I think that you listened too deeply and you listened as Jim, not as a chaplain. I think you went in there with religious feeling but came out of it with something greater. I think that some people are religious in the way that it's organized and orderly and taught. In a way that makes sense to them. But you, you're not like that. You're religious in your own philosophical way. You're kind of a religious empathic." She laughs, delighted at what she's said. "You are a man of empathy, not of God."

"I don't even know what you are talking about."

Miranda sits again. "Think about it this way. When the Prisoner was about to die, what were you thinking?"

"I –"

"You weren't thinking about heaven and shit, were you?"

"No, not shit."

"You were thinking about being in his position. You were thinking about how you would feel if you were in his position. You were thinking about his life and how it turned out this way. You were feeling his pain viscerally. Right? Empathically? Maybe even thinking about Tracy? You weren't thinking, at that moment, about God."

"But that doesn't mean He wasn't there with me."

"And now He's gone? No." Miranda sighs. "He's always with you. He's just different from what you thought He was. You became religious as a penance, not as a calling."

"When did you get to be so smart?"

Miranda grins. "You lose your brain for a bit when you have kids, you know," she says. "But then, suddenly, it comes back to you. Suddenly you can think again. Besides, I was always the smartest in the family."

I stand to look out the window at the light dusting of snow on the ground. It will clear up by the time I leave for work this afternoon.

Miranda stands and walks over to me. She puts her arm around me. Squeezes lightly. "Jim," she says. "You okay?"

"Sure, yes. I'm okay."

"You could go back, Jim, give it another try. It's not like you'd have to do another death row thing, right? That was just a fluke because the other chaplain was sick, right? You could go back to counselling the other prisoners? If you really still want to."

I turn and look at her face. Her kind face, so open and beautiful. "No, I'm fine, really. That wasn't for me. You are right. I'm a religious empathic. I'm happy now, doing what I'm doing."

"Bagging groceries at the Fresh Market Store? You can do more than that."

"I'm making a salary, I have lots of hours. The exercise is good for me. I get to take home stuff that's day-old. I don't have to watch people get killed."

Miranda and I watch the snow blow in the wind.

"Good God," Miranda laughs. "You're eating stale bread, living above a convenience store and working at a kid's job. You're forty-two years old. You have a university education. You've been trained to be a chaplain. Be a chaplain if you want."

"Now you want me to be a chaplain? Now? Make up your mind, sister. Besides, the training doesn't matter. You have to have it inside of you. You are right. I just don't have it in me and I think you are also right that I don't know if I ever did."

"Well," Miranda says, looking around, "at least you get day-old bread. And," she claps, "you said I was right. You've never said that I was right before. I won."

I can't help but smile. I listen to Miranda's footsteps on the stairs and then start to get ready for work.

How can there be a God? Larry's body bucked in the restraints. I felt I could smell burning, but I was in the other room, so how was that possible? The lights flickered. The body bucked again, tensed to the point of breaking. The body. The Prisoner. Larry.

There was a silence in the observation room that was almost deafening – as if my ears had popped. Not a sound. Nothing. Blankness. I watched a man be put to death. A youngish, healthy man. It was as if everyone in the room had stopped breathing.

The doctor came in after a bit and felt his pulse. He was dead.

≫———→

I reach down for the coffee cups and carry them to my kitchen, wash them in the sink, put them in the drying rack. A noon-to-six shift today. Enough to keep my mind occupied for a time. I would rather work twelve hours a day if I could, but they don't need me that much at the Fresh Market Store. After six p.m., the kids from high school come and work until midnight.

The thing is, I'm not sure now if Larry was trying to play me in those last twelve hours. Is it possible he did that? To a chaplain? A man of God? Would he play with my emotions, my faith, that way? Did he manipulate his story slightly to make me believe that Jack committed the murder? But when I came to this conclusion, Larry rejected it. And how dare I think this way, doubt a man taking his last few breaths. Imagining that he spent twelve hours fooling me. Is this what I have become? An unbeliever? Not only in God but in human nature?

I don't know what to think anymore. I am often confused. Lack of sleep contributes to this. The dreaming contributes to this.

As I walk down the hallway and down the stairs to the door on the street, I know that I shouldn't care anymore. What's the point? Who cares who committed the murders? Three people were murdered. Four, actually.

I walk in the melted snow towards the Fresh Market Store. Wave at Mr. Lee. Keep my head down against the wind that has picked up.

Who cares? I keep beat with my feet, walking on towards the Fresh Market Store. Who cares?

I see Larry's eyes before the hood is placed over his head. White with fear. Round and open. Seeing the world for the last time. Focused on the observation room, on the people watching. I see Larry's eyes as they move towards Jack's eyes, as they take him in and then move away from him. Those eyes.

Who cares?

Those eyes find another target, as if searching for someone to save him. He is peering into the observation room and I am watching him, stuck there beside him, not able to move or breathe, just watching, terrified.

Who cares?

I enter the Fresh Market Store.

"Hey-oh, Jim-boy." Mark smacks me on the back as he passes by carrying a box of bananas. "We got a new shipment of poinsettias today," he says. "Put them on the cart near the front, could you? When you punch in."

Who cares? I tread lightly through the fluorescent store towards the employee doors to the back. I take note of the Christmas music and I think about those two boys and what they would have got for Christmas. Their mom probably would have bought them new scooters or a sled. Or Larry would have, if things had been different – I can somehow see him buying them scooters. Or their father, he would have bought them something. That's something a father would do.

And then I stop walking. It hits me in the spaghetti sauce aisle. Blood red jars all around me. Mark waves to me from the front of the store. Points at the cart full of red flowers. The Christmas music is pumped in loud and "Jingle Bells" pierces my ears. Flashing lights above the egg and milk fridge.

Their father. The boys' father.

Who cares?

Surely, he did.

Larry's eyes when they found that man in the observation room. And suddenly, the something that I felt was missing is now making sense. In a foggy sort of way. Larry's eyes. The one thing I was doing was watching him closely. Watching Larry's eyes. In them, a quick dawning. As if the blinds were lifted. A realization. A rapid confusion mixed with anger. That weird "aha" look, as if finally the Prisoner got it. Finally he understood something he hadn't understood before.

That man he was looking at. That was the father. Mona's ex-husband. The one who screamed at her on the phone. The one who made her so angry she bit and scratched and bruised Larry when they made love. He came to the execution. And Larry saw him.

I turn on my heels and begin to walk down the aisle towards the front door. Out past the cart Mark has placed for the poinsettias, out past Mark, who is standing there saying, "What the heck? Where are you going? Jim, where are you going? Your shift just started."

It is dark at the Storage Mart. The snow has stopped. The wind is still. The only lights are the ones in the corners of each aisle, shining dimly down on the hard, frozen ground in small patches. There is a light in the office. A young guy sitting behind the counter. His feet up. I can see him through the window. I walk towards the office and he looks up and waves. Not at all suspicious about some guy peering in on a cold winter's night.

The office is warm. There is a space heater in the corner. The desk clerk is watching the screen but smiles nicely at me when he looks up. He brings his feet down from the counter and sits up.

"Can I help you?"

"I'm looking for Darren Purcell." Darren Purcell, Mona's ex-husband. I read that he now owns the Storage Mart.

"He usually leaves at five p.m.," the clerk says. "But he might be out in his unit."

"His unit?"

"Unit twelve. Next aisle over. He hangs out there at night before going home. Do you want me to get him on the walkie-talkie?" The clerk indicates a charging walkie-talkie on a desk in the corner of the room.

"No, that's okay. I'll just head over to him. You said unit twelve?"

"He doesn't like to be disturbed. He won't open the door for you. You're better to come back tomorrow. He says it's his quiet space. He fired the last guy for knocking on the door."

"Well, I'll see."

"Suit yourself," the clerk says. He puts his feet back up on the counter and returns to watching the screen. "He gets really mad if you bother him. Don't say I didn't warn you. Temper and all." The clerk crosses his arms and shrugs. "Bit of an asshole, actually, but don't tell him I said that. Goes into unit twelve for hours sometimes. And I have to stay until he closes up. Idiot."

I trace my path back to Larry's old storage unit, the murder scene, and stand in front for a minute, looking around. I can see my breath in the air.

I suddenly hear something. A crying sound. Coming from one aisle over.

And there it is. He was here all along.

Sat there, in his storage unit, biding his time. Waiting.

Both men, Larry and Darren, ended up practically living in storage units. Or at least hung out in them. Passed time. Small boxes.

Mona and Darren. Not Jack. Unit twelve. Darren. Mona's ex-husband. Larry said he only came at night. When Mona had left for the day. He knew about Larry and Mona – he must have. The twins would have mentioned their mother's new boyfriend to him. They were everywhere, always present, playing up and down the aisles. They knew what was going on. I walk quietly down the aisle and turn into the next one. I tiptoe towards the sounds. A quiet sound, choking, sniffing. Mona must not have known he had rented this unit, the guy at the desk back then must have filled in the forms. Nighttime only, Larry said, to mourn the loss of his wife, his sons. And then staying on to really mourn their loss. A loss he caused.

Because suddenly I know that the worst thing you can do to a mother is to kill her children. After all, they were stabbed first. The final piece of the puzzle is why he didn't take any of the money. Why Darren didn't just scoop up some of the left-over coffee cans as Larry was off loading his car and take off into the night. Larry's brother, Jack, would have. Of course. But for Darren, it wasn't about money; it wasn't a robbery, it was a crime of passion.

Of course, this is why the children came in behind him. Their father. They would leave the car and come towards their father. Not Jack. They wouldn't come towards Jack. They didn't know him. Or Larry. They had been warned not to talk to him. And the files said the children weren't forced into the storage unit, they came in on their own.

I pause in front of the closed door. I am shaking. Inside is a man who potentially took a knife to his own sons, his ex-wife. A man who did not flinch when Larry was about to be executed. A man who, in fact, left the room just before they pulled the switch – couldn't bother to stay for the killing. As if seeing the end result didn't even matter. As if nothing mattered.

Did Larry realize, at the last minute, in that look he had in his eyes, that he wasn't the guilty party, or even that his brother wasn't the guilty party? Did he know it just before he was killed? Maybe, but I'll never know for sure.

The crying stops. A nose is blown. Loudly.

I turn to leave. Terrified suddenly.

But then I turn back. If Larry was innocent, I have to know. If only to rid myself of the recurring dream, the gull with the arrow through it. If only to sleep.

The door begins to roll open. Slowly. Sliding upwards, winding in upon itself. I see heavy work boots first, and jeans. Knees. I back into the shadows. But there he is, Darren Purcell, looking out into the dark, blinking to adjust his eyes to it. The man is large, heavy in his stomach and thighs, a double chin. A day's growth of beard on his face. Beady eyes. His skin is sickly white, as if he spends too much time indoors. His hair is thinning.

I am there in the dark and he sees me. It is obvious from his expression that he recognizes me, and it is doubly obvious he knows from where exactly. The execution. Darren doesn't move. I don't move. We study each other. Time seems to stretch. And then, slowly, Darren nods at me. He is acknowledging the last ten years. He knows that I know. He knows he has been caught. And then he nods at me and walks out of unit twelve, limping. He leaves the door open and walks towards his car, parked down the aisle towards the front office. He gets in. I am frozen. Stunned. I can't seem to move. And then I come to life.

"Hey."

But Darren doesn't turn back. Instead, he shuts the car door behind him, starts the engine and backs out of his spot. Not once does he look back at me.

I run towards the car. I run furiously towards Darren, pound on the window, but Darren only looks forward, out into the night, and drives away.

"Hey," I shout. "Hey."

The clerk comes out of the office.

"I told you he didn't like to be bothered, didn't I? Hey, he left his door open. He never leaves his door open." The clerk comes down the stairs and begins to walk towards unit twelve. I follow. The clerk has slipped his feet into his large boots and the tongues are out, the laces untied. He trips his way towards the storage unit. I glance down the aisle towards Larry's storage unit.

"Holy shit." The clerk stands there, staring into the lighted room. "What the hell?"

He is just a kid, I think. He knows nothing.

"I mean, that's really weird, you know," the clerk says. "Considering what happened to his family . . ."

We stare into the room. All of the walls are covered with photographs and newspaper clippings. Pictures of Mona. Of the boys. Of Darren with the boys. Pictures of Larry and Mona. Together. Talking. Laughing. Mona slipping into Larry's storage unit. The boys sliding on cardboard in the snow, on scooters between the aisles. Baby photographs. Wedding photos. Newspaper articles that scream *Appeal Denied, Bank Thief and Murderer to be Executed, The Countdown Is On.*

In one corner of the room, there is a chair. A side table. A lamp on the table. Turned off and dark. There is a coffee cup on the desk, steam rising out of it. The chair is facing the picture wall, as if Darren were watching a screen.

The scenario brings to mind the prison cell I sat in with Larry for twelve hours.

"Fuck," the clerk says.

On the table beside the chair is a knife. A large wooden handle, a thick blade. *The* knife.

"Gives me the creeps," the clerk says. "I thought he did the bills out here, you know. Because he didn't want to be in her office. Too many memories or something." The clerk shivers.

"I don't think he was doing paperwork," I say.

Darren was crying long before he killed his family. Larry

had heard the crying for a while. And he continued to cry after he killed them.

"Serious business," the clerk says, releasing his breath. The clerk knows something is not right. "I guess I should call the cops."

Veritas

The irony of all of this is not lost on me. I am sitting in a chair on the deck, a drink in hand. Miranda's kids are splashing about in the river with friends. Richard is refilling everyone's drinks and is carrying a tray of empty glasses into the cabin. Here it is, then, my old, recurring dream come to life around me. Miranda's friend Beatrice has invited me to join Miranda's family for the weekend at her cabin. Everything has that déjà vu feeling, a hazy kind of weirdness that makes me wonder if I'm awake or asleep. Especially after the two beers and the heat of the sun.

And of course, I can hear a seagull. I pinch myself. I am not asleep.

I see Miranda, her mouth open in laughter, talking to Beatrice, both mothers watching all the children who are playing around the water. I hear the gull coming. Solitary. Over the trees. And then down towards us.

I haven't had that dream since the new year. I haven't heard the sound of a crying gull coming at me for quite a while. I slept well on my travels – to Europe and Asia and then India. Six

241

months I was gone, backpack on, wandering the world. Trying to figure it all out. Trying to understand how my faith could be so easily found and then lost, could be strong and then weak. I dropped, exhausted, into hostel beds at night. Was energetic during the days. Taking it all in. Even slept on trains, buses, rickshaws, planes, boats. And not once did I hear the seagull in my dreams.

"Look," my niece, Daisy, says. She is standing on a rock in the river, her small body tan and lean and wet. She points towards the seagull.

I do not want to look. I want to look away. But I force myself to look at the seagull.

"It's like your dream, Jim. Remember your dream?" Miranda turns to her friend, laughing. "He used to have this dream about this seagull with an arrow through it."

The women talk. The kids shout and splash and slip. The river current is strong. The sun is hot. Richard comes out from the cabin.

And the gull flies past us all. Solitary. Crying. Calling. With no arrow through its body. Just a single flying bird.

Then suddenly, beyond that single seagull, the sky is full of gulls, crying wildly, flapping madly and making such noise. Their wings beat hard and I swear I can feel the breeze they create. They are flying low above us, a huge flock of them.

Acknowledgements

My book wouldn't exist without the guidance and support of some very special people: my extraordinary editor, Paul Vermeersch; my initial readers, Edward Berry and Allie Vandersanden; my legal-minded brother, David Berry; Noelle Allen and Ashley Hisson at Wolsak & Wynn; and my agent, Chris Bucci. Thanks to Emily Dockrill Jones for the thorough copy-editing. Thank you to the Ontario Arts Council for the much-appreciated bolt of confidence, a Works in Progress grant. Giant gratitude goes out to my mom, my dad, Stu, Abby and Zoe, who always have my back and know exactly when to put me in my place. Finally, special thanks to the greeter-galore, the one who is so happy he almost dies as he wiggles and groans around the house when I come home, my border collie/basset hound, Buddy. He deserves his name in a book for once.

Notes

The quote on page 211 that begins "O loving and kind God" comes from Psalm 51:1–12, *The Living Bible* (Carol Stream, IL: Tyndale House Publishers, 1971).

The quote on page 212 that begins "When my time has come" comes from the Tibetan Nyingma Master Longchenpa Rabjampa in the fourteenth century. Quoted in Tulku Urgyen Rinpoche, *Repeating the Words of the Buddha*, 2nd ed., trans. Erik Pema Kunsang (Hong Kong: Rangjung Yeshe Publications, 2006), 145. See www.a-good-dying.com/tibetan-prayers.html for more information.

The quote on page 212 and 213 that begins "Now I say to you in conclusion" comes from Martin Luther King, Jr.'s September, 18, 1963, "Eulogy for the Martyred Children." It has been reproduced on the website Martin Luther King, Jr. And the Global Freedom Struggle: http://kingencyclopedia.stanford.edu/encyclopedia/documentsentry/doc_eulogy_for_the_martyred_children/index.html.

The quote on page 213 that begins "I am of the nature to grow old" comes from Buddha's Five Remembrances. See http://www.worldprayers.org/archive/prayers/meditations/i_am_of_the_nature.html.

The quote on page 213 that begins "God of all Creation" I found on the Benedictine Health System website. See Prayers for the Dying: Non-Christian, http://www.bhshealth.org/prayers/140707021014698.

The quote on page 214 that beings "He maketh me" comes from Ezekiel 34:11–24 and John 10:1–21, *King James Version*. See biblehub.com/kjv/psalms/23.htm.

The quote on page 157 that begins "The prisoner's eyeballs" comes from W. Ecenbarger, "Perfecting Death: When the state kills it must do so humanely. Is that possible?," *Philadelphia Inquirer Magazine*, January 23, 1994, as quoted in "Descriptions of Execution Methods," Death Penalty Information Center, http://www.deathpenaltyinfo.org/descriptions-execution-methods.

Michelle Berry is the author of three books of short stories and five previous novels. Her short story collection *I Still Don't Even Know You* won the 2011 Mary Scorer Award for Best Book Published by a Manitoba Publisher and was shortlisted for a 2011 ReLit Award, and her novel *This Book Will Not Save Your Life* won the 2010 Colophon Award and was longlisted for the 2011 ReLit Award. Her writing has been optioned for film and published in the UK.

Berry was a reviewer for *Globe and Mail* for many years, and teaches online for the University of Toronto and is often a mentor at Humber College. Berry now lives in Peterborough, ON, where she operates an independent bookstore, Hunter Street Books. Please visit www.hunterstreetbooks.com.